ANNIE ABBOTT
AND THE RACE TO THE RED QUEEN

First Edition Published September 2023
by Indies United Publishing House, LLC

Cover Art by
Tatiana Villa at Villa Designs

978-1-64456-628-2 [Hardcover]
978-1-64456-629-9 [Paperback]
978-1-64456-630-5 [Mobi]
978-1-64456-631-2 [ePub]
978-1-64456-632-9 [Audiobook]

Library of Congress Control Number: 2023942806

INDIES UNITED PUBLISHING HOUSE, LLC
P.O. BOX 3071
QUINCY, IL 62305-3071
www.indiesunites.net

Prologue

To see the life in all things and feel the life that surrounds you is to know real magic. Annie Abbott has begun to realize the true strength and power of magic. She has learned that magic is real, and it is in everything and everyone, and most of all, it is in her. Until recently, Annie was a junior high school student. She was a diligent student and got good grades. She was happy with her life and thought it was full enough, but then the world, her world shifted.

Living with her father, Michael Abbott, a college professor of medieval history, she discovers that not only is there magic in the world, but that she has somehow inherited great quantities of it from her women ancestors dating all the way back to the warrior-sorceress Morganna Pendragon, apprentice of Merlin the Magnificent.

All her life, her father kept the secret of her power and her identity. As her twelfth birthday approached, her magical self-began to assert itself and she began to realize that things would never be the same. As her ability to channel magic emerged, her father could no longer keep who she was and would become a secret. He reveals himself to her as also having many gifts himself and that he was sworn to protect her. Together with his two best friends, Rafer Tate and Gabe McDonald, they launch on a quest for a mysterious treasure of the ages.

But as they begin, the strength of Annie's gift also reveals her to evil ones, and they pursue her and the three protectors. It is a mad dash to stay ahead of the army of the unclean and find those that can teach Annie how to control the gifts she has inherited. There is danger at every turn, and battles are fought to protect her. All the while her powers continue to grow.

Finally Annie realizes that to be safe, she must go it alone. By her very presence she is endangering everyone around her. In an epic last battle, she summons the powers of the elements and raises an army of trees to defend herself. The demonstration of strength is terrifying both for her and her allies.

She knows that her education must continue but that she must try and do it alone. The great library of wisdom and lore has been sealed for ages beyond counting. It awaits the key to open the door and she is the key. Somehow, she must find the Keeper of the Books of Wisdom and unlock the secrets of the ages. But first, she has to survive.

FOREWARD

"How can I learn everything that I need to in such a short time teacher? There's just too much; I'll never remember all of it."

The druid looked up from stirring the small campfire at his apprentice.

"The knowledge, even the emotion that was gained in a lifetime does not die when the man does. To whatever extent possible, knowledge and wisdom continues beyond the grave. It is there to be accepted or denied by those that come after. Many do not try and find it within themselves as they become involved in an otherwise petty life. They do not seek wisdom but rather pursue pleasure. They never understand that by accepting the gift that lies just beyond their reach, they could have both.

For the few that wish to learn as deeply as they possibly can, they must first learn how to access that gift left behind by their fathers and their father's fathers. They must learn how to negotiate that maze of the hallways of memory and find that gift that was planted within them long before they drew their breath.

They can learn that they are both themselves and those they sprang from. They become them if they can relax enough to look within. But knowledge and wisdom bring with them great responsibility. It is that responsibility that most people do not wish to accept. It would divert them from the path of their own pleasure, possibly direct them toward a life of service.

The knowledge of the past is only as useful as those that wish to add to it, but it carries with it the memories and personalities of each individual that went before.

The memories of our ancestors, each one individually, each one who contributed to this treasure trove of experience, who they were and what they did is there within, all the way back to the 'long fathers' at the very beginning of the new age."

Annie Abbott
and the
Race to the
Red Queen

The Annie Abbott Adventures
Book Two

Isabelle & Michael
Nelson

INDIES UNITED PUBLISHING HOUSE, LLC

The Lady of Vaughn House

A blanket of heavy fog hung just below streetlight level, creating bright glowing halos of white around each one and softening its surrounding light. At the foot of a long downhill slope, a grove of ancient magnolia trees dripped moisture in the cool still air, only their lowest branches visible below the canopy of fog. In the small hours beyond midnight no sounds disturbed the peace. The air was cool and the ground was soft and springy, as it swallowed the moisture from the trees above.

From beneath the shadows of the spreading magnolia trees three shadows were in motion, darting from tree to tree, barely visible, the shadow at the corner of your eye. The three figures were moving quickly. Then separating, they spread out into the open space ahead of them. Moving forward in a crouching run their demeanor one of caution and haste as they hunted up the long incline ahead of them. Moving soundlessly, the hunters searched and listened ahead into the fog alert for any danger. Aware of each other, they moved separately but in the same direction, working their way up the vast expanse of lawn. Objects beyond the fog could not be seen but were felt, as the stealthy hunters melted into the cold mist and their shadows disappeared.

As they faded from sight another dark shape, another moving shadow flowed forward from the deeper darkness beneath the trees. The shadow, darkness against the darker space of the surrounding tree trunks, appeared huge, moving slowly, flowing forward. At the edge of the shadows, it stopped—waiting. A figure more imagined than seen, its presence malevolent, the subject of a children's nightmare. It waited for the three to return.

A wailing police car, its flashing lights reflecting off of the overhead vapor howled by on a nearby street. As it did, the dark shadow disappeared, dropping to the ground, just another shadow beneath the massive trees.

Within moments, all was silence again.

Annie rose from behind the massive dark form of the monstrous dire wolf.

"It's okay; this happens a lot around here."

"I have not walked among the mortals for an age. They have multiplied." Bracken's rumbled voice echoed in her brain.

"Yes, and with each generation, they grow more detached from others and increasingly ignorant." Annie knew that the words were true, even if they were not hers. The voice went on, "But their doom is our doom."

"The elves have moved far forward. Should we follow?" Bracken was wary.

"One last sprint Bracken. We're so close, I can feel it. Should we fight or should we flee? Tonight, if we must, we fight! Let's sprint my friend and catch up to the elves." Annie pulled the hood of her serape over her head and loosened the sword at her belt that she had worn since leaving her father. Leaping astride the great wolf she leaned forward and whispered in his ear, "let's sprint!"

As Bracken crouched to leap into the open space three shadows appeared rushing down the sloped lawn. The three elves slid to a stop on the wet ground, their glowing eyes ablaze.

"Something of power approaches. It is cloaked and we cannot assess the danger." Micah whispered as he and the other two drew their weapons and took a position in front of the dire wolf.

Annie threw a leg over and slid off of the wolf as his hackles rose and he crouched in readiness directly behind the three capable warriors. She took a position at his right shoulder and threw her hood back.

She whispered, "Fight or Flee?"

Bracken's voice rumbled, "Fight first, flee if we must. Spread out. No one can know that we are here. Let none of us be taken… do not allow yourselves to be taken."

She spread her legs and took a fighting stance, she drew the sword and held it at the ready, not sure if she could conjure a warrior to wield it. The four who had sworn to protect her now stood ready to do just that. Their lives and hers, perhaps, hanging in the balance. Patch hovered near her left shoulder, sword at the ready.

Out in front of them a dark spot appeared in the dense fog and grew steadily darker, parting the fog as it approached. The spot grew wider and taller, the closer it approached, moving slowly but directly toward them. No fog surrounded it as it flowed soundlessly down the long grassy slope. As it neared them the last of the surrounding fog disappeared and the shadow was lost in the blackness of the night.

Finally, the elves were not fooled. They knew what it

was now and Micah spoke in a hiss.

"Come no further demon!"

"Hahahaha, quiet foolish elf! You have no power over me." The shadow moved within a few feet of the group and spoke again. "Greetings travelers."

"Who are you?" Annie did not relax one muscle, still in her stance of defense. "Friend or foe?"

"I am neither friend nor foe." The haunting voice spoke from the deep shadow in front of them. "For now, I am your guide to safe passage. There are those near that lurk in the fog and watch. They mean harm for those that they seek. I will take you to Vaughn House.

"Are you a spirit then?" Mink asked, for the elves do not fear the dead.

"I was once Kathleen Arbogast. I am guardian of the Keeper of Vaughn House. We must hurry please."

"You are taking us Vaughn House?" Annie slid the sword away and within seconds once again was a thirteen-year-old teenager.

"Yes, you must meet the Keeper. Now, as quietly as possible mortals, you must follow me; we must hurry; daylight approaches."

"What?!"

"You must meet the Keeper, she awaits."

With that the spirit surrounded by darkness amid the fog began to drift away.

"Follow." It spoke as it drifted up the hill. "Follow."

With the elves leading the way, their vision in the darkness priceless, the small troupe followed the shadow as it drifted up the long slope into the darkness. The fog parted around it as it navigated the fogged, almost invisible campus of Vanderbilt University. Their progress cloaked, muffled in the surrounding damp they cautiously followed the spirit of Kathleen Arbogast.

Within minutes, a building took shape in the darkness muted by the foggy air. Ahead, streetlights winked out in the surrounding areas as they approached each.

As they approached the shadowy house, no lights shown. The windows were black to the outside world. As they approached, they made out the large wooden porch that covered half of the front of a two-story brick house.

"Well that's kinda creepy." Annie betrayed her age as she looked up at the ancient house. "But that's exactly what I would imagine when I think of a haunted house. Dad told me there are more than one or two spirits within, even one of a small child? Dad always laughed about these old ladies who swore there were baby footprints in the dust on the floors. But I've got to say, it does look like that might be possible."

"There is no danger," Bracken rumbled. "There are no enemies nearby, we are cloaked by the spirit that leads us."

As he finished, the front door opened silently; a stately woman, her hair in a tight bun and dressed in an ankle length dress of indeterminate color, emerged and flowed to the front of the porch. She appeared beyond middle age as she addressed them.

"Greetings, travelers. Please come in and take your rest. I am Stella Vaughn, Keeper of the books of Wisdom, long the spirit and soul of Vaughn House. I offer most especially my heartfelt greetings to the Queen of the Fey and our hopes of the Key. I am the Keeper and finally, I meet the Key. The prophesies are fulfilled, and history, legend and fate have arrived at the crossroad. Enter to learn."

A Balance of Strengths

"You are incredibly late. I've been expecting you for a week or more. Did you stop at Dollywood or something? The voice spoke from the darkness within the open door. "Naughty, naughty."

There was no mistaking the voice but there was a collective gasp as Colm McQuinn, the Druid master, stepped out of the front door and strode across the broad front porch. He leaned on the railing, a broad smile on his face holding a delicate teacup in his hand.

"Shame on you for making us wait. I for one am pleased to see you, welcome Bracken my ancient friend, and Micah and you guardians. I'll bet you're all tired and hungry. We began preparations as soon as Kathleen sensed your approach." Then he intensified his stare and focused it directly at Annie, "I think we could all use a nice cup of tea don't you?"

The elves would not enter the house. They much preferred the sky instead of a roof over their heads. Instead, they took positions in the shadows, on guard, facing outward toward possible danger, together a fearsome hedge against those that would do harm. As the sky began to brighten into a grey morning, they became one with the landscape, melting into the surrounding background that surrounded Vaughn House, invisible—lethal.

The dire wolf would not have fit into any of the small rooms of the old house. There was some question as to whether he could have even fit through the wide front door. Instead, as the light continued to grow in the hazy hue of fog, he stationed himself beneath the wooden porch and under the front steps, his great glowing yellow eyes the only thing visible in the darkness cast beneath the slats above. He was perfectly situated to become the subject of any person's worst nightmare should the protection of the elves fail.

Annie, after assuring that all were satisfied with the chosen places of concealment, entered the homely house following the shadows that were Lady Vaughn and Kathleen Arbogast. Inside, in spite of the black appearance of the windows from outside, the house was brightly lit, with lights in every corner and chandeliers blazing gaily. The house appeared immaculate to Annie. There was no dust on the woodwork, no creaking floorboards; the house went against anything she had envisioned when she thought of a haunted house. There was not a single cobweb anywhere in sight. The place looked like it was 'move-in' ready, as realtors are fond of saying, and it was nothing like she had imagined.

Behind her, Colm McQuinn hesitated on the porch, then walked to the front steps, watchful. Satisfied, he sat down on the top step cradling his teacup but still looking into the fog. Then as if speaking into the darkness and fog he addressed the dire wolf beneath the porch.

"Old friend?"

"She is the one. Her power grows as does she."

"The time grows short Bracken."

"She is remarkably resilient; her strength is growing, can she grow in wisdom wise one?"

"The limit of learning is the desire of the student, not the skill of the teacher."

"She desires learning."

"Learning and wisdom are miles from each other."

"I bear the scars of learning; with each scar the lesson of it marks my soul."

"And so it is old friend, and so it is. Shall we roll the dice then? There is much to be gained and much to be lost."

"Gain and loss do not often balance on the scale."

"Yes, of course, for us, gain would be incremental but loss on almost any level would be devastating."

Bracken dropped to the ground with a long exhale as the druid sat down on the top step.

"Perhaps we will not live to see the other side as I expect old friend. I have died before, both in my heart and in my spirit if not in body. She has awakened me. If it is in my power, none shall pass me to do her harm."

"But will she be ready?"

"To fight or to gain wisdom?"

The question hung in the still air as McQuinn reflected on the depth of the question and the silence stretched into minutes. Finally, the druid rose to his feet and put one foot on the top step.

"For all of our sakes, both".

Turning his gazed into the fog for a long moment, then with a sigh he raised his hand and snapped his fingers. One by one the streetlights blazed back to life, marching off into the morning fog. Then putting his tongue between his teeth, he loosed a piercing whistle into the night.

Almost immediately, out of the fog, a silent shadow

dropped below their haloed light. Growing larger and larger as it approached through the air a frightening specter of black against grey. With the silence of its race a huge owl spread its taloned feet and its great wings almost in the face of the druid. Then turning at the last second, it perched upon the newel post at the top of the stairs and fluttered its wings.

The great owl rotated its head in every direction, including behind it. Its great yellow eyes bright in the dim morning light. Then ruffling its feathers again, which made it appear twice its already huge size, it regarded the druid and spoke.

"She has arrived?"

"Yes, she has gone inside Archimedes. I'm glad to see you've decided to join the party. How are you old friend?"

"As well as can be expected. There are far too many people around here for my tastes. They've managed to stunt the rodent population to the point where I'm a mere shadow of my former self."

"You don't look too bad to me."

"Harrumph. I can't just order pizza whenever I feel like it as you can Wizard. People would react rather conversely, I suspect."

"I guess. Well Archimedes? How many?"

"I have counted only eight. They are banded in twos. They are watching the roads to the west."

"Are they a threat then?" Colm asked, trying to assess the danger.

"They might have been, but no longer; the elven hunters have dispatched them. They are returned to the depths. It is good that they keep watch. The elves are fearsome—and silent."

"Greetings wise one." Bracken's rumbled voice

vibrated the floorboards of the porch beneath the druid's feet.

"Greetings True Brother. I saw that you had arrived. You bring with you an important package. You and the silent hunters. How was the journey?"

"It was not without strife. The elves are helpful allies."

"So I have seen. Is there word from any more of your kin?"

"Not for many long years."

"If the need is great, will they come?"

"If the need is great, they will already know of it. Although I was once leader of the True Brothers, they may do as they wish. If indeed there are any of my kin remaining after the long purge of our kind. The need grows by the day. The enemy seems emboldened, and their numbers have grown."

"Will you join us inside Archimedes?"

"I prefer to taste the morning air. Will she be able to open the door?"

"The Key has arrived; we can only hope."

"She is the One. I serve the one. She will prevail." Again, the rumble erupted from below the floor.

"For now, rest old friend. All our hopes and all our fears will be there for us when the sun rises, at least for one more day." Colm spoke to the dire wolf as he met the ancient owl's eyes. "The Grimoire might prove illusive; no matter how illusive that may become, we must above all—show her patience."

The Doorway to Wisdom

Through the small foyer and down a narrow hallway, the glowing form of Stella Vaughn drifted toward a bright room at the end. As they entered, they were greeted with the squeals and laughter of a small child obviously delighted by the arrival of company. Miss Vaughn took a seat in a brightly upholstered wing chair before a wrought iron wood stove and smiled at the child.

"I was such a happy child; I love watching myself as an overjoyed lover of life. I never lost it, but just look at all of that energy! Don't you miss it? Even at your young age?"

Annie regarded the toddler. She didn't understand.

"Wait. You're that child?"

"We should all let our child out to play from time to time, don't you think? It's a bit more fun if you can actually watch the experience."

The priest, Colm McQuinn, entered the room. Annie had never seen him in anything but the long brown robe of the druid. Instead, he was attired in Polo shirt and stylish slacks with penny loafers, his hair was combed neatly, and his beard was styled. Despite herself, it took her breath away for a moment. He was unquestionably gorgeous.

For his part, the druid with a gentle smile on his lips, put his palms together and produced a brilliant blue ball of light which he sent floating into the air around the room while the pale toddler chased it laughing and screaming with delight.

Everyone in the room clapped their hands along with the little one. Everyone except Annie Abbott.

"Wait, she is you? You're her!?"

The laughter continued for more than a minute as the child continued to catch the glowing orb, only to have it explode into sparkling stars that floated to the ceiling like bubbles blown in the breeze and coalesced into another bright blue star and the chase commenced all over again.

At last, the child visibly tired, and the enthusiasm ebbed.

"It is all just a memory Anne of Present. It is a lost thought. A memory of happiness in her current existence of unending death." Patch floated into Annie's face, a meaningful look in her eye. *"It is a joy, if for only a moment. It is the druid's doing. We honor the dead and the spirits who embrace the work of our mission. For them, it is a solitary and lonely work."*

Even as Patch spoke, the child, still laughing with delight, faded into a shadow and then vanished.

"It is both late and early, but time is of the essence." Colm McQuinn stood leaning on the framed doorway. "It is time." He met Annie's eyes. "It is time for the key to unlock the doorway if it can be done. It is time to see if the Key and the Keeper are one at last."

"Wait! What do you mean?"

"It is time, at last to unlock the secrets of the ancients." As the spirit of Stella Vaughn spoke from the chair, she was joined by the visage Kathleen Arbogast who took a position in front of the stately lady and spoke directly to Annie.

"I am guardian of the books of lore. The mistress is the Keeper. Only the true Key may open the door that has been sealed for the years beyond memory. Are you truly the key, or merely one of the imposters of before? You must answer, or you must die, as those of past attempts."

Annie was suddenly very afraid. She glanced, terrified at the druid, not sure that she had heard the spirit correctly. His stern look was intense, his eyes hard, his only response a slight nod of his head while he held her gaze. Annie got the message. She paused. She slowed her breathing and reached back into her memory. She closed her eyes, trying to focus. What were they? Her memory, or her memories? Not hers certainly, but who's and where?

In her mind's eye, an image appeared; a woman, a warrior tall who stood with confidence, her legs spread, her arms folded on her chest. She watched as the tall dark figure met her gaze and slowly nodded—only once.

Yes, the memories, they were her memories and somehow, they were Annie's too. She understood. She could answer the challenge posed by the guardian of the books of lore. She was Morgan Le Fey, at least there in the far recesses of her thoughts. She looked at the druid and nodded and then stepped up in front of the stout Guardian of the books of Lore and squared her shoulders.

"I am the Key."

"Who and who alone may wield the Black Prince?"

This one was a no-brainer, even for Annie, but she answered in the voice and the language of the ancient ones.

"Only The Three as One may wield the Black Prince."

"Who is 'Keeper of the Light'?"

She paused, Allegra had been the Keeper, but now she was part Allegra and part Circe'. As far as she knew no other had been appointed the new Keeper. She straightened up, and again in her voice of power, she spoke.

"Only the daughter of the White Witch and the Spirit of 'The Eldest', may be the Keeper."

"What do you fear."

Wait... what? The first two had been easy. I don't know what I fear, I'm afraid all the time anymore. She didn't really mean, like what I'm afraid of right now did she? 'Answer or die? She can't really mean, like she'd kill me, would she? Nah, but they might throw me out, or make me walk home, or even send me back to school or something. She said the imposters had died. Oh crap!

What am I afraid of? Everything, no I've got to narrow it down. Bears? Yes. Centipedes? Definitely, yes. That's not what she wants, think.

Again the figure in her mind met her gaze; **'Reach out, touch the life in all that surrounds you. Feel the magic. Know the answer.'**

This time Annie answered in her own voice, but she could not hide the trace of a tremble that caused it to waiver slightly.

"I fear failure and disappointment of those I hope the serve. I fear allowing my effort to be less than the need of it. I fear the loss of wisdom and the rise of evil as a result."

The figure of Kathleen Arbogast hesitated confused for a moment.

Then in the voice of the Ancient One, Anne of Present spoke, this time the command, unmistakable.

"Do not question my veracity spirit. I have stood in the fire; I have walked the Paths of the Dead. I have defeated the 'Dealer of Death'. I will know the secrets. I will open the door. I am Morganna, student of Merlin, Queen of the Fey. I am beyond your judgment." And then with a thrust of her shoulders and in her own voice but none the less powerful, "I am Anne Louise Abbott, stand aside."

"Welcome at last—welcome to the Key!" Stella Vaughn sprang forward, skirting the guardian, much more agile than she had appeared to be.

Across the room, Colm McQuinn made a pantomime of clapping his hands and gave her a wide smile.

"Shall we?" Stella moved toward the hot stove.

"Shall we what?" Annie didn't understand.

Stella stepped to the stove, then into it and the brick wall behind and disappeared through it. Then, almost as an afterthought, her face appeared back into the small sitting room.

"I have something to show you, but you must unlock the door."

"How? How do I do that? Nobody gave me the key; I don't have anything to unlock the door. I don't even know where the door is."

"The Key knows the answer and only the Key. I am only the Keeper and as such can only reveal the location of the door. You are the key." Stella again disappeared into the bright red brick of the fireplace chimney.

Annie looked toward the druid. He smiled and walked across the room. Once he stood in front of Annie his dark eyes held hers for a moment, then taking her hand, "Shall we Anne of Present? We shall either be severely burned by the stove or at best bruised by the bricks beyond. Or just blasted straight to hell and how exciting that sounds. Don't you think? Let's leap into the past. Shield and spear? Together again and into the breach!"

He stepped behind Annie and placing his hands on her shoulders spun her around facing the stove and propelled her directly toward the stove and the wall behind, picking up speed as they went. Annie flinched as the brick façade approached her face and closed her eyes as the contact approached.

"Welcome Merlin! Welcome Morganna! Behold the secrets of the ages.!"

Annie opened her eyes. Stella Vaughn stood to her right, her hand gesturing into the depthless room beyond her. On both sides of her shelves of books rose toward the ceiling and marched away into the smoky distance. In front of her, rows upon rows of long wide tables were covered with arcane apparatus and paraphernalia. On each, candles burned, beakers and chalices bubbled, the vapors rising into a haze of smoke above the tables where it hovered, obscuring the ceiling above. Impossibly thick volumes of books lay open on stands on the tables, as quills hovered over the pages. Test tubes emptied themselves into the bubbling potions and returned to long racks of their brothers.

"At last, the masters have returned to their place of comfort and joy. The lock has been shattered and the door has been opened. The wisdom of those of ages past, now at the hand of those that may at last wield the power of the ages."

Annie looked around in speechless wonder, scanning the walls and tables her eyes roving in amazement in every direction at once.

"This looks like something they'd cook up at Disney World. This can't all be real."

Turning toward Colm, she gasped. Instead of a handsome young man, next to her stood an old man clad in ragged and motheaten robes. His beard was snow white and reached to his chest, where it blended with the long strands of his hair. He regarded her with familiar sparkling eyes and smiled a broad grin. Then turning, he strode forward and exclaimed, "Home at last! Home at last!"

As he walked, his threadbare robes revealed bare feet underneath. He raised his arms in both directions and clapped his hands.

"Greetings old friends. I am home at last! Let us stop for now please." Immediately all activity ceased in the room. "I will need a moment to get my bearings. It has been a while since I set many of you to a task, and I don't remember off hand which was which."

"Wait a minute, how did that happen? After all this, we just had to walk through a wall? Couldn't we have done that right away, or years ago even?" Annie stopped. Her eyes widened, her voice had changed and she did not recognize it. "Wait! What's the matter with my voice?"

"There is a time and a season for everything Morganna." The figure of Merlin stepped closer, "You have never been patient, but for once, please? Remember, you are Annie first and before all else. Please be patient my old love."

"What! Why are you talking to Morganna? I'm Annie; I'm right in front of you. After I just opened the door into here? That's so rude!" This time the unfamiliar voice was harsh, impatient.

Colm stepped to the nearest table and picking

something up, he returned and held it up to Annie. "Annie or Morganna?" He held a small bright mirror up toward Annie; "Or both?"

Annie looked into the small mirror and gasped. Looking back at her was a woman, her look challenging, her eyes narrowed in judgment. On her face, streaks of dark red and black had been drawn from above her left eyebrow to her right chin, her long flaming red hair was tied in braids of leather and hung down across her shoulders. Runes of power finely tattooed, ran down the right side of her face from her eyebrow to the curve of her mouth.

Annie stepped back quickly. She looked again at the ancient man in front of her. His eyes were the only familiar thing: kind, soft. She looked down at herself and again was surprised. In place of her jeans and hooded serape, once a gift from Circe' the sorceress, was a long swallow tail coat of the lightest blue, on her feet she wore sharpened silver-toed boots and a long dagger hung at her belt and strapped to her hip. She looked up toward the ceiling and then at the shelves and lastly at the spirit of Stella Vaughn and she felt the familiarity of everything around her; she suddenly understood—she *knew* this place.

"I know this place." Her voice reflected the wonder of the realization.

Then the wizard spoke to Stella Vaughn. "The door has finally been opened my friend. I thank you. Please, at last, may you seek your peace now? We will see you next again on the Paths of the next world."

"And with the door opened. At last—I may finally rest. At long last. Thank you, Merlin, Master of Wisdom, as you promised so it is at last and I am fulfilled."

As they both looked at the regal woman the vision of

her thinned further, and then with a last beatific smile her glow coalesced into a bright shining spot, flashed and vanished.

"Well, both pupil and teacher, shall we see what we shall see?"

"Am I Morganna while I'm in here?"

"Annie, you are always Morganna."

"But now I even look like Morganna."

"I gotta say, you sound like her too." The old man touched a bubbling beaker on the table he was leaning over. Immediately, the ratty sleeve of his robe caught fire which he absentmindedly slapped out on his hip. "Man, she could get seriously scary sometimes," he continued, shaking the smoldering embers onto the floor.

"Scary. Didn't you have a thing with her, or something like that?" Even as she said it, she knew that it had been true. The shifting from herself to Morganna and back was confusing.

"Morganna was a druid in the truest sense. She practiced the art; she studied diligently; she was easily the best student I ever had the pleasure of tutoring. She was ages ahead of Arthur, and he was truly gifted. She was terribly stubborn, but also open to learning new ways of seeing things. When the hard times came, which they did over and over they have come, she raised the armies of justice. She fought always in the vanguard; her ferocity and ruthless nature to those that hated knowledge and wisdom were unprecedented. Her memories are yours, but you must strive to remain Annie. Her strength of character will be difficult to avoid. However, you are correct. I loved her completely, as did many both before me and after me, and for me, that was a very long time ago. So, now it's time to learn.

But you have the advantage because you don't have to learn the things that Morganna already knew, now it's time to learn learn."

"Learn learn?"

"There's the stuff they teach in school." The old wizard stroked his beard. "You learn it so that you can pass their tests. There's a percentage of it that you'll eventually use in real life, but it's a very small percentage. The things that you need to learn, that will serve you the best, you learn on the playground, or the streets." He paused and stroked a long scar on the back of his hand. "Education does not teach common sense. Experience does. Every experience has consequences and every consequence is a learning experience. Common sense is the lesson of experience and the smartest. The true survivors learn the lessons of common sense with the first lesson. Learning is a multilevel experience, but it is only experienced to the extent of the person's interest. Learning learning is about learning what the lesson really meant. The gravity of each lesson, its wisdom, and how to manipulate that knowledge into more wisdom. The only power on this or any other planet—wisdom."

Morganna/Annie turned away from him and strode to the nearest book shelf, her steel toed boots ringing on the flagstones of the stone floor.

"Which one is the Grimoire? I need to get started." Her tongue struggled with the new language of the ancients.

"Cian has the Grimoire, or at least a decoy of it. Only the wise can discern the presence and location of the Book of Wisdom and Lore."

"How will we get it back? Must we attack and wrest it from his control?"

"Why is your answer always force and violence? First, we must find out if it is gone in the first place, then we must discover how he was able to steal it out of these sealed chambers that have been closed even to me, if it is gone. And we must do it before we lose anything else of value."

"You can do that; I'm going after Cian."

"Morganna, as soon as you step out of this chamber you are a thirteen-year-old girl, with thirteen-year-old fears and emotions. She has already earned the scars of lost innocence at much too early an age; ruthless combat and vindictive anger are beyond our needs currently."

"As you say Master." Annie could feel herself relax. "But I will go if I feel the need. Your approval is not necessary." She recognized that at least for now Morganna was mollified, "But for now I need to stock up on potions and poisons at any rate. Where is Archemedes? He knows the whereabouts of many of the arcane substances in here." She paused and looked down the long line of shelved books and then back at the cluttered tables. "Honestly Merlin, how do you find anything in this mess?"

"I have a system," again he stroked his beard as he peered about, "I'll remember it eventually." His bemused face took in the smoke and vapors overhead, "I'm sure I will." The wizard scratched his beard as his gaze wandered over the room, "Archimedes is scouting for the elves. He has not forgiven you for the last time."

"Arrows need to be fletched; his feathers were perfect for the task. At any rate they grew back didn't they?"

"It was not the growing back that bothered him, it was the losing of them."

"I merely relieved him of them. I will offer my

apology if I should see him again."

"I guarantee he will be much more accommodating with Annie than you Sorceress."

"I am a midwife and a creator of potions; any sorceress in me was burned at the stake long ago."

"That was only one of the lives that you forfeited as the witch that you once were judged to be. Actually, not even your most challenging one to the powers and authority of that day, but you have recompensed those who pronounced that judgment upon the midwife, Morgain of the Uplands, tenfold since that time. For a midwife, you have had a rather negative effect on the Christian enforcers of those early years. For now, perhaps we might dedicate ourselves to the endeavor of learning what we can?"

"Merlin my friend, or shall we become more familiar, my friend Emrys? We have had many good times together, but this other person who speaks for me does not share my love for you. What to do?"

"Emrys? Yes, in days while we hid from the light I was also known as Emrys, but in those days long past, Brian Boru walked among the gods of the earth, and Emrys stood at his right hand. I am a shadow and a memory of those valiant days. In the past, we have committed our hearts to each other; I now am troth plighted to the Keeper of the Light."

"The Keeper of the Light you say?"

"The Keeper of the Light and the spirit of Circe', Queen of Aeaea."

"Ah, Circe' truly a woman not to be trifled with. Met your match Merlin, met your match have you my wise one?"

"Time alone will tell."

"For now, I will remember for the girl. For now I

must 'learn learn' again you say?"
　　"For now."

The Ride of the Elven Army

It was hours later as Annie sat cross legged on the floor at the base of one of the bookshelves, a huge book open on her lap as she observed.

"Did you know that the American Meadow Lark does not know how to sing? They have to be taught by their parents. Otherwise, they learn other songs from other birds. That is an oddity."

"Trivial wisdom. And yes, I knew that." Merlin stretched his back and rubbed his eyes; the great book he'd been studying closed itself in front of him. "We need a rest. We've lost focus. It's been a long day already. Let's go get something to eat and maybe a spot of tea." Merlin was already moving toward the door. "Besides, I really need to go to the bathroom."

Annie unwound herself up on to her feet. Until now she had not realized that she was starving. "Wait. Can we just go in and out? Won't the door close behind us?"

"Yes, it will."

"So, we'll be locked out?"

"You are the key. Only the key can open the door, and only the key may re-enter."

"Well I'm starving. How long have we been in here

today?"

"Today? Annie, I'm pretty sure it was Tuesday, maybe Wednesday morning when we first breeched the doorway. It is probably Friday, maybe Saturday by now. The pendulum swings much more slowly in here than it does out there. Time moves much more quickly among the mortals. Their pendulum swings much more quickly."

"Three days! I've been in here, like—three days?"

"More like three-and-a-half."

"Three-and-a-half days! I haven't eaten in three-and-a-half days? That's insane. Get me out of here. I think I must be dying of starvation."

With a subtle hand gesture the wizard waved toward the only blank wall in the room. "I'm right behind you."

"You mean I could have done that anytime I wanted to?"

"You are the Key."

"I think I may be starting to resent you Merlin."

"So you say, young one. So they all have said—sooner or later."

Annie rushed toward the wall but stopped just short. "This will take some getting used to." Then putting one hand out in front of her, she pushed toward the wall and melted into it. The druid priest was only steps behind her.

Arriving in the parlor, in front of the wood stove, they were greeted with a darkened room. No lights shone like before. The room air was cold. There was no welcome warmth from the small wood stove keeping the room cozy. The cast iron stove stood cold, with no trace of a glowing ember.

"The Keeper and the Guardian of the books have departed. The house now fully belongs to the

University." The druid observed, once again in casual dress and penny loafers, "They can search in vain for their evidence and trace, but the presence of their spirits has departed. Wouldn't I love to be a fly on the wall when they try and measure the energy that was here only days ago."

"Okay, that's fine, but is there anything to eat."

"We'll have to forage. I can send Archimedes to scout, but we'll need the elves too."

"Don't they get hungry?"

"The owl provides for them and Bracken. We need human food and he doesn't do that." Colm stood next to her in the dark. "But I bet he knows where to find pizza."

"Pizza! Oh my gosh! I haven't had pizza in forever." Annie shuddered as she gripped the arms of the druid and in a deep feminine voice said, "I might not be as mad at you if we can get pizza!"

"Don't do that! It's hard enough to separate the two of you. Just be Annie out here, please."

"Sorry. I didn't realize that I could do that."

Stepping out of the house and onto the front porch they were immediately greeted by a grouping of the warriors. In the dim light of the distant streetlights, the great dire wolf stood at the foot of the stairs, his gaze fixed on those already on the porch. The owl was in his customary perch on the newel post, also transfixed. On the porch were four elves. The first three were the travelers, companions of the One, the fourth was a new arrival. All eyes were on the fourth elf who lay on the porch floor as another knelt, cradling its head. The other two leaned in, their posture signifying alarm and concern.

"What is this then!?" The druid rushed forward.

"It is Ash. She brings word from the south." Micah's face never left the fallen elf. "We believe her wounds to be mortal."

"We mourn our valiant sister. She brings word and a foreboding." Mink spoke with obvious emotion.

Colm McQuinn dropped to his knees next to the injured elf. "Ash! Oh, I am so sorry Ash, I honor you my comrade and my friend. I can ease your pain if you wish."

"Greetings wise one." Ash voiced, a pained whisper. "No please do not trouble, my pain is but a small matter now." Ash gasped. "I bring tidings—at great cost. They are most dire." Another gasp. "You must—you must prepare." Her words tapered off and her eyes rolled up in her head. She took two shuddering breaths before her glowing eyes returned and focused on the druid's face; her hand gripped his sleeve. "I have traveled through fire and water. I have finished my journey."

"Yes, my friend; please. Then rest you will have in the land beyond the Mountain of Smokes."

"Those of the Underworld have grown strong. They manipulate the world that is beyond ours, they bring uncertainty and distrust. They foment anarchy and hate. Their successes are growing. They hope to resurrect Balor the Evil One in mortal form."

"I understand Ash."

"The Red and the White are disarmed and taken captive." Ash raised her head in emphasis. "The Red Queen rides to their rescue. At her back ride the Elven Kings of Old. The fight has begun." The stricken warrior paused as she gasped for her breath. Continuing she looked over the druid's shoulder into Annie's eyes. "The need is for the One, Morgaine of old, once again."

Then again, she held the druid's eye. "The need has

become great. The last word of the Red Witch as she was taken, *"The world once again calls for the Shield and the Spear."*

The elf shuddered and her eyes closed. Then with one last incredible effort. "To have lived to see the rise of the One and the force of The Three is a joy beyond my hope. I die fulfilled in my mission." Then with one last sigh, she was gone to the ages.

The elves bowed their heads as the druid solemnly closed her wide eyes. The dire wolf bowed down on his paws. A long silence followed.

The owl spoke, "The witches of the Red and White have been taken. Cian indeed has overstretched his reach if he thinks to hold the two of them."

"There is something else; I can sense it." The druid, still on his knees next to the fallen elf examined her carefully, looking at her many wounds and touching her at the points of the seven spiritual connections. Finally, he placed his hand on her forehead and closed his eyes. "Ah, yes. Yes, I see. Thank you, Ash."

"What is it? What do you see?" The dire wolf rumbled with interest.

The druid remained silent for a long moment as all leaned in to hear. Annie fidgeted, not sure of what she should do, stunned by the death of someone who had once been so close to her.

In a voice that did not match his own, he spoke, "There is a traitor. The traitor is one that has been close to us all. They have given up the Red and the White. It is by that very hand that Ash has been taken from us."

"Who? Who is this vile creature? They shall die by my own hand I vow." Micah could not hide the hate and grief from his voice.

"I'm incredibly sorry Micah, I know how dear Ash

was to you. But I cannot see beyond that. There is something else first. The Elvin army rides, and we are too few. How many? How many does Garnet bring at her back and do they ride to their destructions? The Books of Lore must wait. We must find The Three and go to their aid."

"I'm sorry too, all of you; I really liked Ash." Annie stepped forward and put a hand on Micah's shoulder. "You two, I could tell you kind of liked her especially. I'm sorry."

"Yes, I will have to get word to the children."

"The children?"

"Yes, Ash was my long mate. We have children together, many children. They will be heartbroken. As am I."

Archimedes, his head constantly on a swivel, spoke, "The Three will be weary, but they must be located. The light will come soon, but the hunt must begin immediately. Who will go?"

"I will seek The Three." Bracken climbed the few steps and placed his massive paw on the shoulder of Micah. "I must be away, and I must finally seek my brothers. Once I discover The Three, I will hunt to the north. I must find them if still they are; the hammer has come to the anvil, and the need is great. I must raise my kin, if kin I have left. But first, I will seek The Three." Bracken spoke in a whisper, the emotion clear in his strong and usually brave voice. "I mourn your loss my ally of old."

"How many? How many ride Micah, do you think?" Colm, his countenance grim he spoke to the darkness beyond the house.

"The Lady Garnet long ago pledged her aid to the Red Witch in time of need, she will ride with the full force of the Mountain of Smokes. The Red Queen wields the fire of the mountain itself as her weapon of war. Woe to those that will hope to stand against her. Her riders will sweep north in a vanguard as wide as a man may walk in one hour, wider than the shadow of the sun from one hour to the next."

"We must rendezvous with her before they come against Cian." Colm rose and walked to the top of the staircase. "If he has the ability to disarm the Red Witch and White Witch, they must be prepared. Their journey will be days upon weeks; they must arrive as rested as might be possible."

He turned and faced them, "The Shield and the Spear must delay those minions of evil until that can be achieved. We must stand against the tide until they arrive."

"Wait! The Shield and Spear thing again? I didn't like that the first time." Annie had been listening intently but this caught her completely off guard. "This sounds like an even bigger deal! Is that the only answer, the Shield and Spear thing?"

"The Red and White are captive." Colm turned toward Annie. "That means that the Keeper of the Light has become a fugitive; she will not have the strength even with those that remain of the thirteen, to resist Cian. She will be at great risk. With the loss of Circe' and the Colors there is no one else. If the forces of integrity are to have a ghost of a chance, they must be allowed to marshal their forces against the evil that wants to replace it. The Elven Army must have the time against greater odds. They have wagered everything in this last roll of the dice. We must stand for them; we must buy them the time that they must have—even should our own lives be forfeit Annie, we must buy them those precious minutes.

It is why we are who we are. It is why we are created."

"Forfeit? You mean, we, you and me? Forfeit? You mean killed? We'd be killed!"

"If that is what it takes to slow their march."

"Nope, no thank you. C'mon, I'm sorry. I'm sorry Micah; I'm sorry everybody. This is too much. It's too real. No, no… no. I can't." Annie backed away from the group waving her hands in front of her, most especially the small lifeless form that lay on the floor in front of her.

"Your father fights; he fights to the death that you may live." Micah rose to his feet and advanced on her. "I fight, with or without my wife. I fight because I must. It is not a choice or because I enjoy it. I fight for my children and my children's children."

"We ask nothing for ourselves, only that our children may live in a world of sunshine and hope." Mink stepped forward next to Micah. "We no longer fight with the hope that we will see it for ourselves."

Archimedes walked along the banister of the porch railing, his great yellow eyes fixed on Annie's. "You can refuse. You can run. You can hide. You can find the deepest hole in the ground and pull the hole in after you, if you will. The darkness that is spreading in our world and the world beyond ours will find you. Maybe tomorrow, maybe next week, next year, but find you it will. And while you hide, all you will be able to think about is when will it find you and knowing all along— that it would." The owl swiveled his head to the darkness beyond the house. "The great one that weaves the webs of our lives wove yours long ago. Hide if you must; it will not alter the events that march toward you at this moment. It will only prolong the pain of the final moment."

"Stand and fight, or run and be overtaken. I will fight, and I will fight until their darkness is returned to the night." Bracken's voice was rough. "I will see you soon, on the other side of tomorrow." With that he sprang away into the darkness. From the darkness his rumbling voice reached her brain. "Always I will be your friend. You are the One."

"I think a little pizza and maybe a gigantic chocolate shake might be the next more immediate requirement though. How about we have something to eat and then maybe give the rest of this a little time to percolate into our thoughts?" Colm stepped up to Annie and put a comforting hand upon her shoulder.

"Pizza! I love pizza! With anchovies please." Archimedes' incredibly deep voice sounded enthusiastic.

"Nobody invited you Archimedes."

"I distinctly heard Anne of Present request my presence in the absence of her valiant protector Bracken. Isn't that correct Anne of Present?"

"Um… yeah… I guess. Do you even eat pizza?"

"With anchovies? Assuredly."

"*I also like pizza. With jalapeno peppers and extra cheese please.*" Patch hovered in front of Colm McQuinn.

"We do not eat 'pizza'. Are we traveling soon?" Micah stepped forward. "There will be need for haste. We will arrange transport." Micah smiled, "Something discreet perhaps."

Pizza and Questions

Annie had to admit that middle of the night pizza, in a small dive pizza bar on the outskirts of Mt. Juliet, Tennessee really hit the spot. The chocolate shake that they had picked up just a couple of blocks off of Music Row in downtown Nashville only minutes before also was memorable. She was starting to relax, the events beyond the Door of Wisdom almost an afterthought, the death of Ash now buffering into memory. She tried to relax into the seat but the plush leather bucket seats refused. The constant belching of the fairy seated on the dashboard didn't help either, as she consumed one beer after another.

After shifting one more time, she sighed and in the dim dashboard light of the Maserati, she looked ahead beyond the long hood and chewed thoughtfully.

"Are you going to eat that last piece?" Archimedes spoke in his haunting voice from space behind the seats.

"It has fish on it! Eww! No." Annie wasn't too tired to express herself fully.

"That was excellent! It has been a long time since I had pizza indeed." Patch moved to the armrest between the two seats. *"Is there perhaps any of that last beer left druid?"*

"About a half-pint perhaps, maybe a little more."

"Hand it back then." The small fairy hefted the tall bottle of bitter beer, maneuvering it and then tilting it back. After a long pause punctuated by the sound of tiny swallows. *"Alas, gone too soon."* She wiped her mouth on her arm and belched loudly. Then handing the bottle back to the druid who was just finishing his own, she leaned back and scratched her stomach. Raising her gaze, she spoke, *"Well Anne of Present?"*

Annie had been trying to focus on her shake and her pizza but she knew that this question was coming sooner or later but still she did not have a ready answer.

"Let's see if I understand, okay? I know you guys are old hands at this. You've all been through this before, right?"

Patch spoke for the others. *"No Anne of Present, with each time it is new again. We have all paid the price for our efforts in times past. Some cursed to live on and others to not."* She paused looking meaningfully toward the druid and then back at the owl behind her. *"Some of us have outlived the times of peace to these times of today. It is a pity and cruelty for those of us who have waited for the rise of the One and the hope of the righteous. As it is for the others who were forced to rise again from the graves of those past selves."*

Annie looked across at the druid who was avoiding her gaze, and then turned to look directly at the small fairy.

"But the Shield and Spear thing? Does this happen every time? I mean; does it always come to that? Isn't there some easier way? Wait. No wait, just a minute. It's never succeeded in the past, has it?"

She thought for a moment. "No, wait... never; really? And now it comes down to me? This Key thing, this Shield and Spear? It's all come down to this. This?"

Annie rubbed her suddenly damp palms down her pants legs. She fidgeted, trying to look at the oncoming sunrise, to look anywhere else. No, no, she had to know.

"Do any of you remember? Ummm… I don't know if I know what I mean, but do any of you remember? You know? You know, the last… um… Annie?"

She asked, not sure that she wanted to know the answer. Not sure that there even was an answer. Instead, she focused down the long hood of the Maserati, hoping that there wasn't one.

There was no sound for a long moment in the car. Colm McQuinn quietly put his empty bottle down and twisted the key in the ignition. The powerful machine growled to life and slowly pulled away from the curb. The sleek car maneuvered down the deserted city streets until it entered the Interstate and veered west and into the darkness beyond. The silence within the car stretched on as time stretched out with it. With each minute, as the signs of civilization faded into the rear-view mirror behind them, Annie's discomfort increased.

The car's engine calmed to the hum of the tuned exhaust as the speed increased and the shining mile post markers passed in ever shortening intervals. The broken center line striping blended into a flashing strobe of yellow light. In the lights of the dashboard the face of the druid appeared to grow tighter; the shadows beneath his eyes grew darker and his cheeks narrowed. At last, the streaking vehicle raced off the highway and on to an anonymous off ramp braking only enough to fishtail onto a long lonely stretch of two-lane rural road and race on.

After several miles of winding darkness, the car slowed and pulled onto the grassy shoulder. The druid released the steering wheel only long enough to turn off the car's engine and return his knuckle whitened grip to the steering wheel as the car's inhabitants were instantly plunged into the darkness and cold of a growing February morning.

In the silence that followed the engine slowly ticked itself to sleep; the windows began to fog over and the owl in the back roughed his feathers and sighed. The silence stretched further until it was beyond discomfort. Then finally, in the intense quiet of the cold Tennessee morning at sunrise, the harshly whispered voice of the druid priest sounded loud and discordant in the closed space.

"Yes."

Yes

"Yes?" Annie hadn't forgotten the question; she just wanted to be sure that 'Yes', was the answer to that particular question.

"Yes. Yes we knew the last 'Annie'. We have known all of the 'Annies'. We have known them for generations upon generations. We have watched as their promise failed before it could manifest. We have suffered when their courage was insufficient to stand against the darkness. We have watched as they struggled. We have watched as they failed. We have watched as they passed through the veil, the cost of their failings." He paused and turned his now gaunt face toward her. "And each time we have loved her," he paused and sighed, "and each time we have died at her side in one way or another."

"I was but a thistle bud when the last true seeker appeared. But she fell victim to her power and sought treasure instead of riches. Thus she perished in the flames of her own fire." Patch floated forward and perched on the dashboard in front of Annie. *"There have been others. Those that wished to be Seeker, those that pretended the substance of the One. They foundered before us. We have lived in fear of the next Seeker*

who was not so and we have lived in hope for the next that may be the true. Since the true Morganna, our ferocious queen walked among us, there has never been one such as you. The responsibility for your safety is beyond your ability to believe, but it is a responsibility that we gladly accept."

Archimedes spoke from behind Annie, "We have known many and just as I have assisted those many, I have died with them as well. Their attempts for success were sometimes heartfelt; and sometimes driven by ego, or greed, and fairly often by the direction of darker agendas beyond them. None were successful. They paid the price for their lack of personal substance and passed from this earth as a result—as did we, the result of our trust in her."

"With the appearance of each new Seeker, we rose once again. Our task always to protect her and test her. You, Anne of Present, have surpassed those tests a hundred-fold. Your power, even at these early stages, is beyond anything we remember." The Druid leaned back against the car door and smiled across at her. "It is even a little terrifying."

"Wait. You mean every single one. Every single one since the last confirmed time that Morgan Le Fey stood before anybody, they all failed?"

"The last nine-hundred-seventy-two times. Yes, we have known the last Annies, every one of them. You however, will be the last."

"The last?"

"Cian has risen beyond our greatest fears. He has found a way around us. He now lives in the world beyond ours; he has become powerful among the mortals. His success there will seek to end us and our world. He would close the door that we guard so diligently. He would do so that we can no longer return him to the darkness where he belongs. If that happens their world will fall as well—eventually. You will be the last, win or lose, the last Annie—ever." The dark face of the druid appeared almost as a mask of death from the other side of the car in the low light of early morning.

Patch flew into Annie's vision, *"Cian cares nothing about the mortal world. There is no gain for him there. Their attention span is so short that they will adapt to almost anything, even that of servitude. He wishes only that we too pass from this, our world, and he wishes to hold the Key and powers of our queen, Morganna of Old, Anne of Present. He wishes for our demise but your life as one of servitude."*

"I'm sorry. I'm sorry." Annie leaned across and touched the hand of the druid. "Somehow, I can feel your pain. I can feel all of your pain. I don't even know how that happens, but I feel it. Now it's my pain too, oh and it hurts my heart to know that you suffered so much. I'm so, so sorry, but even though this gets more real every day, I don't know what to do. Every single thing that I learn, that I learn every day, gets scarier all the time."

"It is beyond scary young one."

"No, come on! You guys are talking about me dying if I don't do all of this stuff just right. Come on you guys, I'm thirteen-years-old. I have trouble deciding whether to wear the socks with the dinosaurs or the ones with the green frogs. I'm supposed to be this almighty woman from the ages past and instead I'm looking at a zit on my forehead in the mirror and wondering if bangs might have been a better choice. I can't save the world; I can't even take care of myself. Come on!"

"When The Three rose against Cian I looked for someone, a champion probably at least twice your age. I never expected it to be the daughter of Roison of the

West March because I was looking beyond her. But The Three gathered near her. I admit, you are young in years Annie, but there has never been any one even once who expressed the incredible and remorseless ferocity of Kehlen of the Twisted Teeth, the Taker of Souls, much less hold her powerful personality in check. There has never been one that has walked the Paths of the Dead or faced the Dealer of Death, much less lived to tell the tale. And you have defeated her, perhaps the greatest foe of our lives, ever. It is the stuff of legends, and you have done all of it in the span of a few short months. You have spoken among the Fey, you have been accepted as one of the thirteen, and you have witnessed the death of Circe' the Eldest and her rebirth. You understand the language of the ancients and can speak it. You have opened the door to the Books of Lore. You are the One Anne of Present—and then some.

"We stand beside you, though it may be the last time or perhaps the first time of the next age. You are our hope. Even as the Red Queen rides to the north, her armies marshaled behind her; she comes to stand at your side. For the first and perhaps the last time, the greatest force of the Fey, those that carry the spiritual strength of this world and that of the one beyond ours. The greatest force of our kind since Brian Boru and the hosts of Tam Lin fought the gods of evil ever to assemble will marshal forces behind the teenaged queen, our teenaged queen, the queen of all of us. We will bear arms in the name of Anne of Present. We will bear arms against the rise of evil. We would fight with or without hope, but now we will stand, our combined strength focused, our talisman in the forefront, Anne of Present, Warrior Queen of the Fey, for one—

last—

time."

Annie unlatched and threw open the door. Jumping out she thrust her arms in the pockets of her parka and stomped off up the road ahead of the car and into the fading darkness.

"She took that rather well I thought." Archimedes observed.

"Archimedes. She's a kid. She hasn't had hundreds of years to get used to this."

"Well, if any of us is going to live to see the other side, she had better catch up in a hurry. That message of Ash should be enough to support that theory."

"The elf's message was one of caution. They have always been among us, but it is a terrible price we pay when we relax our guard. They are clever and concealed until the moment when they emerge and can accomplish the most damage." He looked at the owl meaningfully in the rear-view mirror.

"You no longer suspect her, do you wise one?"

"There is none other more clever, cruel and most of all patient than the 'Taker of Souls'. I don't fear Annie; I fear 'The Taker' waiting, crouching within her, waiting for Annie to lower her guard. I fear her strength overpowering an unprepared opponent and I fear the combined power that she would obtain if she did just that. She lurks; I know it. I will always be a little on my guard; that is my wisdom."

"Yes, it is a heavy price. The Red and the White both taken and powerless. That is unprecedented and a dark foreboding. Will he perhaps send them through the veil?"

"I don't pretend to know the plans that Cian may be

hatching, but I know he will not let them go peacefully if that is his plan. He will wish to take his pleasure first; he will wish them pain above all else because that will please him most. He will take his leisure with it and he will be diligent."

"Can they be rescued?" Archimedes sounded skeptical

"Say the word, and I will marshal those of the Glen in the Woods, and those of Wind River Mountain. We will fight for their freedom." Patch was starting to feel the effects of the beer.

"No Patch, Cian would like nothing more than for us to charge against him without the organized strength that we might muster. No, first we must help that young girl out ahead of us to find the strength of her ancestors and somehow not lose her mind and soul in the effort. Before anything else, first—we must save Annie."

Hammer of Stone

The sun had risen above the trees in the east and began to warm the interior of the bright red car. The passengers sat silently, dozing in place—waiting. It had been a long night. The minutes had ticked away beyond the next hour as the silence grew. No birds sang, no chickens crowed in the frigid morning air. Around them the empty fields of harvested corn stretched in every direction. No one stirred—they waited.

In the distance a figure appeared, fogged breath puffing out at intervals. The figure approached, walking with purpose, long fast strides closing the distance rapidly. Inside the car, a small fairy looked up with a sharp intake of breath. At last drawing beside the car Annie grasped the car door handle and yanked it open. The druid, who had been leaning against the door while he dozed, fell backward out of the door and hung upside down, his head only inches above the dew frozen grass. His eyes wide he flexed forward far enough to make eye contact.

"Hello Annie! Good morning." He tried to smile as he regarded her from his upside-down position. "How was your walk?"

"Forget that!" Annie fumed at his upside-down face. "You never once mentioned that this was the last time. You made it sound like we were going to study— learn learn—you never once told me that I was not expected to live to see the other side of all of this, that you weren't either, that none of us were! When? When were you going to mention it? When were you going to tell me that I was born to die?"

She backed up, waving her hands.

"No wait, don't try and answer. You pretended to be my friend. You pretended that I would be protected. You, you…" Annie stepped out to the middle of the road and stared into the distance. Then in a meek and quiet voice, "You made me like you, all of you. Now I can't… I can't stand the thought that I will lose you. Any of you. I can't, I can't and somehow, I have to… somehow, I have to find a way to make it not happen. It's unfair; you ask too much."

"I know Annie," Colm finally levered himself back up into the seat and swiveled his feet out onto the ground. "It's a lot. It's more to take in than this moment can handle. It's more than anyone who had a lifetime to accept it could absorb. No one ever expects to come to the crossroads of their lives with so little preparation. No one expects when they must choose the course of their futures, especially when they least expect it and it has such dire implications as yours does.

"But even at this point, you must admit that your appearance has accelerated the events that shape the future. You are the catalyst of the future. Whether it will continue in this age, or whether it will advance into the next, your influence will create that. But now; now you must decide. Anne of Present or Annie Abbott, junior high school student."

Annie had not turned to face them yet, but now she swiveled and with her fists clenched she angrily squinted at the three in the car. As she did her eyes suddenly flamed hot, bright red as the tendons in her arms stretched from beneath the skin.

"You guys… you guys!…"

"It is the final test Annie. You must decide. It is the final moment." Colm rose to his feet and stepped forward, his hand on something in his back pocket, his demeanor no longer benign, "You must declare your intent."

Annie looked up into his dark eyes. There was no enfoldment, no warmth, they were opaque to any reflection of emotion. He held her gaze in unrelenting watchfulness.

"I… I think I choose…," Annie looked away, "I choose to be…" The red in her eyes flamed bright. "I choose to be…", and then they faded as they slowly turned back to blue. "I choose to be your One. For as long as I can. I will do what I can to protect my Dad, but also to help my new friends."

The druid sighed and his shoulders relaxed, his hand moved away from the dagger at his belt. The fairy now seated on the roof of the car relaxed, sighed and sheathed her sword. The great owl ruffled its feathers and swiveled his head in all directions and looked toward the druid. Then with his long sigh, Colm regarded Annie.

"I am the embodiment of Merlin the Magnificent, it is true. But at one time, I stood at the right hand of Brian Boru, the last great king of Ireland and my liege lord. You should know what comes to stand beside you. You need to know that I am not just a chemist or a teacher. You should know the Hammer of Stone."

"What… what does that mean?"

Patch zoomed from the car and suspended in front of Annie, her voice was breathless as she drew her sword.

"The Hammer of Stone is lost to the ages. No one who could wield it walks the earth today and even if they were here at hand in this moment, the Hammer is lost, destroyed in the last great battle. There are none of those that warred against the hounds of hell in ages long past. They passed away long ago. You should not try and fool her with tales of glory and strength when we have so few weapons already."

It was Colm's turn to step out into the abandoned road. He walked to the far shoulder pulling his Polo shirt over his head in the cold wintery air and turned to face her.

"Warrior of old, warrior today, fighter of renown, show her my way!" He chanted in a shout toward the rising sun and he reached for the silver medallion that hung suspended at his throat.

In a flash that reflected the brilliance of the morning sun back in her eyes, Annie beheld the warrior she had first seen on the night of the Shield and the Spear, the night of Circe's final battle, the night she had first met her true father. Before her stood a mighty man, his face painted in colors of battle, his kilt and belt the plaids of the king. In his hand he brandished a mighty war hammer. He twirled the hammer in his heavily muscled arm as if it was almost a trivial thing. Then he swung it high over his head and brought it down on the pavement of the road. The reverberating vibration of the impact immediately turned the paved road surface into vibrating gravel that spread away into the distance in both directions.

"He wields the Hammer of Stone!" Patch's voice could

not conceal the awe. *"I did not know."* Patch hovered in front of Annie but faced away from her. Instead, she faced the terrifying visage before her, her tiny sword drawn and her pose one of defense. *"The Hammer of Stone may be wielded by only one of them. One of the 'Terror Fighters' of old. It was thought that those passed from the earth years upon years ago. It was believed to be lost to the legends. Truly, he must be last of his kind. The fighters that fought at the front, that fought to the death—to defend the last great king."* The fairy's eyes never left the warrior, and she did not relax a single muscle.

Suddenly, from over her shoulder the great horned owl swooped to the ground in front of her, his wings spread wide facing the visage that wielded the hammer, shielding Annie.

"Step back Annie! Stay behind us!"

Patch spoke again over her shoulder, *"It was thought the last fell at the feet of the final king, Brian Boru, in the futile defense of his king's life. It was at the end of the last age long ago. Here stands the last, the last of the ferocious Berserkers of old."*

"The Berserkers!? I thought they were a myth." Annie whispered, both frightened and awed by the figure in front of her that seemed to simmer in the morning sunlight. "My Dad talked about them. He thought they were cool, like he admired them but I thought it was just stories they used to scare the peasants in olden times. Weren't they all Vikings or something?"

"They were Celts, one of the seven nations. We thought them gone from this earth in the long years of the past. That I have lived to see the legend of the Hammer alive and before me. It is a true wonder to me." As the gaze of the fearsome vision shifted so did the fairy's position as she continued to shift and keep herself between him and Annie. *"Trust*

them not. The Berserker fights with a passion beyond his own recognition. The ferocity of the Berserker is a blind weapon. He fights what lies ahead of him, regardless of the odds that he faces, regardless of the foe. His only desire, to destroy."

Archimedes' strident voice, "If we tell you to run Annie, get in the car and go! Go as fast as you can!"

"Lilith said that the druid was no warrior. Wouldn't she have known?"

"The Hammer of Stone fights, the Berserker only wields the weapon because he must. The Hammer knows its foe, it is the Hammer that they fear."

As the first rays of the morning sunrise struck the face of the painted warrior, he again touched the silver star at his throat and faded back into the shirtless druid swinging a small keychain on his finger with a tiny hammer on the ring.

"Ye gads, it's cold out here!" Colm hurriedly pulled his shirt back on.

Archimedes had moved forward.

"A little too theatrical for me. You could have just told her you know."

"I don't know what you mean Archimedes. Would you have believed me?"

"I make it policy to never believe anything wizards or witches tell me at face value. It's a good way to lose tail feathers, I have learned."

"Touche'. Did we finish all the pizza? Is there any left? Now I'm starving again."

"Alas, the pizza and all the rest of the beer lies at the bottom of the selfish fairy. Apparently, she is completely unschooled in the social graces."

"I looked to see if anyone wanted any more. You all seemed preoccupied with other things. The first rules of the warrior; eat when there is food, sleep whenever you can and fight when you

must. Patch is a warrior.”

“The next time, perhaps we should lock you in the trunk until everyone has had all they want.” Archimedes ruffled his feathers and glared at the fairy.

“Perhaps you will try that, and perhaps you will lose more than a few tailfeathers.” Patch waved her sword at the owl one last time before returning it to its scabbard.

“You mean, you have that, um, that monstrous thing hanging on a keychain in your pocket?” Annie was beyond being surprised anymore, but she was incredulous at the casual way the druid handled the terrifying weapon. “Really?”

“Well, I can’t just leave it in the cup holder now, can I?” He winked at her. “Let’s get back in the car and get the heater going. We can talk once we’re all thawed out.”

In a matter of a few short minutes, while the car was content to purr quietly at the side of the road, the heater had responded and the car poured heat into its interior.

“So, you’re Merlin, and you’re Colm McQuinn and now you’re some freak-show warrior that we’re all afraid of? How many other people are you hiding inside of you? Am I supposed to trust you when you’re that guy?”

“Nope.”

“Nope what?”

“The Berserkers were so uncontrollably savage that even their own people did not step in front of them. If the Hammer of Stone appears, all would be wise to stand behind it, never in front. It is a corner of my mind that I cannot see into, or control it, nor can I expect it to be able to be controlled.”

“But you were one once?”

“Long before I was Merlin, when I was still in my apprenticeship, I was known as the man named Emrys. I was young, and I was always anxious to learn, to experience the next thing of interest. Because I was descended from royalty, I was educated by the finest druid tutors, but I wanted to learn beyond the books and scrolls of that time. I wished for the secrets that the druids kept hidden. Even though I was of royal blood I had accepted an apprenticeship with them, but it wasn't enough. I wanted more. I wished to go beyond the craft of wisdom. I had read about the secret of the warrior but could not find what it was. I asked the masters to open the door beyond them.

"At first they refused thinking that I was just too young and foolish but I persisted and they finally honored my request. I stood the transition; I took the medicants they offered and disappeared into the sea of fire and fume. I suffered long in an agony of total awareness. When I emerged beyond the travail still alive, I was gifted the weapon that I had earned while within, I became the hand of the Hammer, and I assumed my rightful place at the right hand of the King."

"But he died."

"Yes, slain by the hand of Kehlen of the Twisted Teeth. She struck him down even as I struck her. My effort was in vain, and my master suffered to his mortal death."

"And you and that hammer thing just disappeared? Is that why Patch didn't know?"

"It is not just me that failed that day you know. I stood at the right hand of the king, Brian Boru, but there was an equally fierce warrior on his left. And in that moment, both failed to protect him."

"Who? Who was the other one? Who was standing on his left?"

"Why Annie... it was you."

One Mad Witch

Annie's eyes couldn't have gotten any bigger. Her head snapped back and her knees smacked the underside of the dashboard. Again, she unlatched the door, stepped out and slammed it behind her. Colm jumped out on his side and faced her across the roof.

"No! No!" Annie's hands were buried inside of the serape as she yelled into the distance. "I don't want to die. That's what you're trying to tell me isn't it? You're trying to make me see what's going to happen to me." She looked up at him, his face now in the morning sun. "I know that's true; I can feel it even if I don't remember it. I've already died? No. Wait."

She clenched her hands at her sides and paced the length of the car and back. Her face that had been anxious before, now became a mask of horror.

"Now I feel the pain. I... I... remember."

She fixed her gaze on the ground at her feet as a vision of memory returned and played out in her mind. In a deeper voice, she remembered,

"No... no, no, no, I watched as the mighty Hammer fell. I see... I can see as one after another arrow finds its mark, but still, he fights on. I watched it...as his strength faded and the… and the hammer fell; as he was overpowered, as he fought to his very last breath. I… I see him look up to me as our eyes met. I was… I was shielding the king! I couldn't go to his aid." Now her face reflected the anguish of the memory. "And then… and then I died too. I felt it… I… Oh my god… I can feel it… I… I died." She could not help the tears that splashed from her eyes and fell into the gravel between her shoes.

From across the roof of the car, as tears rolled down his own cheeks, the druid watched as she suffered through the sensory memory of her own death. He had watched her die then, as their eyes had met, as they had died together. And now perhaps, he must do it once again.

Her sobs continued, impossibly loud in the still country that surrounded them. "Oh god! You… you knew all along. You saw my future from the day I was born. You knew it would come to this."

"No." Colm spoke quietly, "No, I hated the thought of it coming to this. I had hopes that we could somehow avoid this moment in time. I wished another fate for you." He turned and looked up the road for a long moment. "I believe we can alter this path. I believe that we may avoid that ultimate fate. I have to hope that is the truth, and above all—I believe in you Annie." He turned and faced her again. "I believe in your goodness, and your capacity to love. I believe you are the One because of that very fact. We will win—we will win because we must."

Once back in the car Colm executed a 3-point turn and drove back to the freeway and again turned the car west. Annie turned her face to the window as her sobs continued. As the miles rolled by her sobs turned to hiccups and then finally her chin sank to her chest and she fell asleep leaning against the door.

"The chess pieces are moving. The game is in the balance but we are at a disadvantage."

"Yes," Archimedes voice seemed sad. "Yes, we are blind to their movements and blind to our own."

"The Fomorians of old rose from the sea, but also from the depths of the Underworld. The forces that we oppose will be already assembled when they set foot on the land. They will be fully capable immediately. But where? Where will they come from and where will they assemble?"

"They will come from the sea as in days gone by. They should be met on the beaches and thrown back to the fishes." Patch's voice was stern and angry.

"Easily said my friend, but unless we are mistaken in our calculations, or we pick the wrong beach. What then?"

"Then we track them."

"We must face them on two fronts. Remember, Cian is now in the mortal world. He is creating havoc, and he will not miss the opportunity to turn those people and their world upside down. He is rising in power, and he is starting to command media attention. The mortal world looks for a savior that won't interfere with their lifestyles. Cian is the perfect individual for the job. He will be their savior in exchange for their freedom, and eventually their lives. And they will gladly give it to him.

"Those that will come from the sea must be dealt with to be sure, but we mustn't be distracted from the real target. Cian must be returned to his realm above all else, and no sacrifice will be too great to accomplish that."

"As it was then, so it is now as well. Woe to us."

Archimedes leaned in between the two bucket seats. "Not to cause additional concern, but where exactly would we be going at the present moment?"

"I can sense some things, and I can divine other things. Also, I read the newspapers. The weather in the west has been increasingly unpredictable and the incredible number of wildfires and drought there give me suspicions that is where their influence is growing the strongest. My feelings tell me to go west. The Red Queen comes from the south; she can read the signs as well as I can, but she cannot follow the shoreline, there are too many riders that charge behind her. Along the coastline the way becomes too narrow for a host of that size. She will come through the central valley and I believe she will make for the redwoods before she turns to the east. The redwood forest is a deeply spiritual place and an ideal location for them to rest and regather their strength. We must try and intercept her before she makes the decision to turn east. We're going to need to hurry, and we have to try and cloak this vehicle. Please wake her up. I'll need her help to do it."

"I don't think she will be in the mood for that sort of thing." Archimedes immediately moved to a safe distance beyond the reach of Annie.

"She is a warrior, she will answer the call of duty." Patch dropped onto Annie's shoulder and leaned carefully close to her exposed ear. She cupped her hands, took a deep breath and in a surprisingly loud and deep voice yelled, ***"Hey! Wake up! Wake up. We need assistance here."***

Annie's head snapped alert but not before it banged against the passenger window. "What? What's going on? Ow! Where... what." She blinked her eyes trying to stare in every direction at once.

"We need to cloak this vehicle and we need to do it now!"

"So?"

"So do it."

"What, how? Why are you asking me?"

"Imagine that you just don't want to talk to anyone, that you don't want to deal with anyone, not even see anyone." Colm alternated between watching the road and glancing across at Annie.

"I feel that way already, especially about the people in this car."

"Good, now just direct that around us too. I need to make some time. I kinda' need you in a bad mood if you don't mind."

"No problem! If I wasn't in a bad mood I am now!"

"Thank you, Anne of Present, we appreciate your willingness to help."

"I'm never speaking to you again Patch, I thought you were my friend. I'm going to be deaf in that ear from now on!"

"Please focus Anne of Present; he is already speeding; we must not be detected. The road will be long. Time is not our friend."

"He's already speeding? Wait, let me see." Annie leaned across the console in the middle of the car, "Oh my god! You're going one-hundred-and-thirty! That can't be right. Are you trying to kill us?"

"I'm in a hurry Annie, please? I will try and maintain the most of it, but I'm driving so I can't devote my full attention to it. Can you just think about not wanting us to be seen or pursued? Please."

"I'll try, but you guy's social technique needs work. Seriously."

"You complain much. Will this continue for the

duration of the trip? Or can we hope that the whining will eventually run its course?" Archimedes threw gasoline on the already hot fire.

Annie had enough. Something inside snapped. Her vision narrowed and was tinged in red. She felt the air rush into her lungs and her heart pound in her ears.

"You miserable excuse for wisdom; I've ripped your tailfeathers out before. This time it will be your head I tear off!"

"That's the spirit! Is that all you got?" The druid dove in where the owl had left off.

"You… you… I will have your head on a platter; I'll feed you to the wolfhounds. You motheaten, smelly, pretentious, …***potion maker!***"

"You act like a child. Are you going to be one forever?" Patch hovered in her face.

Annie's face reddened and her fists clenched, she gritted her teeth as her anger mounted. She reached for the Elvin Star on her chest, but her robes were not there; instead she touched the shoulder of her parka. She closed her eyes and shrieked as loud as she ever had in her life.

It was like a rocket had suddenly ignited behind the Maserati. The car threw itself violently forward. Even as the RPM's of the engine dropped to a gentle purr, the speed rose in a steep slope, sweeping past one-hundred-fifty, and then rose steadily beyond the last number on the now obsolete speedometer and pegged itself against the little post beyond it. Even the sleek fuselage of the super car could not quiet the howl of the wind screaming past them.

Colm McQuinn gripped the steering wheel with both hands and smiled a satisfied smile.

"That didn't take as much as I thought it might."

Archimedes observed

"What you did that on purpose? You were trying to make me mad? You were trying to make me bring out my angry power? Now I really am mad. Really mad!" Annie brought her hands forward, palms outstretched. Again, the car lurched forward even faster.

"Easy Anne of Present, any faster and the wheels will lose contact with the road. Easy please." Colm had never left the left lane of the Interstate Highway, but now with the increased speed, cars that appeared as spots on the horizon flashed past in a matter of seconds.

"Why? Why should I? Should I die again, and again and again, in some battle that we can't win? Or should we die in a twisted pile wrapped around a telephone pole? I can't decide which one I'd prefer more." Anne's hands, palms outward, never lowered from aiming out through the windshield as she screamed her rage. The car began to drift back and forth in the lane as the rush of air lifted the chassis off the ground. In response, Colm released his grip on the steering wheel. He crossed his arms and twisting, leaned back against his door.

"You're right. Your choice."

Annie's anger continued to simmer, she looked across at the druid. She wasn't really angry with him; he was trapped by the same fate as hers. She looked at her friend Patch as she hung onto the rearview mirror for dear life, her body stretched out in a straight line behind her. She wasn't mad at her either. And she didn't really care one way or the other about the owl behind her. Looking up, she saw the car veer hard to the right as if by itself and cross the lanes toward the shoulder. Almost in a panic she looked across at Colm who continued to lean against the door with his arms folded, watching her.

"Okay! Okay," She turned her hands to the left and

the car veered back into the far-left lane. "Okay."

"Perfect! Now, just keep that up for awhile please, we need to cover a little over two-thousand-miles, and we need to do it right away." Colm sat back up, turned to face the windshield and took hold of the steering wheel. "Welcome back Annie, thanks."

Annie was beyond falling for any sentiment of gratitude after the way they had just baited her into a fierce temper tantrum. "Yeah? Whatever."

"We need more than a teenaged pout please. I need you mad, and mad as hell would be even better."

"Would you stop!" Annie slammed her hands on the sloped dashboard. "I'm not pouting, I'm mad. I'm really mad at all of you, and I'm mad that I'm supposed to be handling all of this. I'm not pouting."

Again, the car lurched even faster forward.

"You don't have to be so mean."

"You're right, I don't. But until you step up and start brandishing your force on purpose, I am limited in my abilities to resurrect it. Help me Annie. We need speed. We need to rendezvous with the Red Queen before she comes against the marshalled strength of Cian's minions. I must stand between her and them. I must stand so she can conserve her strength for the last. The last sprint as you said, the last conflict. She must be warned and shielded until then. I need haste; help me Annie. Please?"

"Wait? You're the Shield? Didn't you say that we had to face them together? The Shield and the Spear? Didn't you say that?"

"I am the Shield, as I have always been. I am he that goes to the front, and I am the one that delays the onslaught. I am the first bastion of the defense of the Queen. I must stand when no one else can."

"So, I don't understand. If you are the shield, the… Berserker? You are supposed to stand alone against all of these terrible creatures that you talk about?"

The druid spoke in the sudden quiet of the car's interior, his face set and his jaw tightened, never taking his eyes away from the road ahead, "Yes."

"Where? Where am I then?" The rocketing sports car began to slow. "If you have to stand in front of all of them, alone. What am I supposed to be doing?"

"Annie, the legions of the Red Queen, a sea of incredible Elvin warriors are charging north. I am sure they are coming with all the speed they can muster, spurring their mounts to the limits of their endurance. They ride to the final battle, the battle for their very existence. The mightiest Elvin queen of many ages, daughter of the mortal knight Tam Lin and her mother, the then queen of the Elvin realm rides at the forefront; in her hand she wields the Hammer of Iron. She rides with all haste. She rides to stand at the right hand of the One. She rides to stand at the side of the Queen of the Druids. She is the last of her kind, and she rides to stand with the last of our kind. She rides possibly to her ultimate destruction, but she rides none-the-less. She rides to stand for one last time; the Red Queen rides to stand beside you— Annie. She rides to stand beside you."

"I know. I've known. I knew almost from the first time that I fought for the three 'Witches of the Colors'. I knew. I somehow knew in the back of my mind. I never thought about it until now, but somehow—I knew." Tears sprang from her eyes and streamed down her face once again. "Somehow… somehow I've always known. Why? Why? I'm just a kid. Everything—everything; everything that I've ever known, that I even cared about is gone. It's been taken away. My dad, my friends,… sniff,… my life even. It's all gone. It's too much! I can't even tell how sad I am anymore."

Somehow, I'm supposed to believe in magic—witches even. Then my dad gets shot and dies even. Then he's not dead after all. These warrior guys show up, and they're all of a sudden my friends. Then I meet the scariest person that probably ever walked the earth, and she's my friend too. And then… then she… dies. Circe' dies, sob, while I watched, she died. And all the time I'm running away, from one place to the next, running for my life if you can believe it. And in the middle, somewhere I find out I'm a witch too, not just any ordinary witch either. I'm supposed to be the bad-assest witch that ever lived.

"And now… sniff… and now… and now, I'm supposed to be some kind of general in a war to decide whether the world that all those people that I didn't know existed until a year ago will end or not. I'm alone; I feel alone in a world that isn't supposed to be real but somehow is. You guys expect too much."

She stopped, turned her head toward the window and wiped her eyes with the sleeve of her shirt. The car had slowed to less than one hundred miles per hour and continued to decelerate. No one inside of the car responded. Their gazes focused everywhere but on the young girl curled in the passenger seat.

"I miss my Dad. I miss my house… I miss my bed. I just want to wake up in my bed and get up and get ready for school. I want to sit in the cafeteria and talk to my friends, and eat… and eat… tacos, and… and Cheez Whiz on crackers. I… I… How do you think I'm supposed to do all that other stuff? How can you think I'm even going to try to do all that other stuff."

A stern voice spoke loudly in her head. A voice she recognized—but didn't know. Powerful.

"You must rise sister! We, your sisters, stand beside you; we stand behind you. Trust the life that surrounds you; feel that vibration of life that surrounds you. It is here for you in your need. The Red Queen rides to ambush and the time grows short. Seek the wisdom of the ancient ones, long forgotten. Seek the forgotten sister's message and the mark of the druid."

The Message of the Sister

Annie had been leaning forward, stretching her seat belt tight across her chest as she complained to the others. The sheer force of the voice that had shouted in her head dropped her back into the bucket seat. It took seconds before her eyes regained their focus. In that time, the car's speed had already dropped almost thirty-miles-per-hour and continued to decelerate. Annie's breath gasped in and out as she forced herself upright. She knew that no one else had heard the voice; it had been meant for her and her alone.

In almost a whisper, *"Seek the stones, and feel their life. First before all things, feel the life in all that you see and touch. Only then will the steps to the great mystery become clear to you. Seek the stones, that bear the mark."*

"Colm, stop the car! Now!!"

Colm at first looked across at Annie but the look on her face told him she was serious. Pulling the car into the right lane, he slammed the brakes and the car left a long black streak on the pavement as it squealed to a stop. With a long sigh, he turned toward the young woman, but she was already out of the car. Colm threw open his door and skirting around the front, he approached her.

"Annie? What?"

"Wait… wait." Annie stood as still as she could and focused.

'Seek the forgotten sister's message and the mark of the druid'.

"Wait, Colm, the time is short, I feel it, the Red Queen rides to an ambush, she rides to ruin and I must seek the stone." Annie stamped her foot in frustration, "I have to think, but my brain is too busy. I can't focus on what I need to."

Again, she paced the length of the car and back again, "Do you have any magic, any magic that can help me to see the something that is right on the edge of my thoughts?"

"Actually, I do. But it's the fairy that you need. She has other abilities besides just being annoying."

"That's enough out of you… wizard. What? What is needed of me?"

"Annie is at the threshold of a memory she can't chase down. It is apparently important enough for us to have had to stop along the side of this busy road Patch." He paused as several cars and trucks blew past them at high-speed on Interstate 40 causing them to be buffeted repeatedly with each passing one. "You've helped her with sleep before, and you've helped to calm her when times were dire. Can you help to relax her enough to allow her to find that place in her thoughts?"

"I am only one, she is large."

"Patch? Please?" Annie pleaded.

Patch paused as the next semi-tractor and trailer roared past and she was blown about. Then she flew in front of Annie and hovered directly in Annie's face.

"Anne of Present, I can help you but the work is yours and yours alone. Feel me, think of nothing but of me, feel me and feel what I offer."

With that she placed her tiny hand on Annie's forehead and closed her eyes.

Suddenly Annie had visions of tall grass meadows and autumn leaves that floated down a calm stream. It was such an entirely different thought than what had been going on in her mind that she staggered backward, and the vision was gone at once.

"Anne of Present, you must try to focus."

Again, Patch placed her hand on Annie's forehead. In her mind, butterflies flitted among late blossoms and fat bumblebees breezed by with buzzing zooms. She heard the sound of bubbling water as it ran over smooth stones and the delicious smells of dry autumn leaves and dew on grass. In spite of herself her eyes closed and smiled dreamily. Sighing, she drew a deep breath and then… and then… she remembered!

"Seek the stone, seek the druid's mark.", she whispered breathlessly.

"It is close! Seek the sister's message. It is for only the One. I remember! Thank you Patch! How do you do that?"

"I show you my happy memories. I can show you other ones if you like, but you would not enjoy them as much I expect."

"No! No thanks Patch. I can imagine, you're a warrior, right? No thank you, that was quite enough."

Patch smiled a wry smile, *"I am a warrior yes, and I have seen much in my six-hundred eighty-seven years, five months, and eighteen days. Many of my memories lie close to the surface, and some should never again see the light of day. Patch will fight until the need to fight is no longer, but always… Patch will remember."*

"So?" The druid opened his arms and looked at

Annie.

"Back in the car, take the next exit that you can and turn left!"

"South?"

"Turn left, I don't know what direction that is. I just know that is the direction we need to go."

"As you wish, Anne of Present."

Once back in the car Colm merged back onto the Interstate but within a half a mile an exit appeared and he slowed and exited. At the top of the incline a smaller rural road running north and south greeted them. With no hesitation he turned left and accelerated as the road wound off across miles of winter barren farmland.

As the miles disappeared in the rear-view mirror, he kept his eyes pointed out through the windshield but cast glances across at Annie.

"Are you sure Annie?"

"I'm sorry Colm, I'm trying to concentrate. This feels right to me, I think. At least it doesn't feel wrong. It shouldn't be long, I'm trying to feel that thing that is inside of me, but I only see a little bit of."

"What is your need Little One?" The gentle tone of Roison of the West March whispered in her ear.

"Mother. I seek a message, but it is very far away and very close at the same time. I know it is there, but it is a faint whisper. Mother, can you listen for it with me?"

"Yes, my sweet child, I hear it clearly. Listen with me."

"Turn here!" Annie's voice was shrill and as she shouted her hands slammed into the dashboard. **"Right turn!"**

"Good grief!" Colm McQuinn yelled, his eyes as big as frisbees as the steering wheel was pulled from his grasp and the car did a perfect 'four-wheel drift' into the road that crossed just ahead of them, and the tires again squealed in angry protest as it accelerated away from the intersection.

"Do you just want to drive, or can I have the steering wheel back now?" Colm struggled to slow his breathing and heart rate. "What is that? You spoke the language of the ancients! How? How do you even know that?"

And then after a few calming breaths, he added, "Good grief, that scared the crap out of me!"

"It certainly surprised me as well." Archimedes was just untangling himself from Patch in the far corner of the space behind the seats.

"That was not enjoyable." Patch was getting aggravated after another feathery encounter with the owl's breast.

"I was talking to my mother. She doesn't speak English, thank you."

Again, Colm looked across at her with wonder. "You were speaking with your mother? Roison of the West March, you can talk with her?"

"My mother? Yes."

"You can do that whenever you want to?"

"No, but she seems to know when I need to."

"You can walk the Paths of the Dead whenever you need to. Holy Cats! When I took you there that first time, I had no idea that you could do it at will."

"I can't do that...*at will*. Like I said, my mom knows when I need to talk to her. She's the best. I..I..I wish I could've... you know... got to know her. You know?"

"I knew your mother; she was kind and incredibly giving. You would have liked her Annie, and she would have loved you. You are very much like her." And then he added, "She was my cousin you know?"

"Really?"

"Really. So where are we going?"

"I have no idea."

"What?"

"I don't know where we're supposed to go. I just feel this is the right direction. I can't explain it."

"Okay. Any idea how far we're supposed to go?"

"Turn at the next corner, left."

In a few more miles they approached a sign that indicated an upcoming left turn. As they approached the intersection, a large National Park sign in the shape of an arrowhead, had an arrow below it indicating a left turn for the Shiloh Battlefield Visitor Center. Colm turned left.

"Yes, let's hurry. Speed up a little please."

"It's not going to be open yet Annie. It's still pretty early.

"We're not going there; we're just going to park there."

"But the parking lot won't even be open."

"Figure it out. You're Merlin aren't you?"

"Touche' But then what?"

"I'll let you know."

The parking area was generous, but closed. The wintery morning light played across the empty landscape from the chained entrance gate. The visitor center sat at the farthest reaches of the parking area, mocking them from the distance. Colm paused at the barricaded entrance and looked across at Annie.

"Keep going, just a little further."

Colm drove forward on the small access road beyond the locked gate.

"Here! Stop here!" Annie threw her door open and even before the car had come to a full stop, she was out of the vehicle and jogging off at a tangent to the road.

Colm shut the engine off and stepped out of the car. First, he leaned across the roof as she continued and he watched in wonder. Finally, he shrugged and followed.

"Archimedes, she's got too big a lead on me, follow her and don't lose her for goodness sake. I'll catch up if I can."

The great owl launched himself out through the door that Annie had left open. Rising in a majestic arc he then dropped to within inches of the ground and swept away in pursuit of the girl. The fairy was not far behind him. The druid sighed and dropping the car keys into his pocket skirted the vehicle, closed the passenger door and trotted after them in the ice cold of the February morning.

"As if things weren't crazy enough already, now where the heck is she going?" He mumbled only half out loud.

After a fairly long jog he stopped to catch his breath at a point where the trail veered deeper into the woods and a smaller fork appeared in the trail. At the entrance were two signs describing the trail and what the traveler might encounter. There were several points of interest on this particular trail, the most important, and the one that claimed a sign all of its own was that of the Shiloh Indian Mounds. A lesser sign showed the whereabouts of a mass grave of Civil War dead. Colm puzzled over the two signs, which one? Which way did she go? Both had promise, but what kind of promise was anyone's guess.

The owl dropped down and roosted on the nearest placard in front of him.

"She has passed the graves of the soldier dead, their bodies have departed, but their spirits live on. She is running now." The owl swiveled his head to look back up the trail and added with a sigh, "she is running quite fast actually. Patch is with her. She races to the mounds of the ancients."

"Oh dear! Can we trust them?"

"Only you can know wise one; she's got a good lead. I cannot tell if the spirits of those dead are active but you should probably pick up your game a little; she's a lot faster than you, old man."

"Easy now; bird. I've just been pacing myself that's all."

"Well, get a move on. I don't know if she'll stop when she gets there or if she'll just keep on going."

"I'm on my way."

A full ten minutes later Colm pulled to a stop next to the owl and fairy and dropped his hands on his knees, winded after the long run. Thirty yards in front of them Annie knelt on the ground, digging frantically with her bare hands.

"What is she doing?" He gasped between breaths.

"She appears to be digging." Was the considered response of the owl.

"I can see that, geez, I was hoping for a little more information than that."

"She ran to this spot. She dropped on her knees. She began to dig. You now know what we know." Patch's eyes never left the young women as she hovered with her arms crossed.

Colm walked the last thirty yards and approaching Annie, placed a hand on her shoulder.

"Annie?"

Annie shrugged his hand away roughly. "It's here, but it has slept. I must awaken it. It is here. It is here." Her voice was almost frantic.

"Annie, this is a National Park. You aren't supposed to just go around digging holes wherever you want to."

"It is here. She is here."

"She is here?"

"Here!" Annie's voice was victorious, "Here!"

Below the frantic digging a small grey surface had appeared as she struggled to uncover more of it. Colm, surprised, dropped to his knees and began to clear the dirt out of the deep hole that Annie had already dug. Slowly it emerged, a stone, no larger than a large dinner platter, oval in shape but with one end forming a point. Scrabbling to clear the edges and lift it, the two worked feverishly. Finally, lifting it out Colm brushed and scraped the remaining dirt from the rough surface of the stone.

There were intricate carvings on both sides of the stone. An eagle, a badger, and a fox were easily identified. Turning it over the opposite side told a different story; several runic characters had been painstakingly but roughly chiseled in the surface, and near the tip of the point of the stone, larger than the other carvings, separate and clearly preserved—the mark of the druid.

"Well I'll be. How can this be?" Colm stared at the stone in disbelief, rocking back on his heels.

Annie dropped back on her heels as well, winded, regarding the stone. Only now able to look at it rationally. "What is it?"

"You should know that Annie, you're the one that dragged us halfway across the state to dig it up. But at least it appears we have one of the Druid's Stones of legend. This is a complete mystery to me. The druid brotherhood does not always communicate with each other very well, but the placing of our stones is one thing that is so important we must not harbor it as a secret. This is doubtless a very old one. These mounds are more than a thousand years old, but this stone is relatively shallow, only a few feet deep. It might not have been placed here by the mound inhabitants, I am sure. It's the fourth one that you've unearthed that I, actually none of us, had any knowledge of. A complete mystery, and then some."

"Seek the forgotten sister and the mark of the druid. That was the message that I received. What does it say?"

"I can read the runes, but I don't understand the pictographs."

"Well, c'mon, what does it say?"

"It says, 'They are coming.'"

"What else?"

"Nothing else, just, They are coming."

"Let me see that thing. Is it heavy?"

"Not really, but its heavy enough. Here."

The druid hefted the stone toward her but then because of the remaining dirt and grit, it slipped from his hands and fell to the ground. Annie had been reaching for it but now she knelt next to it, looking at the carvings carefully. Slowly she reached out a finger to trace the mark of the druid.

"They are coming! The undead and the unclean rise from beneath us. Those that poisoned this earth and drove away our people. They are coming once again! Their numbers cannot be counted; they rise from the depths. They seek to destroy the warriors of justice. The Three are lost."

Annie's eyes had lost their focus as she spoke with the voice in the stone, but now she looked across at her friend. She suddenly had a vision of a vast horde pounding north in a raised cloud of dust, their mounts sweating, their weapons burnished in morning light.

"They ride to ruin. The Red Queen's army. It rides to ruin."

"That make no sense. They are not; they could not be attacked yet. They aren't anywhere near a rendezvous point."

"Let me see the other side again please?"

The opposite side of the stone displayed four weather worn caricatures. The fox, badger and eagle were easily discerned, but the fourth was almost worn away and difficult to make out. Colm tilted the stone in the sunlight trying to see what it might be.

"It's a tree, but look how high up the trunk rises before it starts to look like a tree. That's totally odd. There aren't any trees around here that look like that I don't think. Another mystery."

Again, Annie pointed a finger and traced the outline of the tree. And again, the stone spoke through her, ***"Seek the Sentinel among the forest of the ancients. She maintains the watch and awaits the One. You must feel her life and seek her wisdom. The Unclean will seek her out; their hate for her kind burns hot. She will be among the first to fall."***

"The forest of the Ancients?" This time it was the druid's turn to rock back on his heels, perplexed. "The Redwoods! Do you mean the Redwood Forest Annie?" He looked across the stone at her, his confusion showing on his face.

"We have to go to the 'Forest of the Ancients'. We have to seek the Sentinel. Go as fast as you want Colm, don't worry, I'll help. We have to hurry." Annie's voice only moments before sounding terrified, now sounded urgent. She felt the need. She felt that she was needed, but the need was far away.

All Haste

Back in the car again, Colm McQuinn wheeled around in a wide U-turn and headed back in the direction they had just come. As they once again approached the visitor center parking lot they saw a large black SUV blocking their exit, parked crossways in the roadway, sitting ominously silent. Blue police lights flashed across the radiator grill and windshield. The Maserati crunched to a halt on the gravel road and waited facing it. There was no movement from the police vehicle as water vapor coiled up from the tailpipe of the idling car in the frigid air. Those in the red sports car waited as the tension rose. They were alone in a desolate landscape.

Suddenly there was a hard tap on the window glass on Annie's side of the car.

"License and registration please." The voice was muffled by the window glass.

Everyone inside jerked in surprise, so engaged in watching the idling police car they had not noticed the approach of someone from another direction.

"License and registration please." The bright morning sunshine framed the silhouette of the figure at the window, throwing its features into faceless shadow. The only thing clearly visible; the bright gold badge on the left breast of the heavy police jacket. "Please lower your window ma'am."

Annie fumbled with the window button, finally lowering it only an inch or two, she asked.

"Yes sir?" Annie struggled in a hurry to comply.

"I am officer Mink, ma'am. I'm here with your police escort."

"How on earth!" Colm jumped from his side of the car. "What in the name of the Queen of Aieia are you guys doing? Did you steal that car? Where did you get that uniform Mink?" Geez, if we weren't in trouble before we're going to be now." His voice sounded accusatory as he skirted the vehicle and embraced his warrior friend.

"No worries wise one, we signed the vehicle out from the motor pool at the State Patrol Headquarters." Micah now approached, similarly dressed but with sergeant stripes on his winter jacket. "We are on special dispatch from the Governor of Tennessee's office."

"What?!" How does that work?" Annie was still struggling with their arrival and appearance.

The three elves stood together in front of Annie; even as she looked, their appearance began to shift, changing. Instead of the tall slender warriors, there stood three police officers. The sergeant was a middle aged paunchy looking veteran, the other two seemed younger. The one on the right sporting a jaunty mustache which he twirled with one hand while he winked at her.

"Things are not always as they appear, and sometimes, neither are we Anne of Present. Shall we go?"

"Yes, let's hurry please." Said Annie.

"And where would that be, exactly?"

"West. For now, just west," was Colm's response as he exchanged eye contact with the three elves.

Once they had re-entered the Interstate, he reached across in front of Annie and dropped the glove box door open. Reaching in, he withdrew a cell phone and powered it up. As the light on the display glowed alive, he turned to Annie, "A little faster please?" as he pointed out through the windshield.

Annie threw her hands forward, palms outward. Immediately, the two humans were thrust back into the leather of their seats. The small fairy, who moments before had been hovering in front of Annie, was thrown toward the back of the car and directly into the feathery breast of the great owl. The owl in turn was forcefully thrown into the very back of an already too small space where both exploded in a cyclone of soft feathers and profanity—uttered in more than a few different dialects. The police car, its lights flashing, struggled to keep pace and then gradually faded into the distance behind them.

"Steer for me for a minute please Annie."

Annie didn't hesitate, turning her left palm outward, the car immediately vaulted into the left lane, and then impossibly, picked up even more speed as Colm punched in a phone number. The flashing lights disappeared in the rearview mirror.

"Hello? Yes, this is Mr. McQuinn. Yes, that Mr. McQuinn. Yes. Yes, as soon as possible. Hmm... hold on." Colm squinted at a passing milepost marker bright in the morning sunlight. "Um, let's see. I'm still about twenty miles east of Jackson, so I can be in Memphis in another forty minutes. "Yes, yes I understand it's about ninety miles, yes. We will be there in forty minutes. I expect you to be prepared. Okay? Alright, there will be five. Yes, five." Colm muted the phone. "Annie, ninety miles, forty minutes," and pointed meaningfully out through the windshield.

Annie nodded and again, just as the fairy and owl were starting to untangle, they were thrown back into the boot, with another hoot from the owl.

"Yes, same as per usual. Yes, cash disbursement. No. Are we good? Good." He ended the call and immediately thumbed the power button turning the phone off. Then rolled down the window and threw it out into the gale force wind screaming past them. Once the window was back up and the maelstrom inside the car had receded, he reached into his pocket and produced an ornate pocket watch. Spinning the dials on the side he adjusted the hands, then pushed a button on the side. He returned the watch to his pocket, turned and looked down at the dashboard, "Well what do we have here?" as he took the steering wheel in both hands.

"What? What was that all about? That's the first cell phone I've seen in almost a year. Who did you call?"

"We need a faster ride. This slow coach is starting to bore me."

§§§§

Thirty-seven minutes later, the bright red Mazerati wheeled up to a private gate far in back of the Memphis International Airport. A guard at the gate stepped out of the small hut that he waited in and approached the car, a clipboard in his hand. As the driver's window rolled down, he leaned down and spoke.

"Good morning. Oh! Mr. McQuinn? Nice to see you sir; they told me you would be arriving soon; I hadn't expected you quite so quickly. Please, I'll get the gate open in just a tick." The guard straightened up and looked down the length of the snappy sports car. "Nice ride. Is it new? I've never seen one like this."

"Not new Oscar, vintage. It will still outrun anything on the road."

"Wow! You remember my name? That's amazing sir! I haven't seen you in a long time; I don't think. I can't believe you remember my name."

"Important people are always worth remembering Oscar. Don't you think?"

"Yes Sir!! I most certainly do. Thank you, sir."

"Now I must apologize Oscar, this one time… it is important that you do not remember."

"Sir?"

Colm reached out his hand for Oscar to shake. As the gate guard took his hand, the druid stated.

> *"Things said, things remembered.*
> *Memory or fantasy, none can say.*
> *People come and people go,*
> *in this life's long flow*
> *Events of today, or none can say."*

"What?" Oscar released his grip and looked down at his open palm like something should be there. Walking to the gate, he raised the red and white striped bar, opening it. With a smile, he waved the Maserati through. As the car sped up he lowered the bar back down, turned and reentered the guard shack, switched on the small television on the counter, swiveled the small dial on its front and found the "Price Is Right". Dropping onto a stool he leaned forward and smiled into the television screen.

As the small television blared inside the tiny room,

suddenly, with a puzzled look he looked up and out the window, momentarily confused. He looked out at the closed gate and the driveway; something was just a tickle of a thought but not really there. Finally, he shrugged and returned to the television and let it go.

Axel

Once through the gate, Colm hung a hard right and powered the car along the perimeter fence for almost a quarter of a mile. At a small Quonset-like building they slowed. The shed looked decrepit, rust bloomed on the sides and vines had grown over the windows. The wide sliding doors stood open and as they watched, a small tractor towed a sleek Lear jet slowly out from inside.

The tractor driver reached behind the seat and unhooked the tether from the plane, then swung it in an arc and parked it in the shade inside of the steel building. The Maserati followed it in.

Jumping down off of the tractor, the driver of the tractor broke into a trot approaching the car. Once his feet had touched the ground Annie was amazed at how short he was. He was less than three feet tall, but even for that, his pace was quick as he approached.

Colm opened the door and stepped out to greet him.

"Hello Axle, long time no see. Everything ready?"

The short man removed a well chewed cigar stub from the corner of his mouth, "Yes sir! It's a pleasure to see you again sir."

Annie climbed out and turned to face the small man.

Patch was right behind her. She examined the arrival. The man, although short, was incredibly wide across his shoulders and built powerfully; his eyes had an unusually wide shape, with a large nose and ears almost huge in comparison to Colm's. They also rose to a point. The stub of the chewed cigar protruded beyond his shaggy beard and his thick forearms covered with thick course hair were massive.

"He is one of the honored ones." Patch whispered in her ear. *"He is of the dwarven race that the 'Taker of Souls' hunted almost to extinction for sport. A capable ally, he is no friend of the minions of Cian."*

Archimedes spoke from between the two bucket seats. "He is also an excellent pilot but I would not mention to him that you harbor the Taker within you."

"Seriously? How does he even reach the pedals?"

"In a few minutes you'll see for yourself Anne of Present. I hope he has laid in some snacks. I haven't flown with Axle in one hundred years, two months and twelve days. In those days he piloted the bi-planes of the British during the Great War. I was privileged to fight beside him, as his gunner. We had some high times together he and I. To fly in a dogfight with him against the Fokker Triwing planes of the German Army was to experience the lust of battle in its purest. It will be good to greet my former comrade." Patch glowed in anticipation as she could not contain herself any longer and darted toward the dwarf.

The expression on the face of the dwarf changed from one of gruff welcome to one of awe and shock.

"Patch! Oh... Patch my old friend! Is it really you?"

"Axle!" The two embraced, their joy obvious. *"Axle! Many miles my friend. Many miles. My thoughts and heart have often returned to our time together."*

"As have mine, a good team we were. A difference

did we make. Yes, all those years before, and now again we must face a dark curtain that threatens."

"Yes my friend, but we bring with us today a great gift. Your cargo today is precious like none ever before Axle, we bring with us—the One."

"So you say?" His bushy eyebrows raised in surprise, "Truly? Is that possible? Do you jest? If you do Patch, it is not amusing."

"Time is of the essence my friend, we must hasten, but yes, we bring with us the most precious thing that has walked this ground in ages upon ages. She is in truth —***The One***." Colm spoke as he opened the door of the imposing airplane and lowered the small cabin staircase. "Please, we will have time for talk once we are airborne."

"I filed a flight plan for Duluth, Minnesota. I trust that will suffice?"

"Yes, but as soon as you clear the airspace drop below radar my old friend and turn west. All haste, Axle. History hangs in the balance; she has spoken with the eldest and bids us to hurry."

"Word has come of the passing of the torch. It is truth? The Eldest has succumbed?"

"Yes, sadly. But another has taken up the mantle, yet we must shield her until she finds her strength and wisdom."

"Where to then wise one?"

They both paused as Annie's door swung shut and she stepped away from the car. She looked too young, she looked too fragile in the morning light, nothing like the strength and wisdom that they might have hoped for, yet somehow she also radiated power that they both could feel. She demanded their total attention just standing there.

The druid spoke almost distractedly as he watched

her. "Uhm… West."

Traitor

"Really?" The dwarf Axel's eyes got even bigger. "She's just a skinny kid!"

"Oh, but what a kid. And you better not say that in front of Michael," Colm spoke out of the side of his mouth still looking at Annie. "She's his daughter.'

"Michael! Really? He was here only a few days ago; Raphael and Gabriel were with him too. And a really big dog. He didn't say anything about a daughter."

"*What!* The Three were here? When?"

"Well let's see, today is Donnerstag, so…" Axel counted backward on his thick fingers. "Mittwach, Dienstag, Montag, Sonntag… it was Samstag last. They stopped for the night on Frietag, I gave them what supplies I had and they left at the first light of Samstag." The dwarf stroked his chin as he remembered. "They also went west."

"So, they left here last Saturday. Did they say where they were heading? Are they still on foot?"

"They are driving my pickup truck. I have my Volkswagen yet, it is easier to get into than the truck was for me, and it's turbocharged. Also, there was room for the dog. I do not recall why I thought it was a good idea to buy that truck in the first place. Glad to be rid of it really." The dwarf tapped his jaw in reflection, nodding his head as if in agreement with his own thoughts. Then as if coming back to the present, he looked at the druid. "Yes, yes, they are driving."

"Did they tell you where they were going? Anything Axel?" Axel's face looked blank, "Did they think they were pursued? Come on Axel, did they say anything?" Colm's voice was elevated, stressed because of missing The Three by so close a margin. "Axel?"

Tapping the side of his jaw again, the dwarf looked away and thought. "Yes, there is something. Something that the Wind Warrior said. What, hmm, what?"

Then again, his eyes went blank, "Nope, nothing. I'm mistaken. There was nothing said."

"Axel!" Colm stepped forward, his face imperious. He had seen that empty, vacant look before and he knew what it meant. He made eye contact with the dwarf. "Tell me."

"He said something to the Guardian. The Guardian agreed. What was it, my brain, my brain is too full. I heard but did not remember. I am sorry wise one."

"Stand fast man of stone! I must know what you would not remember." With that he placed one hand on the forehead of Axel, and one on the back of his head. The cords in his forearms rippled as he increased his grip.

"Where? Where is the memory Axel?"

"I... I... don't know. Wait! No, no... wait."

The druid closed his eyes in concentration as the dwarf struggled in his grasp. Finally he spoke as he looked into the mind of the dwarf and saw what only he could see.

"Ahh, I see... there is the Mariner. Oh! He has been

injured."

Colm spoke through his concentration. Despite himself, Colm smiled, while his hands never moved. The dwarf dropped to his knees, still struggling.

"His hand, hmm, yes but bandaged with skill. The Guardian, yes, he will drive the truck... the Wind Warrior... the Wind Warrior stands facing the breeze. He is turning—turning in place. He turns to each of the four powers, but leans last to the west. He speaks to the Guardian."

Colm paused, frustrated, searching for the rest of the dwarf's memory.

"What Axel, what does Rafer Tate say!"

"I..I..can... can't... No! I don't remember!"

"Axel, freagraidh tu, freagair mi fior, an fhirinn chi mi, no fear brathaidh bithidh tu. Chì mi do chridhe, chì mi cò thu."

(You will answer, answer me true, the truth I will see, or traitor you be. I see your heart; I see who thou art.)

Axel's body contorted as his struggle played out across his face and it drew back in a snarl of pain, and his back arched. His eyes rolled back in his head, and finally he blurted out,

"Seek the Sun Road. My ancient brothers await." Axel tried to rise to his feet but instead staggered backward several steps and then fell onto his bottom on the ground, his eyes vacant.

Oh, I'm sorry old friend. I got a little carried away." Colm approached nonchalantly but malice dripped from his voice. "It's the stress you see. I'm no good with stress. Worse these days than I used to be."

"He has always been prone to over-excitement." Archimedes dropped to the ground next to Axel and placed a taloned foot on the dwarf's arm, digging his dagger-like talons into it. The dwarf winced while still rubbing his head. Colm leaned forward and offered him a hand up.

"What does it mean?" The sun road? Who's ancient brothers?" Annie had rushed up from the car when she had witnessed Axel being thrown back from the force of the druid pulling his reluctant memory from him.

"I don't know yet, but right now we have a much bigger problem."

The fairy dropped down and with one well aimed kick she struck the dwarf in the forehead with surprising force knocking him flat on his back. Then with sword in hand she stood upon his chest, ***"Where would you have led us, 'old friend'? Away to the ends of the earth, or to an ambush that awaits us beyond the next hilltop?"***

As she spoke the druid bent over the fallen dwarf, his face set in anger. "We will have your confession one way or the other, *friend*. Will you tell us?" Colm scowled down at him, the ferocity glowing in his eyes, "or will we have your soul?"

"Wait! What is happening?" Annie approached, alarmed, "He's a friend, right?"

"Appearance-wise yes, but there is another one here as well. Our friend Axel is not all he appears to be, or so it would seem." Archimedes' taloned fist tightened on the arm of the dwarf as blood began to seep out around them.

The druid, clothed in smoke, lightning crackling within storm clouds in the bright morning light. Without preamble he reached and grabbed a handful of the dwarf's shirt and pulled him into a sitting position.

"Aon chothrom, aon chothrom leis fhèin! Seall do ghnùis, no bàs a'd' aghaidh !

(One chance, one chance alone! Show your face, or death you face!)

The dwarf looked into the flaming eyes of the druid priest and smiled.

"You are all dead! You cannot escape; you are trapped; we have trapped you. Here you will die and I will have victory and praise from my master. Ha-ha. Ha-ha-ha-ha..." The dwarf drew a breath as blood began to seep from the corner of his mouth, "Ha-ha-ha-ha.." Then suddenly, his eyes saw no more and his breath stopped as he sagged back against the arms of Colm. The druid lowered him to the ground gently, placed a hand on his forehead and bowed his head. Suddenly, a shadow escaped and swiftly disappeared in the morning sunlight.

Terror in the Air

"Is he? Is he… dead?"

"Not for the first time today it would seem." Archimedes' tone was somber. "He was a good man once."

"No, but the rest of his memory is masked. There can be no doubt, I could feel it even if I could not see it. His passing is of great despair, but it did not occur in this moment."

I don't understand. He was already…?"

"Yes Annie, he was 'already'; they had taken him. He was no longer himself. He was left here to delay and trap us." He sighed and looked down at the dwarf, "To be honest, I thought he seemed much more polite than how I remembered him."

The druid held his chin as he considered.

"I'm sure that they will be on our heels in minutes! Everyone on the plane, I'll bring Axel. Hurry!"

"What? You're bringing him with us? Like that... you know... that?"

"Yes, like 'that! Get on the plane! Hurry. Somebody's going to have to fly this thing and he's all we've got."

That stopped Annie halfway up the short ladder into

the plane. She looked back with her eyes opened wide.

"C'mon Annie, move it. Time is of the essence." The druid struggled under the weight of the unfortunate and very heavy dwarf in his arms.

As the Lear Jet door hatch lowered itself into place the druid laid the inert form of the dwarf onto the long bench seat inside the cabin and knelt next to him. Even before he was securely placed, the twin turbine engines began to whine into wakefulness.

Annie looked around the luxurious cabin, with its leather bucket seats and carpeted floors. She had never imagined that she might someday even see something like this, let alone ride in it was beyond her imagination. This was a long way from the humble house of a college professor's daughter.

As the sound of the engines crescendoed, she glanced into the cabin of the jet and all she could see was the feathery wings of the fairy flitting back and forth over a countless array of dials and gauges. With one last glance at the druid kneeling beside the fallen dwarf, she stepped up into the cockpit. The tiny fairy continued to flit from switch panel to the next, flipping switches and watching digital readouts.

"What are you doing?"

"Sit in the right chair Anne of Present. Put on those headphones."

"Seriously?"

"Seriously… yes Anne of Present. It is time for you to step out of your very nice self! It is time for some illegal and perilous activity. We must escape; we must fly; the traitor has given us up. Put on the headphones, we must take off and you must gain the clearance. Only the dwarf can truly fly this machine; I can only start it on its way. The druid must do his skill diligently and you must secure ground clearance for take-off, even if we

can only reach the trees beyond the runway. We must escape. The alarm has been raised. **The traitor has been uncovered**.*"*

"The traitor?"

"Betrayer of those who guard the One. Perhaps even the assassin of Ash. Yes, but no."

"No?"

"The druid will determine if the dwarf has betrayed or if the dwarf has been betrayed as well."

"As well?"

"Put on the headphones Anne of Present. I am going to start the engines, perhaps you would fasten your safety belt as well. Oh and apply the brakes under your left foot when the time comes please."

Patch threw two separate switches and immediately the engines powered on with a deep thrum. The plane's twin engines howled into life and then they started to roll forward.

"Put your foot down on the brake pedal Anne of Present. Now, thumb that switch on your right hand,… no… above that one… yes...push it up."

In Annie's ear a businesslike voice spoke. "Lear Jet, approaching Y to Y1, identify call number."

"Call number?"

"Yes, identify Lear Jet, you are approaching one-eight left. This is tower control, identify."

Tell him you are Tango Golf dash three five six." Patch hovered next to her left ear.

"Tango Golf three five six? What's that?"

"Acknowledged Tango Golf 356, good morning, proceed to left Y, Y one, one-eight left. And hold."

"Tell them 10-4."

"10-4"

Patch alternated between the left side of the steering yoke and the right, steering the jet as it taxied along a long concrete taxiway that skirted the maintenance sheds and veered toward the Memphis Airport proper, never slowing down as the turbine engines continued to whine

"Can you fly Patch?" Annie belted into the co-pilot's seat was starting to understand just how serious their predicament was about to become.

"Don't be silly Anne of Present, Patch is a fairy, and not even a very big one at that. I could not possibly fly this machine."

"Then why? Why are we taxiing down the runway, in what is probably a stolen airplane, with a dead guy in the back, and a talking owl, and… and… that we can't hope to take off in?"

"We can take off Anne of Present." Patch stopped her activities, hovering in front of her for a moment she made eye contact with Annie, *"I did not say that we could fly."*

"Oh. Oh…," Annie looked at the fairy and at the ground swiftly rolling past and the reality of Patch's words sank in, "oh."

"Exactly. You must put your feet on that pedal on the floor Anne of Present, under your left foot. Push it down and the plane will roll more slowly. Push it harder and the plane will stop—probably."

"Probably?"

"I don't know how to fly an airplane, only how to start the engines and push the throttle. We are a team Anne of Present, at least until the end of this runway." Patch threw her shoulder into the right throttle lever and then the left one increasing their speed on the runway below. Looking back over her shoulder, she smiled, *"It is exciting is it not Anne of Present."*

"Exciting!? Patch I'm freaking out here." Annie put one hand on each side of her head, "We're about to explode in a ball of flame at the end of the runway Patch; this isn't exciting. This is a nightmare." She swung her head from side to side, looking out the windows, "Oh my God, I'm about to die!"

"Not if the druid is skilled in his craft perhaps. Who can know." Patch shrugged without looking back at her. She continued to concentrate on pushing buttons and steering the plane.

"You are second in line Tango Echo 356, please tighten it up a little."

Until she heard the tower's voice in her ears Annie had not realized that she was trying to push the brake pedal through the floorboard. As she relaxed her thigh muscles the jet again rolled forward. A large commercial jetliner was just ahead of them and appeared dangerously close in the windshield before she thought to push hard on the pedal again and the plane lurched to a stop just in time to avoid a collision.

"How's it going back there Colm?" Annie shouted over her shoulder. "I'm going to need some help here— uhm—pretty soon." As she watched the big commercial liner rolled into position turning onto the runway and without hesitation its engines roared and it raced forward and out of their vision.

"Tango Echo 356 you are next, proceed to One Eight Left and await cleared for takeoff."

"Hold steady Anne of Present." Patch appeared in Annie's terrified vision. *"Patch is a warrior as are you."* She moved forward a few inches and furrowed her brows.

"I am brave as are you. We are valiant as we must be, hold steady Anne of Present, none can divine the last moments of our breath." She stopped and placed her hands on her tiny hips and threw her chest out.

"Stand ready, hold steady. When they give us the

signal we must go, it is perhaps our last great act my Queen. But go we must! To glory or to death, only time will honor the moment."

"Tango Echo 356, hold in position. I repeat hold in position."

"They told us to hold in position.'

"Why, we are next. Something is wrong.' Immediately Patch flitted from one side of the cockpit to the other peering out of the windows.

"Ladies, we are detected. Police vehicles are approaching from behind, with flashing lights no less.' Archimedes waddled up into the cockpit. "I thought you should know, there are quite a few actually."

Even as the owl spoke, the first flashing cars came into view through the front windows. Patch did not hesitate; in swift movements she threw her whole tiny weight into the twin throttles.

"Release the brakes Anne of Present! It is time that we fly! None of us must be taken, fly or no we must give them a last defeat! Release the brakes!"

Annie released the brakes and the jet careened out onto runway One-8 Left as Patch shoved the throttles far forward and the little Lear jet roared ahead, pounding down the pavement beneath them, rumbling louder and louder.

"Ayieeee! I fight to live, I live to die!" Patch screamed in defiance, her sword held high in one hand, as the flashing barriers at the end of the mile long runway appeared ahead of them and the plane's speed caused it to begin to weave from side to side. ***"One last flight, one last fight!"***

Annie's face was drawn back in a grimace, her jaw muscles so tight that her lips pulled back from her teeth. She was too terrified to scream as the barriers with their flashing lights rocketed toward them.

"Get out of the way Pixie!"

The thick form of the dwarf vaulted into the left seat of the cockpit, snapped three switches and then drew back on the wheel. Immediately the jet's nose rose pointed into the winter bright sky and the G-forces pressed Annie deep into the seat.

"Come on baby! Come on! Lift your pretty little butt up for ol' Axel!" His thick arm bulged as he yanked back on the steering column, he shouted, "C'mon you overpriced piece of junk! Just once; do for ol' Axel!"

The dwarf, with a fresh cigar clutched in his teeth was pulling the steering column for all he was worth. The rumbling of the tires on pavement abruptly stopped and the perimeter fence of the airport flashed by, seemingly right outside of the window. The jet barely cleared the barricades and the perimeter fence as it gained altitude.

Axel braced his feet and continued to pull with all his strength against the jet's resistance.

"Come on, come on… up, up, UP!"

The nose of the plane was pointed directly up at the sparse clouds as the plane shot up in a severe acute angle. With one bare toe, the dwarf flicked a switch and the landing gear ground up into the fuselage and their speed increased as multiple lights began flashing on the control panels.

"Tell that priest to get up here. I need some longer arms in the other chair." Then glancing over to his right for the first time, he blinked his huge eyes, "Hey! Who's the kid"?

"Axel, let me introduce you to my friend, Annie Abbott." Colm McQuinn shouted as he climbed the steep floor, pulling himself into the cockpit by grabbing onto the door frame with his hands. Once there he shooed Annie out of the seat. Annie immediately slid, skated and ricocheted back into the cabin, landing in one of the soft bucket seats.

Taking the co-pilot seat, he buckled in and put on the headphones.

The dwarf's head almost twisted off. "McQuinn! That's not funny. Who's the kid?"

"She is the One, Axel, my recently deceased friend; she is the One."

"Yeah sure, and I'm the Queen of England. Look they're gonna scramble jets out of the Tactical Air Wing here in minutes, there aren't any defensive weapons on this useless limousine. We're gonna need a plan. Hopefully, one better than your last one."

Turn around Axel, I'll request landing clearance. Go back to the airport and land this thing. You're right; that last plan wasn't a very good one. I don't want us to get shot down if we can help it."

"What, you—we—we'll all be arrested as soon as we open the doors."

"Not all of us Axel. Just some of us."

"That's crazy, that's not a plan that's insanity. They're not takin' me without a fight that's for sure."

"You are correct there." Signaling the others to come forward he spoke. "Patch, find the boys; bring them to us if you can. Archimedes, now you will earn your bread and butter. Find The Three, think about the Sun Road. Maybe you can outrun them if it's not too far. We are going to need them—and soon."

Placing on the headphone set, he thumbed open the microphone, "Tower this is... um... Tango Echo 356 requesting permission to return to the airport. We have overpowered the kidnapper and have retaken the airplane. Hello? Does anybody hear me? Hello?"

There was a long pause while the people in the control tower dealt with their panic.

"Tango Echo 356 that is a relief. Come around to 360 degrees and descend to three thousand feet. Traffic will be clearing ahead of you. Is anyone a pilot that is with you?"

"No sir, I've done some flight simulation video gaming though." Colm winked across at the dwarf, who grinned around his already soggy cigar.

"This not the same thing Tango Echo 356. Please hold on for a few moments."

There was another long pause, this one much more than a few moments. The dwarf grinned his amusement and snapped open a lighter and lit up his cigar, while he steered the aircraft with his right foot and adjusted controls with long muscular arms.

"Sir, do you see the two levers in the center?"

The voice in the headphones came as a surprise after the long wait.

"Um, yes." Colm winked at Annie again.

"Very slowly pull those back toward you a very small amount. It will reduce your speed so you may start to descend. Please sir, only a tiny amount and gradually. Reduce your airspeed. Relax, we'll get you down, don't worry, you'll do fine. Do you know how to lower the flaps sir? Do you know how to do that?" Then as an afterthought, "You'll be fine; we're going to get you down safely."

"Good, cuz' I'm so scared I'm about to wet my pants." Colm grinned over his shoulder at Annie, who had just arrived back in the cabin, she almost choked. Her eyes couldn't have gotten any wider.

"Descend to twenty-five hundred feet, hold at three

six zero. Do you see the small guage about halfway up the console? It is the same one on both sides, that's the compass. You look at it like a clock. Three six zero is the top of the clock, you're doing just fine. We're bringing you in on the longest runway we've got, three six 'C'. Plenty of room to stop, and your model Leer should have automatic braking and shut down, so if we can get you on the ground, you'll be golden. Just take a few deep breaths now Tango Echo 356."

"Um – 10-4."

"Roger, 10-4. Start glide path to three six 'C', reduce throttles descending through three thousand to twenty-five hundred. You are ten miles out. You are doing fine, there is crosswind of twelve miles per hour, be prepared to correct."

The whistle of the jets dropped.

"There will be a thumb switch near the pilot's left hand for the landing gear. Throw that switch. You will get a green light above it when it locks in place. Tell us when the light comes on."

Again, the dwarf, flicked the switch with his big toe. Immediately, the whine of hydraulics of the landing gear folding out was followed by a dull 'crump' of it locking in place and the green light on the dash flicked on.

"The light came on."

"Excellent, now not much longer. You are doing an excellent job sir. The runway ahead is clear, but you are not descending on a good glide path. You need more flap and to get the nose up a bit more. We have you on visual now. Do you see the runway?"

"Um, I think so. Hold on." Axle made a few adjustments, and at first the plane bounced, tilted and wobbled then rose higher before settling again in a glide path. The nose of the plane now more elevated. Colm continued, "It's the middle one, right?"

"That is correct sir. Steer for the middle runway. You are doing an excellent job. Just a few more minutes now."

Axle looked across at Colm, "They're watching on radar, I don't want them thinking you're a pro or anything." He wobbled the plane once again just for good measure and then let it drop a quick thirty degrees with a good bounce at the end.

Colm gave him a thumbs up.

"This is tower, easy now, that was too severe a drop. All of your adjustments should be slow, slow and steady. You are cleared, continue to descend. You have the ball, the runway is directly ahead. As soon as you clear the perimeter, throttle down as far as you can. Glide in from there and pull back on the flaps sir. Keep the nose up. No matter what else – keep the nose up. Relax now, and hold steady." Then almost as an aside. "Emergency services are standing by; good luck to you sir."

Within seconds the outer perimeter fence of the airport flashed underneath them as the engines went almost silent and the plane continued to glide.

"Plenty of crosswind. I guess we should bounce this thing at least once though, just to sell your lame story priest."

With that the landing gear contacted the runway with a hard bump, then rose again only to bounce again and slew to the left almost off of the tarmac. Airborne again it drifted back over the pavement. The dwarf looked like he was enjoying himself but everyone else had forgotten to buckle their seat belts in the excitement, so they were bounced about the cabin with many 'oofs' and 'umpfs'. Finally, the plane settled into racing down the runway unabated for almost half of a mile, racing past numerous fire trucks and emergency vehicles arranged along both sides of their route. All of which, their lights flashing, pulled onto the runway behind them and raced in pursuit.

Finally, he threw the reverse thrust on the engines and the plane quickly slowed and again the passengers received a few more bruises.

Coming to a full stop, he left the engines running and turned to the druid.

"You'll come for me, once you get this sorted out right?"

"Right my friend. But for now," he raised his right hand in a fist and punched the dwarf, hard in the jaw drawing blood.

"That was a good one, you've gotten better than I recall." The dwarf licked his bleeding lip and grinned through bloody teeth.

"Just for show I'm afraid, good night my friend. See you soon. Remember the devil woman."

"What?"

Colm tapped the dwarf's temple and Axel's eyes rolled up and became vacant. He collapsed onto the pilot's seat.

"Okay, everybody. You have your assignments. As soon as the doors open, Patch you'll be able to leave unseen. Archimedes, wait until the forensics team is finished. See you all soon. "Annie; one sec!"

Colm stepped up out of the cockpit and stepped close, looking Annie in the eye. "We have just overpowered an evil dwarf and prevented him holding you for ransom or being forced into slavery. You are my kid sister Raven D'Argo's, and I am Doctor Jason D'Argo's. Don't ask, I've been around for awhile, at one time it was necessary. Anyway, I'm Jason, you are Raven.

We are fabulously wealthy. You are also breathtakingly beautiful, fastidiously reclusive, and of course, the darling of magazine covers all over the world. Perhaps, just for a bit, you might want to brush your hair. Maybe, a little more. Maybe?" He wagged his head and shoulders back and forth and winked. "If you know what I mean."

At first Annie looked at him with a blank stare.

"Here, close your eyes Annie. Don't open them until I say."

"I don't think we've got time for silly games Colm."

"Close 'em!"

Annie dutifully closed her eyes and started ticking off the seconds. There was a knock on the outside door. her face pleaded but she kept her eyes closed. "Hurry up Colm, please."

"Okay, open them."

"What?!"

Instead of the Colm McQuinn she knew, dressed in slacks and a polo shirt that was somewhat the worse for wear, a mature man dressed in a natty navy-blue suit and tie stood only a few feet in front of her. His beard and hair were trimmed perfectly, with a small strip of grey that swept back on each side. A set of round black framed glasses completed the picture.

"How?"

"I need to look differently than I normally would. In this realm, we look like who we are. In their realm, out there, outside of this plane, we don't. We look like what we want them to see, or like in Patch's case, she looks like nothing at all to them. I am showing you what they will see when the door opens. You can see it because you are human, mortal—For now.

"For now?"

"You should give a little thought to your back story. Unless we can't help it, no one should see 'Annie' before we want them to. Let's see what you got, shall we." He followed the statement with a tilt of his head and a shrug of his shoulders while he raised his eyebrows.

Annie looked at him just as another knock came at the door. This one sounded more like someone knocking with their fist. Colm reached past her and pushed the button. The door began to open. With a look of panic in her eyes, Annie turned and hurried through the cabin and into the restroom at the far end and slammed the door behind her. Colm smiled after her, then raising his hands behind his head, he stepped into the open doorway.

Raven D'Argos

"Yes, that's right." Colm McQuinn was seated in the open doors at the back of the ambulance. "Yes officer, we were supposed to charter a flight to Duluth, Minnesota. It was not supposed to be our usual pilot, something about some 'family' thing he had to attend. I think his daughter was getting married or something. He could easily have fit our flight into his schedule but obviously he thought it wasn't worth his job. I'll fire him as soon as I finish with all this foolishness of course."

Colm swept his stylish hair back in a slow-motion cascade of color and ego.

"At any rate, this new pilot was supposed to be adequate. It's only a few hours flight, so I didn't think anything of it. He seemed okay until he threatened us and then made us sit in the back. I was taken completely by surprise, and then he just took off without any clearance, I guess. But Raven knew exactly what to do. I guess she deals with a lot of that paparazzi stuff. She took care of it right away. She's had years of self-defense and kickboxing, you know?"

He paused and watched as the EMTs carefully lowered a stretcher down the steep steps from the Leer jet. A white sheet covered the form of the dwarf, his head restrained by an oversized neck brace and safety straps secured him to the stretcher. As they wheeled him to the second ambulance, his eyes opened and he moaned, "She's a monster, don't let her escape. It was her, oh, my head, oh… don't let that monster escape. She's… she's the *DEVIL*!"

With his eyes still on the stretcher as they loaded it into the back of the vehicle, Colm continued, "It was all Raven; I was useless officer. She's been taking martial arts most of her lives… er… I mean life. But me, well, you know… I don't do any of that stuff. I was, you know, just afraid."

"And Raven?" the policewoman with the notepad in her hand. "She's alright?"

"She was frightened. She is no innocent, but she was not prepared for this sort of thing at all officer." Colm McQuinn/Jason D'Argos winked at the woman. "If you know what I mean. I think she might have needed a minute or two to try and pull herself together. I guess she acted out of reflex, but she's just trying to get herself together, I'm sure you'd understand."

"Yes sir, I probably would have the same reaction." The police officer seemed very interested in keeping eye contact with the handsome man. For his part, his brows lowered and he increased the intensity of their stare. The officer stopped writing and put her pen back in her shirt pocket, content to just hold eye contact with the druid.

"I'm sure she'll be out in just a few moments. Perhaps you'll not question her too forcefully."

"No sir, I would never…"

"Oh, and here she is now."

All eyes turned toward the figure that suddenly

appeared at the top of the airplane's staircase. The breeze across the airport blew her fiery hair into streamers of red across her shoulders. Her long black swallowtail coat hung below the tops of bright black leather high heeled boots that laced to her knees. A blood red leather corset encircled her waist and extended out over her hips where it covered the waist band of black leggings that disappeared into her boot tops. Above the coal-black of her outfit a face of alabaster white was highlighted by almost iridescent blue eyes, which were highlighted in severe black eyeliner and black lipstick. Raven D'Argos had arrived on the scene. Every single person on the scene drew a collective breath; if they were not already standing, they rose to their feet.

"Where's the limo?" Raven quickly pulled out a pair of designer sunglasses and pushed them up her nose. "Jason! Jason! I swear to god if this is one of your ideas of a stupid joke, or some publicity stunt! Where's the limo! I can't be out in the sun and wind like this! I'm gonna burn! Or worse, my skin will chap in this wind. I have a show the day after tomorrow!" She drew her arms in, "And it's cold!"

As she ranted, she began to descend the narrow stairs in her high heeled boots. Two of the police officers quickly moved to assist her balance. She ignored both. As soon as those boots reached the pavement, she stalked up to the druid seated on the tailgate of the ambulance and finished her rant as she arrived at the toes of his shoes.

"Don't you even care about me?" She finished leaning over within inches of his surprised eyes and lowered her sunglasses to make eye contact—and winked. "No, don't bother answering that, of course you don't."

"Ah… Ahem… I'm sorry Princess. The officers wanted to ask us a few questions about that awful man."

"Oh! I can't even think about him. He was sooo creepy." Spinning on her heel she faced the young policewoman. "He smoked, officer! Can you believe that? He actually smoked a cigar. So vulgar." She finished with a small shudder. Then looking around her she again addressed the druid, "Where is the limo, Jason? Why are we still waiting? Shouldn't we be going somewhere else?" Annie looked around at the group that had collected around them. "Maybe someplace a little more interesting than this?" She pulled her sunglasses down and again surveyed her surroundings. "This is positively bleak."

"Any moment now, Raven." Colm consulted the watch from his pocket and pushing down the button on the side of it, he continued. "It should be any moment now."

"Sir, this is a crime scene. You cannot leave until we have finished with processing it. At least until we have questioned any witnesses and gotten their statements."

"I couldn't agree more officer."

"Um… Sergeant."

"Yes… Sergeant, I couldn't agree more. After all, you have to do your job. Raven can tend to be a little impatient—petulant actually."

"Hey! I know what that word means. I am not petulant; you're just being mean, I didn't do anything just by asking and now you're telling her? That's not fair. Not fair, not fair… NOT fair!" Raven D'Argos stomped her signature Prada boots on the tarmac for emphasis. The State Police Sergeant was dutifully impressed by both her station in life and her petulance.

"No Miss Argo's, it's alright. I understand completely. These things can seem so mundane, but... but... if we don't do our job. That horrible man might go free."

"O M G! Really! That's totally wrong!"

"I agree Miss Argo's, that's why we try and ask all the right questions and not waste your time."

In the momentary silence that followed, the sound of a high-pitched police siren started far away but rapidly approached. On the perimeter of the airport property a long border road ran along the inside edge of the fence. On the road, two vehicles were approaching at high speed. The first had emergency lights flashing. The other vehicle was dark, long and black.

Skirting the perimeter, the two fast moving vehicles did not slow down as they approached. Instead, they burst through the loose police line that had formed around the Leer Jet and stopped short at the tail of the aircraft. Everyone was transfixed as the unmarked police escort with its lights still flashing took position on the side of the black SUV. The doors opened and three officers stepped out and took positions in front of the two cars. The front doors of the black Suburban opened.

On the driver's side a tall man stepped out. As he straightened up from the car, he rose to an impossible height. Standing next to the tall car he still dwarfed it. He had to stand seven feet tall, Annie thought. He was dressed in an impeccably tailored suit and wore designer sunglasses. His incredible height and the vast width of his shoulders made it hard to notice his dapper appearance.

"Why that looks like the Governor!" Colm McQuinn chortled.

"It does?" Raven asked, looking at the figure.

"It does?" The deputy sheriff asked.

"Sure, looks just like him." Colm fixed her with a steady gaze. "Just like him; don't you think?"

The next person stepping out of the right side of the vehicle did in fact look just like the Governor of Tennessee. He appeared somewhat out of focus in the clear morning light, like observing him through a dark screen, but he waved and shouted above the noise of the airport.

"Jason? Jason! What in a goddamn hell of blue blazes is goin' on?"

"Hey old buddy." Colm called back, "There's been a bit of a dust up. Got it all sorted out now, but you know. These folks. Your folks, just doin' their job, so we seem stuck."

"That so?" It was a long slow, 'that so', spoken with a deep whiskey voiced man of power and authority as the dark figure approached at a slow walk, the giant right behind him.

He fixed the young sergeant with a critical stare.

"That so?"

"Yes; well no sir. There has been an attempted high-jacking of an airplane and kidnapping sir. We're just following protocol… um sir."

"That so?" His voice had dropped the friendly smile that went with it.

"Um, yes sir. We have a suspect in custody, but we're taking these people's statements. We're holding them until we finish."

The Governor dropped his sunglasses and stepping closer to the sergeant, he looked her in the eye.

"That so?" His voice had deepened even further and now had a hint of malice.

"If you're willing to vouch for these folks then no

sir."

"That so?'

"Yes sir."

"Well alrighty then." He said cheerily and clapped his hands together. "You folks pile in the back with me."

Like all things quiet, you don't realize how noisy it has been until it isn't. And then the silence is profound. The interior of the luxury car was decidedly less noisy than the busy airfield that surrounded it. As the limousine silently drew past the wide-eyed police and emergency technicians, it seemed a surreal slow-motion event. Only the large man in the front seat carefully watched them as they drove past, led by the police escort vehicle.

"Thank you, brother. I hesitated to contact you, but the need seemed to call for it."

"An enjoyable excursion brother. Introduce me if you will. Those elves of yours are an absolute riot. Comedians for sure."

"Annie Abbott, I would like you to meet one of my brethren. This is Ethan Greyhame, or Ethan the Wise, druid priest of the seven tribes and one of the original seven of the order. Ethan, my friend, you know of her already, but here before you lies our hope."

"Indeed, it would be hard to mistake her for anyone else; the fey speak of her daily."

"Wait. You're a druid? Like Colm?"

"There *are* more than one, you know."

"I guess I knew that, but I didn't grasp it."

"He is not as much fun as he once was, our Colm. But that little bit back there more than made up for it. That poor policewoman is going to lie awake tonight wondering what exactly she just experienced. Isn't that right little brother?"

"A little bit of fun for certain, but a delay nonetheless. And by the way, everyone is little next to that monolith in the front seat Ethan. I have not seen Thomas in more than a few lifetimes. How is it that he has landed on your doorstep Ethan? I'm almost afraid to ask."

The immense man turned in the seat, lowered his sunglasses and offered a hand for Annie to shake. In a deep baritone voice, he spoke, "I am Thomas."

The eyes that regarded Annie flamed bright red in the subdued lighting inside of the car. Annie gasped and recoiled.

Thomas, Bringer of Death

"What! He's a Fomorian? Oh my god, you're a Fomorian!"

"Yes, I am of the dark ones." He rumbled back.

"But... but..."

"Easy Annie, Thomas is our friend and has been for many generations. He has pledged himself as a protector of the wise."

"A protector of the wise?" Annie was pushing herself as far into the corner of the back seat as she could get still not trusting the huge visage that had turned his attention back to driving the car. "What does that mean?"

"Thomas has been one with our cause since he was first aware. He is the most ferocious individual I have ever known." Ethan Greyhame spoke with a smile. "He has demonstrated repeatedly and why I am so thankful that he is on our side."

"But..."

"Thomas is known far and wide Annie. He stood against the tide when no one else could." His eyebrows lowered as he met her eyes as his narrowed. "In ancient days, like us, he stood at the foot of the king. He was the first of his kind to war against the evil, and he has earned our respect—and our trust."

It was Colm's turn to reply. "Think back Annie; you know this guy." He turned in the seat and regarded Annie. "Thomas will be in your memory if you think back. I can help you remember if you'll trust me." He slid closer to her. "Would you be willing? Can you trust me?" He looked at her with concern, "Let's do something, if you will?"

"I'm pretty sure that never ends up working out very well for me these days."

"This one could answer a whole bunch of your questions."

"You always say that, and it always just brings up more questions." She looked up at the sunglasses in the mirror, sighed, "What do I do?"

"I want you to remember one more time. Not try. Really remember. You have met before; you and Thomas and I want you to remember, I want you to remember- Thomas," Colm reached across the seat and placed his index finger on her forehead. Annie couldn't help herself, she closed her eyes. She didn't know what to expect so she tried to relax and concentrate.

"Remember…", his voice changed in tone and began to fade into the distance, "remember Annie, … remember … remember 'Fear-giùlain a' Bhàis.'"

As if in a dream, Annie's thoughts spoke to her, *'Fear-giùlain a' Bhàis? What was that supposed to mean? Remember what?*

"Take my hand my love, come. It is time. It is time that you remember. Roison of the West March spoke in her mind. *"Come dear one, I will go with you."*

"Mother? What?"

"My language is your language bu ghràidh, (dearest). It is

the tongue of our ancestors. Take my hand and remember."

"The language of the ancients? Okay, and remember? Remember what?"

"Yes my love. Remember."

Annie felt as if she was sinking into a deep hole, slowly at first and then faster and faster. Finally spinning in a long freefall. She eventually felt her motion stop and she opened her eyes.

"Steady my love, I am with you. Remember."

She stood on a high hill in hot sun. Below her in all directions the bodies of fallen soldiers lay in tangled masses. The toll of death uncounted, the loss of souls immeasurable. Yet still those she fought continued to surge up the hill in numbers uncounted. The sound of their hatred deafening, as she recognized the few that stood beside her.

She felt herself brace for the onslaught. She felt herself shake and loosen her already tired right arm and again raise her shield onto her left forearm. With her sword she struck her shield three times. It was answered by similar staccato responses from behind her, other swords on other shields, three times.

"I am ready, bring them on!" She heard herself scream, but no longer in English. Instead in the language of the ancients.

"Do not worry my left hand, there are plenty for all of us." A strong voice from behind her shouted.

"Hail my king, I stand at your side perhaps one last time."

"I am strengthened by your valor. I shall do my best to deserve such a sacrifice." He struck his sword against his shield three times.

The first wave of attackers crashed into the line of defenders; the clash of iron on wood deafening. Annie strode downhill swinging a great sword in both directions. The defenders who had been on the verge of being overwhelmed rallied at her arrival and their ferocity returned.

But the numbers were too great. Slowly they were pushed back up the hill, backing up as they fought furiously. The sun beat down on them, its heat combined with the sound and fury of the battle. She felt the intense fatigue in her shoulders and legs. She was now fighting out of desperation to return to the king. She fought knowing that who she fought for was more important than who she herself was.

Her shield had sprouted arrows as she used it to hold off more than one attacker at a time against her sword. The first arrow to hit its mark took her left leg out from under her. Forcing her to drop her shield as she struggled back to her feet. With her weight on her right leg she raised her sword and faced downhill. Behind her, her king bellowed, "**Chan urrainn do dhorchadas buaidh a thoirt air an t-solas!**"

(Darkness will never triumph against the light!)

She turned and quickly limped the remaining distance to the top where her king fought. Her leg hindering her ability to move and to fight. She felt as another barbed missile struck its mark in her left shoulder and she saw that arrows had already found their mark in him, the mighty king, Brian Boru. He was bowed but not defeated; he fought on. She arrived at his left side almost simultaneously as the Berserker backed into their small circle as well facing downhill, forced back by the tide of attackers. Together they repelled the current attackers and forced them downhill where they gathered to brace for their next assault.

Hails of arrows landed among Annie and the

defenders of the king. More than a few found their mark. The Berserker dropped to one knee as he pulled a dart from his shoulder. Once again, he rose to his feet and lifted his mighty hammer. Again, a hail of arrows arrived and again he fell to his knees. Standing again he faced down the hill as the next wave of attackers charged, screaming their hate. One after another the arrows found their mark and with each hit, he staggered backward a step. Finally, the wave crashed against him. First, he fought on his feet, roaring his battle cry and swinging the mighty hammer. Then he fought from his knees. At the very last he turned and looked directly at her, meeting her eyes as he disappeared under the wave of the murderous attackers.

In horror, Annie felt the pain of loss in her mind and in her heart. With a scream of hatred she launched herself into their midst. She had a brief glimpse of the warrior king, Brian Boru as he fought on, arrows protruding from his chest and back. She struggled to stand until she no longer could. She felt the many wounds as each one took its toll on her but without their pain. Finally, when she could no longer hold it any longer her sword dropped to the ground and she drew her dagger one last time. But the fight was lost and the world went dark around her.

"Be still child, be still. I am here, be still." The calming voice of Roison spoke quietly in her ear.

Then there was only silence and darkness—seemingly endless silence—and darkness.

Suddenly she felt movement. She was moving—swiftly bouncing, jouncing along. As she struggled to understand, she couldn't seem to come up to the surface. She was not asleep, but not awake. There was movement beyond her eyelids but her eyes felt as if they were glued shut and would not open. When she tried to move her arms, they would not respond; she could not feel her legs. She was trapped in a nightmare of paralyzing silence as the journey continued, endless movement in an airless space.

The journey continued, seemingly endless and occurring in what seemed like only one moment, all at the same time. At last, all movement stopped. Even with her eyes shut she could feel light shining beyond her eyelids, and she could feel the ground that she was suddenly lying on. A cool breeze brushed her face and she took a deep breath of air that smelled of freshly mowed hay and spring flowers. She opened her eyes to a bright spring day and a giant armed warrior standing over her.

Immediately she recoiled, reflexively she groped for a weapon, forcing herself into a sitting position. The giant did not make any attempt to defend himself or to injure her. Instead, he leaned down and handed her a goatskin filled with liquid.

"Drink." It spoke

"What is this?"

"Water—Drink."

She had no weapon; she had no escape. There was nothing except open fields in every direction as far as she could see. She took a drink. The water was cool, refreshing. She took another drink and felt it revive her. She instantly felt more awake, alert.

The tall visage stood with his back to the sun, his immense frame blocking the light and heat, shading her while she sat on the ground. Looking up into the sun at the immense height of the giant his features were cast in shadow and she could not see his face clearly.

"Thank you."

In response he grunted, "You thirst, I give you drink. No more, no less." The voice was impossibly deep.

"Thanks. What is this place? Where are my kinsmen?"

"Gone. They are gone."

"Gone?"

"They are no more."

"What is this place then?"

"Beyond." It rumbled back.

"Beyond?"

"Beyond."

She turned and looked in every direction. Beyond… beyond. "Are there no others then."

"I came for the One. I have brought the One beyond."

"Is this beyond the veil?"

"It is the Elysian Field, the place for only the most heroic; only the brave may come to the Elysian Field."

"I'm dead."

"Yes." The great figure bent at the waist and leaned in close. "But no. I am—'Fear-giùlain a' Bhàis'." His eyes flashed red as they met hers.

"The Bringer of the Dead, you have brought me from beyond hell and the Paths of the Dead?"

"Yes, to live again when your time is ripe."

"Thank you, Fear-giùlain a' Bhàis. You are one of the unclean yet you have rescued me."

"I choose honor over evil. I am Fear-giùlain a' Bhàis."

"Thank you once again. That name is what you are, do you have a name as well?"

"I am baptized Tomas."

"Tomas? Thomas?"

"Thomas… yes."

"What now Thomas?"
"Now? Now the raven must fly again."

The Road to the Sun

Annie felt Colm McQuinn's finger leave her forehead. Suddenly she recognized the controlled air environment inside the big SUV and the movement as it sped down the road. She opened her eyes and looked at the two men. They both regarded her with concerned smiles on their faces.

"You have remembered Thomas. It has been a long, long time since when you first met him, but you and all of us owe him a great debt of gratitude. And now you see why he is our friend."

Annie looked from Colm's smiling face to the sunglassed eyes that regarded her steadily in the rear-view mirror. They held her gaze for several seconds.

"We have walked the Path, and we have been to the place beyond evil and climbed to the Elysian Field." Thomas' voice was a deep rumble that felt more like vibration than sound. "I came for the One."

"Th… th… thank you Thomas. Is it too late to say that now?"

"You have thanked Thomas many times over the ages. Thomas is Protector of the Wise," Colm held her eyes for the last part, "and he is also Fear-giùlain a'

Bhàis. When all was lost, when there was no longer hope, Fear-giùlain a' Bhàis' was there. He was there to rescue, to save the world," he leaned across and deepened his gaze, "he came for you."

Annie's eyes widened, "He's done it more than once." She looked again at the sunglasses in the rear-view mirror. "Come to get me, I mean."

Ethan spoke earnestly, "We had not seen Thomas for many years beyond years, and he slowly became the stuff of legends, and a fantasy to many, the wraith of ultimate darkness. With his new appearance we know that things have changed. By his presence we know that there is unrest in the Underworld, and that it is rising. Thomas has stood at the gates of hell and held them shut, sometimes only himself alone. But when he reappeared, we knew that the time of trials is upon us once again." He leaned across Colm and met her eyes, "and we know that we are going to need him again."

Annie gulped and looked away but somehow her eyes were drawn back to the sunglasses in the rear-view mirror. As she gazed, the great head nodded—slowly. She looked someplace else, anyplace else. She looked out the window and watched the skyline of the city as it rolled away.

"Where? Where are we going actually?" Anything to change the subject.

"Thomas has been reluctant to leave our area for several generations," Ethan continued, "we haven't been able to budge him. We haven't been able to understand it, but recently the fairies and other fair folk have also started to feel a shift, a change in the threads of life around us all, but it has also been hard to understand. Then two days ago, The Three arrived and confirmed our worst fears."

"What! You saw my dad?" Where? When?"

"Hold on. Hold on. This part is important and then we'll get to your father."

"What's more important than my dad? I need to know he's okay. C'mon please?"

"He's okay. They all are okay. But they are moving fast and they are dragging a ton of evil behind them. They're followed constantly and fight in front of themselves and behind. But they are all healthy and fit, strong. Their time has come. The time of The Three has come. At last."

"But where are they now?! I want to see them!"

"Gone I am afraid." He caught Colm's eye and said, "Going to the 'Road to the Sun'. 'We must meet with the ancients and join with them once again'. That's what he told me."

"I'd heard that before Ethan. Do you know what the Road to the Sun is? I have no idea myself."

"Oh you poor little Irish boy. Perhaps if you spent more time learning about where you live now, instead of remembering where you used to live, you'd know already."

"Noted. But for now… what is it?"

"The 'Going to the Road to the Sun' is a mountain road that runs through Glacier National Park and climbs high through Logan Pass. There is a mountain near there called Mountain of the Sun that legend tells the deity Sour Spirit goes to and from heaven when his people are in need. There is a connection point there, so it is said. It's in Montana, Colm, surrounded by hours of wilderness in every direction. They left the day before yesterday and it's over fifteen hundred miles."

"So? Beyond our reach, for now."

"Indeed."

"Wait a minute!" Annie sat bolt upright. "Wait… Why did they come here? Why didn't they just go as soon as they got the truck from the dwarf? Why come to Memphis, it's not on the way to Montana, is it?"

"Why… I don't actually know why. I didn't think about it before."

The sunglasses in the rear-view mirror regarded her and again he gave a slow nod. She understood. She reached forward across the two men and touched the shoulder of the huge driver. And again Annie intoned the prophecy, "They are coming! The undead and the unclean rise from beneath us. Those that poisoned this earth and drove away our people. They are coming once again! Their numbers cannot be counted; they rise from the depths. They seek to destroy the warriors of justice. The Three are lost."

"It's what she read from the stone."

"Stone? What stone?"

"About a hundred miles east of here. She made us pull off the highway and then to the Indian Mounds at Shiloh. She found one of the Druid Stones buried there."

"A Druid Stone!? Here? In Tennessee?"

"That is the fourth stone that she has found that I had never known of. This one was enlightening; the one before was terrifying." Colm leveled a hard stare at Ethan, "It was the binding stone of Lilith."

"What! You're kidding! Where?"

"Near the Dell of the Red Witch no less, but let's not get too far off the main track here. The stone of the mounds gave us two clear messages. You've heard the first, Annie can you repeat the second?"

"It said to seek the Sentinel in the Forest of the Ancients."

"The Redwoods of northern California," Colm spoke assuredly.

"Not necessarily."

"What do you mean, 'not necessarily'."

The escort police car slowed and then turned into a gated entranceway. Thomas steered the big, black Governor's SUV in as well. At the end of a curving drive, a massive brick Georgian mansion stood at the top of a small rise. It's size and beauty could not have been argued, and Annie gasped.

"You live here?"

"Yep, for nearly a century now. Tennessee constitution only allows you to serve two terms so I had to change my identity every several years before the next election. I'm a lot better looking this time than I was last time though."

"This time?"

"Yep, my last two terms I was an ancient and quite crotchety fellow. You can't imagine how difficult it can be to act that way for eight years. This Ethan rendition is a lot more energetic. I'm kind of liking it so far."

"Why? Why are you even doing that? You're a druid right, you don't need to be governor, do you?"

"Why? Goodness! Because it's fun. Why does the White Witch love to create illusions that scare people? Why does Colm McQuinn pretend to be some twenty-something stud, when he's actually older than I am?" Ethan leaned across and winked at her, "And just between you and I, that's saying something.

Colm had only been listening with half of his attention. Finally, he spoke up, "Okay Ethan, why the 'not necessarily?'"

"There's more than one 'Forest of the Ancients', and one of them's right underneath us Colm. Didn't you ever study anything about the U.S. of A.?"

What do you mean? California is the only place where the giant redwoods grow. Right?"

Yep. But there are old things wherever you look in this world and our world. Right?" Ethan winked at Annie again. "And there are things even older than old, actually really ancient."

"So why is there more than one Forest of the Ancients?"

"Because old chum, there's one right under your feet."

"In the ground?"

"Come on, let's get something to eat, get you two cleaned up and maybe a little well-deserved rest. When was the last time you slept Annie?"

"Slept? Gee, um, I not sure."

"At least six or seven days if I'm counting it correctly." Colm counted off on his fingers, "A few more than that for me. It's been a bit hectic lately Ethan, but you're right; we need to rest."

"Well I have to say Annie, for a *mostly* mortal, you are doing amazingly well. Seven days! Impressive. But you'll get better at it soon."

Turning to Colm, "As good as done my old friend. Welcome to the little house I built back in 1933. Welcome to Wills House, still my home but now owned and maintained by the State of Tennessee. Let's get you some food, and then let's find you a bed."

The door next to Annie clicked and opened slowly. Looking up a narrow smiling face with glowing green eyes greeted her.

"Greetings my lady!"

"Micah! I thought we'd left you behind! I am so glad to see you. Can I hug you?"

"We reserve the display of physical affection for long mates and newborns—but for you I will gladly return your embrace." As Annie hugged Micah, the other two elves stepped around the SUV smiling shyly.

"We met with Ethan the Wise once we could no longer keep pace with the red vehicle. The dwarves have maintained an outpost near here. They knew of the druid. He wields the levers of power and he assigned us escort duties. We are united again my lady, to protect and serve." He gave a friendly salute.

"Micah—, again! I told you, I do not hold the levers of power. But I have plenty of oversight, just not power. I am a politician, not a strategist. Let's get these two some food, a bath and to bed. We will talk tomorrow, and even though the day is still young, these two need to let it go for now and rest. I feel that there is an energy that follows us," he turned and looked back over his shoulder. "A negative one that is in pursuit and saps their energy. While they rest and strengthen, will you watch for them?"

"As we have pledged, so we will continue. The One must be strong and rested as the Red Queen rides to war. We will watch."

Thank you, friends. Tomorrow will bring hard decisions. But for now, they can rest." Then he added grimly, "For now, I need to go into town." Ethan frowned, and then continued in a tight voice, "If I'm not mistaken, there's a dwarf that is going to need to disappear into thin air." He turned and looked down at Annie, "And I am going to need to clear my schedule for the forseeable future; and as soon as soon as possible."

§§§§

At the foot of the great mountain the market had just opened for business. People shuffled from stall to stall, selecting among fruits and vegetables while birds sang in the rainforest canopy overhead. The sun shone brightly and the people smiled to one another.

At first, a small vibration caused glasses in the cantina to tinkle. But the vibration grew, and vases and plates began to shake and were quickly snatched to safety by the shopkeepers and the sound of distant thunder grew in the sun bright sky.

Sweeping down from the smoking mountain a great cloud of dust, as if blown by a gale wind, poured out into the lands below, racing to the north. The thunder continued as the land beneath the people's feet shook and trembled. On and on the noise and vibration continued as people were stopped in their tracks and forced to grab trees or tables to keep from falling. It was minutes before the thunder finally faded.

The people looked meaningfully at each other and made the sign of the cross. The small church bell began to toll. The old church would be very full this Sunday.

The legend of old had risen once again.

The Council

A deep sigh sounded in Annie's ear, disrupting her sleep. As she slowly rose through several layers of sleep to the surface of consciousness, she realized she had been hearing the same deep sigh while still asleep. Without opening her eyes, she squinted them more tightly shut and flounced onto her other side, away from the brightness of the windows and punched up the pillow. She relaxed, sinking down into the pillow, but the deep sigh came again. Cautiously, she cracked one eyelid. The first thing she saw was a fairy standing less than a foot away with her arms crossed and a scowl on her face. The fairy immediately seized the moment and stepped forward.

"It is time for rising. The day has arrived and is passing. How can you waste this precious time?"

"Patch, I'm tired. Just let me sleep a little longer."

"Longer? It is tomorrow, yesterday has come and gone. Today is the tomorrow of yesterday and still you sleep."

"What? I don't even know if I understand what you just said." Annie rubbed her eye with heal of her hand.

"It is tomorrow. You slept away the yesterday, and yesterday's evening and night. Now it is tomorrow and it is not

early tomorrow. The breakfast has past, and the luncheon has been served yet still you linger, lazy in your responsibilities."

"Responsibilities?" Annie rubbed her eyes again and stretched. She closed her eyes against the light from the high windows and looked wistfully at the pillow she had just left behind. "This bed is seriously comfortable."

"Ethan the Wise has had almost one hundred years to get his house just the way he likes it. Of course, it is comfortable. For mortals at least. There is no 'extra food' and they have almost no idea about what good beer should taste like."

Annie sat up in bed and stretched again. Then scratching the haystack of hair on the side of her head she smirked and said, "So you've been raiding the kitchen larder soldier?"

"I have merely requested additional rations. They have been stingy. And now it will be a long time more. A Council of the Races has been called. They are waiting for you."

"What are you talking about?"

"The convening of the races has been called. Only once in my seven-hundred years, eight months and nineteen days have I witnessed another. It is a rare occurrence to be sure and this time I am asked to represent. As are you Anne of Present. You must arise or there will be no dinner served anytime soon."

"The races? What is that?"

"The races of our world have been called and much is to be discussed. The warriors of our worlds must decide a path. You must speak for the witches as there are no others."

"Wait. The witches are a separate race? Aren't they just normal women? Who are the others?"

"We are all 'normal' Anne of Present." Patch gave here a stern look, *"There are various depths of understanding that cross the races of man and magic. The race of Men, does not delve these levels 'normally'. Those that do, come to the other side transcended to a different level of existence, and a different*

form of being. The witches represent one such. The elves are another and there are also the dwarves." Patch puffed out her chest and added proudly, *"And I will speak for the fairy realm."*

"I'm not much of a witch." Mused Annie scratching her head.

"The druid's bring two of their kind to the council but only The Three can represent themselves."

"Yes. I suppose they are a pretty unusual, …WAIT! What do you mean? The Three? The Three are here?"

"The Three have been returned. Archimedes has performed a great task, they are pursued to this very door and now we are all prisoners in this 'seriously comfortable' fortress as you say. The council must convene—or it will become our prison."

"My Dad? My Dad's here? Here, like here in this house?"

"We shall never eat another bite before starvation sets in if you must ask me to repeat everything I say to you. Yes, The Three arrived at first light this morning, the minions of Cian close behind them. Now they know the whereabouts of all of us and most especially you Anne of Present." The fairy took a step forward and drew her eyebrows down. *"Most especially Anne of Present, they know the location of you."*

Annie threw her legs over the side of the bed and dropped down onto her feet. "You could have just said that my Dad was here." She hopped around the room on one foot as she tried to struggle into her jeans. "He'll know what to do."

"I have given you all of the information necessary and I have given it in the order of its importance Anne of Present."

Annie turned toward the fairy ready to argue with her but then sighted herself in the mirror behind Patch and gasped, "Oh! I need to brush my hair. I'll be downstairs in a little while. I look awful."

"Yes. You indeed appear unkempt. Perhaps Raven would be a better choice. Or at least a more immediate one?"

"Raven?" Annie cocked her head to the side and smiled at the fairy, "I hadn't thought of that."

"Well that does not come as a surprise." The little fairy smirked.

"Come on Patch, be nice. I'm still tired you know."

"I will tell them that you are on your way."

"No, hold on. I'll come with you." Annie gave a final look in the mirror and turned to face the fairy. The fairy smiled, satisfied, Raven D'Argos radiant and goth, smiled back at her. She reached for the door handle, "Let's go; I'm ready."

Fires Built

Stepping out into the thickly carpeted hallway, they walked to the top of the stairs and turned.

"She is coming!"

The raised voice of Link spoke from her post at the foot of the long staircase. Behind them Raisa, the second elf guardians came up behind them.

Immediately, the doorway to the foyer crowded, filled with the jostling of heroes of the races, their eyes all fixed on the figure at the top of the stairs. Their attention and focus so intense that it dizzied Annie and she felt her knees weaken and she stumbled in her heeled boots. Grabbing for the banister to steady herself, she missed her grasp and pitched forward, teetering on the top step until her balance finally failed and her heel caught in the carpeting. Almost in slow motion, she pitched out into the vast space of the chandeliered foyer below, even as Raisa reached out for her.

Her eyes widened in horror, her arms flailing, a scream grew in her throat as her vision blurred and her speed increased. But before she could gasp or scream a great force struck her, stopping her in mid-air— suspending her there. Then, slowly and gently, she was returned back to her feet, once again at the top of the staircase. With her hand on the banister this time but her heart beat still pounding in her ears, she caught her breath and looked down at the throng below. Every face reflected fright and horror save one. Standing to the front of the throng stood a tall man, burly and rough, his bearded face stern, his right hand raised toward her, his left hand on his right wrist steadying it. As she gazed down at him, he lowered his arms and smiled.

"Dad!" Annie's voice trembled and she started down the staircase trying to hurry, but this time watching her step.

"Easy Annie. I can wait." Michael stepped to the bottom of the staircase and raised a hand to steady her as she approached. Several of the observers were shoved aside by a monstrous figure that pushed through from the back followed closely by a smaller shadowy figure in his wake. Out into the chandelier's light of the foyer the tall, wide form of Gabe Macdonald and Rafer Tate emerged and joined him at the bottom of the staircase, making the room seem much smaller than it really was.

"Guys!" Annie arrived at the bottom of the stairs and threw herself into her father's arms. "Oh Dad!" Tears burst from her eyes as she buried her face in his chest, breathing in his aroma, unable to hug him close enough. She sobbed, "Oh Dad. I know. I know now what you didn't want to tell me. Oh… *sniff*… oh Dad, I've been so scared."

Mike Abbott hugged her back and lowered his forehead to touch the top of her head.

"I know Annie, I am sorry. I didn't know how." His voice was choked as he added, "I didn't know if I should."

"Now that is a look! I must say, an improvement to

be sure." The Great Horned Owl spoke as his great wings fairly brushed over the heads in the doorway and landed on the corner post. Cocking his head at a right angle he regarded Annie, "A little less make-up perhaps, but otherwise I like it."

Annie smiled despite herself, "Archimedes, you found them and brought them back. Thank you!"

"Archimedes got us back here to Mills House alright, but it turned into quite a race at the end. Going to the Road to the Sun is going to have to wait; it looks like we are stuck here for a while."

"And that's why the council has been called. We are all in the same shoebox here and all roads out are blocked." Ethan Greyhame strode into the room, "But the council's business will need to be short and sweet. Less talk, more action is needed or I am mistaken."

"I think we all agree to that," Rafer Tate stepped around Michael and wrapped his arms around Annie. "I bet you're hungry though, aren't you? Maybe just a little Annie?"

As if on cue, Annie's stomach rumbled loud enough so that everyone close by heard it. Annie rocked back and met Rafer's eyes, who smiled back at her. She gave him a bemused half grin and winked, "Thanks Rafe."

"Everyone, down to the meeting room, we'll rustle up some grub for Annie. In the meantime, let's go, time is of the essence." Ethan directed them to the elevator near the back of the house.

§§§§

As they exited the elevator onto the lower level, they entered a large open space, enclosed in glass. In the center a long highly polished wooden table extended from one end to the other, surrounded by at least thirty chairs evenly spaced. The darkened wood of its' surface reflected the light of the setting sun from the windows that lined one side of the room. There was nothing on the long table from one end to the other, except for one place at the far end. Somehow in the time it had taken for her to descend in the elevator, a complete place setting rested on the table, surrounded by several covered dishes.

Recovering quickly Annie said, "Well, I guess I know where I'm supposed to sit," and she moved around the window side of the room and walked to the far end.

"Everyone please find a seat; there is no seating chart." Ethan addressed the group, "Sit where it pleases you."

There was a general whisper of chairs on carpet and shuffling of feet. The soft murmur of brief conversations and apologies for trod on toes. As the members all politely found a seat, Annie scanned the participants. The three elves sat directly across from her and smiled. Four swarthy dwarves took seats with two on each side of the table but left a space between themselves and Annie and the elves. Gabe MacDonald with his wide shoulders occupied two spaces next and Rafer Tate sat next to him. Patch settled onto the table directly in front of Annie and began to raise the lids on the various dishes. Michael Abbott strode around the table and took the last vacant seat next to Annie.

Several chairs were left empty between the Rafer Tate and the distant end of the table. Colm McQuinn, dressed casually, but all in pure white, took the last seat on the side opposite the door. Leaning back with his arms folded he gazed down the table with a calculating look. Then he leaned back far enough so he could see

Annie and smiled from the far end and winked.

Next to the doorway, the giant Fomorian, Thomas, ducked his head to enter the room and leaned against the wall just inside, his arms also folded on his chest. With his sunglasses still on in the sunlit room, it was impossible to tell if he was looking at her or somewhere else.

Finally, an aged hooded woman in a robe of gray shuffled into the room. Without looking up or any greeting, she pulled back the last chair, closest to the door and took a seat. Her face hidden within the hood once seated she folded her hands on the table and made no other sound as she looked straight down at her hands, the hood the only thing visible in the last rays of the setting sun.

Colm McQuinn threw a quizzical gaze at Ethan, who raised his open palms to him. Gesturing for him to be patient.

Finally, a silence ensued and all eyes turned toward the head of the table where Ethan the Wise stood. From her seat at his left Annie looked up at him, surprised at the visage. Gone was the posture and face of the youthful and vibrant Governor of Tennessee. In his place was a tall lean man, well beyond his middle years with lengthy gray hair and creases of age and experience covering his face and electric green eyes that surveyed the room. It was a face that radiated authority and strength yet still somehow resembled the Ethan Greyhame she met yesterday at the airport.

"Greetings friends. These meetings are informal; you may speak freely. We do not have any reason to favor anyone's opinion over anyone else's. Our purpose is to make a choice of direction and whatever action we can provide with our combined strength. We have only one agenda, and it is one that is passed down to all of us from generations upon generations—vigilance.

"We have seen the age of today, our age, reach a tipping point. We must decide whether to refuse our role in protecting the world beyond ours and allow it and our own to slide into pettiness and the squalor of lost integrity. Or to fight against it and protect the flow of life that is the magic of everything in our world and theirs; that is the very life that surrounds us. Now because of this and many other influences, the end of this age and beginning of the next is upon us. We have the will to strive toward making it a golden age, but only time can judge if we have the strength. Much of that will depend on what we agree to today in this very room." He paused and surveyed the room. "It is my fervent hope that our discussions will be constructive and the efforts that follow our decisions are effective. In this room today, we will make decisions that will affect every single one of those in our world, and the world beyond ours. We must choose wisely—and justly.

"Some of us here gathered have witnessed the rise and fall of the gifted in long ages past and are aged in the match of those long years. And some of us are young by comparison. Some of us here are young enough so that they have not yet realized or come into their full potential."

He glanced down at Annie who returned the look with wide eyes and a mouthful of cheeseburger. She gave a small sideways smile to those down the table facing her and wiggled her fingers at them. Some of them returned the gesture with smiles, others did not.

"Even Patch here, in her eight hundred years…"

"Seven hundred years, eight months and nineteen days."

"Yes, in her almost eight hundred years, has only witnessed one moot such as this in her lifetime, and only once in that lifetime was it necessary. We all know what is at stake, and we all know what chess pieces are moving and which are not. The Red Queen rides north as we speak, and we must anticipate her aid. But we must also not overestimate the strength that she brings. It will be up to we few to prepare and be at the ready.

"Not all warriors bear arms. Not all of us are warriors in battle, but each of us brings individual skills that can help to stem the tide that only wishes to destroy, to steal our sunshine—to create an existence of fear and despair in the mortal world beyond ours. We must marshal our strengths and skills my friends. We must create a united front and we must muster the strengths of those we few represent. Shall we begin?"

"When our Queen arrives with the forces of the kings of old riding behind her Cian and his rabble will feel the full strength of defeat and she will banish him and all that follow to the darkness beyond death!" Mink stood up and spoke defiantly, leaning forward with both of his hands on the table.

"That may be true, and we can hope beyond hope that may be possible my elven friend, but what would be the cost of that victory? How many of your brethren would pay for the dawn of this new age. Every life lost, every soldier who does not return home is too high a cost, but cost there will be." Ethan the Wise spoke from his seat at the head of the table. "We will fight when the time comes, each one of us will fight with such skill and weapons that we have, and for now we must prepare the ground ahead of us. We must work to minimize such a loss, and we must achieve small victories in the meantime. Above all else, we must be in agreement and we must do it quickly."

"I agree," Colm McQuinn stood from his place at the foot of the table impeccable in his white shirt and pants. "Each of you possesses a unique knowledge of the ways of life and each of you sees the magic in all that surrounds us; indeed without that magic some of us would not even exist." He looked down the table and smiled at Patch who was eating a french fry from Annie's plate and not paying any attention to anything else. "Because of this we have the ability to walk between the worlds. Those of the vile underworld cannot do so without difficulty because although they are somewhat magical, they deny the very existence of the beauty, the magnificence of creation and in turn they are weak as a result. They make up for that weakness in sheer numbers. They have those numbers because it is easier to be selfish and evil than it is for us to maintain the balance of truth, the constant awareness of the threads of life. These threads, the magic that surrounds us and is constantly weaving in and out of our lives is what makes life worth living." Around the table many heads nodded in agreement. "And it requires an instant awareness if and when these threads lose their resonance. The harmony that plays the music of magic, we can feel the discordant note. Right now, that tone is out of tune with our world, and we know that sorrow and tribulation are upon us. We must act and act quickly."

One of the four dwarves stood next and bowed to the two druids. "We know what you are talking about wise ones. We who delve the earth have felt the rumbling below us. The Fomorians have taken control of many lower levels and we grow uneasy. The longer they continue to build their strength, the less they fear our defenses and there have already been small battles and skirmishes. We must have reinforcements and in exchange we pledge our own battle-ready forces to the cause. The tones from afar speak of conflict at many entrances. The dwarven fighters stand ready, the history of their strength and ferocity is known to all here, but we alone are too few against them.

"Right now any fight will favor the dwarf nations. In the close quarters of the caverns, we are at an advantage. We know the ways of the roads and highways of the underground, and we know how the stone and the rock will assist us. Those of evil caste do not hear the tones as we do and could not understand even if they could. We are ready, but coordination with those other races here is necessary."

As if on cue, the light beyond the western windows dimmed suddenly as clouds thickened over the setting sun. Sleet began to pelt the windows tracking sideways across the panes of glass propelled by a sudden wind.

The dwarf spokesman hurriedly sat down, a fearful look on his face.

As one The Three rose to their feet, Raphael and Gabriel stepped behind Michael and placed a hand on his shoulders. Immediately the three images of the ancients of old stood before them. Michael glowed from within his massive chest, his face impossible old, his gray eyes alive, the visage of capable leadership, Gabe the massive warrior with dark leather bands surrounding huge biceps and eyes aglow and Raphael, a wavering vision of wind and storm, his dark eyes flashing. Each of them nodded to each person at the table but paused when they came to Annie. As one they bent at the waist and bowed. Michael spoke.

"The time of discussion has come over late. The battle is joined and we have already fought many with our will alone. Those that would delight in the downfall of life as we know it, the fabric of life that we know of as magic, have risen once again. They walk our earth and the world beyond ours. These most recent skirmishes have taken place in the mortal world where magic has begun to fade. Many of the beasts of the earth, many of the essential plants have been rendered extinct as the magic of life is drained all around us.

"The Fomorians are losing battles but they are winning the war. The earth continues to warm, weather becomes increasingly severe. Wildfires, drought, and famine are increasing as they draw magic from the world around us. Whatever we decide we must act immediately, the mortals talk and argue even as their boat continues to sink. And now the Fomorians are learning the secrets of diplomacy. They are gradually replacing lawmakers, governors, no offense intended to the governor of Tennessee," He nodded toward Ethan, "Senators, congressmen, even running for presidencies in many countries around the world." He scanned the room and placed a massive hand on the table, "And they are winning!"

"So what... what do we do ancient one?" The dwarf leader asked meekly.

"We fight."

Before Michael could answer a quiet voice caught everyone in the room by surprise, wide eyed they all turned in that direction. Colm McQuinn sitting next to the figure recoiled, rolling backward in his chair away from the source of the voice.

Slowly the gray hooded figure rose to its feet and with head still lowered, a cascade of white hair hid the face. From the sleeves of the robe, long gnarled fingers emerged and slowly drew back the hood. As the hood was drawn back the gray of the robe shifted and swirled as a sweep of colors swept from the hood to the floor. In place of the worn gray, the robe had become the deepest forest green.

There was a collective gasp from everyone. Annie's mouth dropped open in midchew, eyes wide gaping. Before them stood Allegra 'Keeper of the Light'. The dark streak in her long blond hair now gray, her eyes no longer young, instead looked out through a veil of great knowledge… and distress.

"We fight."

Battle Lines

"Allegra!" Annie shoved back her chair and stumbled around the table in her haste, but as she approached she stopped. With one hand over her mouth, "No! No!" She reached out and took the long gray strand in Allegra's hair between her fingers, "It's too soon! You're changing… you've started the transition! So soon?"

"These times require it Annie and I will answer the call." She placed a gentle hand on Annie's wrist. "Allegra will fade as she must. But friends and sisters we are, and always shall be."

Annie slowly stepped forward and they hugged, holding each other for a long moment.

"And look at you! What's all this?" Allegra held Annie out at arm's length, "You look absolutely smashing girl! Is this what you're going with now?"

"Too dramatic?" Annie looked down at her boots.

"Too dramatic would have been a full-blown Morganna darling, so no, this is good; just right. And you do look great—really great. Besides, just for this once, I think I just nailed the dramatic thing," she winked. "Don't you?"

"Ladies. Please?" Ethan at last spoke quietly.

Those who had had risen to their feet reclaimed their seats. Annie sat in the previously unoccupied seat on the left of Allegra still holding her hand. She smiled across at her father and shrugged, apologizing for not returning to sit next to him. He smiled back and nodded that he understood.

"Good. Now to business and first, a bit of an apology." He surveyed the room and sighed. "As soon as Colm messaged that the need for assistance was coming to us here. I requested the dwarven warriors to locate Allegra. With their swift help, the tones of the ancients were sounded and she was brought here only hours ago through the secret ways that they know. Now the moot of the races is filled and we may truly meet in agreement. We of course are too few here alone to resist the onslaught of evil coming toward us in an ever-rising tide. Therefore, it will take every ounce of our will and we must plan our moves carefully so we do not squander our strengths. This means that we must use magic—and we must use it like never before."

Every face that had been registering stubborn determination now switched to one of confusion.

"Yes." Colm McQuinn stood at his seat. As he did, his appearance began to shift. In a brief blur of spinning grey lines he turned toward the group. Now instead of the handsome young man in white there stood an elderly man robed in the pure white of the wise, ramrod straight, long grey hair cascaded over his shouders and a long beard extended to his chest. He continued in a harsh whisper; "Yes, magic like never before. The magic of malice."

"I agree, but life and magic are the same thing. How can we direct life to our will It is all well and good to speak of using power that is not ours to use; it is another thing entirely to do something like that." Gunther, the leader of the dwarves turned toward Ethan.

"Don't misunderstand my friend. I did not say we should engage in evil actions. I said, "like never before." Every one of us at this table is here because of magic. The wonder and power of it is limitless as long as one sees it, lives it and makes it their own.

"For some, their existence itself depends upon magic." He paused to look down at Patch, who stood up and drew her sword in response. "They dwell in the world of fantasy and legend that surrounds all that live, but many are afraid to acknowledge. For them the mortal world and the limitations it imposes make no sense to them, and they would never be able to understand it. For them a discussion of mortality and those things important to the people who live in the mortal world sounds like jibberish and makes no sense.

"There are also those who live separate and apart from the races of man and their pettiness. The dwarven nations have long existed unbeknownst to others. Keeping to themselves, but ensuring the flow of the aquifers, the recycling of resources and a guardianship of the earth itself, the dwarves have long maintained the watch of the underworld.

"For others it has been a journey from the ages long past in the service and study of the magic of life itself. The knowledge and wisdom somehow passed through the molecules of each new member, never the same, but always the same, we who are doomed to look forward and cursed to remember our past.

"And finally," he nodded to The Three who were still standing, "those that are ancient beyond time. Those that serve at the hub of the great celestial timepiece. Those that are charged with the preservation of magic, life and all the power that is a result. Those that we honor by keeping our own pledge.

"Lastly, are those that though mortal are aligned with the power of magic and grow strong in it, channel it, and direct it to the protection of all living things; they are the mothers of our earth. For them, the power courses through them, creates wisdom within them through the generations of their craft. It is they that we must support, for only with them can we direct our efforts. It is only through them that our plans and schemes may be successful. For us, who wish for victory, we must rely upon the witches in this the final conflict of our age." He gazed down the long table at the two women seated at the end. "Let us lend our strength to those who go at the forefront of our endeavor, the Red Queen, daughter of the mortal warrior, Tam Lin, who rides to our aid," he nodded to the radiant Allegra, "The Green Witch, Keeper of the Light, and the rise of our new hope; and" he looked down the long table at Annie, "the Blue Witch, Queen of the two worlds, Anne, Keeper of the Long Promise."

"Whatever we decide at this final hour, let us be prudent, rational and above all else trust in we few. Few we are truly, but our power is mighty."

As he finished he turned to the grouping, and his eyes lit in blazing white.

At the end of the table, Colm McQuinn rose to his feet, no longer a young man. Before them instead stood Merlin of Old, Hammer of Stone and his eyes burned bright as well.

One by one the others stood, the elves in full battle array their luminous green eyes ablaze weapons at the ready. The four dwarven warriors rose as one, battle axes and heavy hammers drawn, surrounded by darkness, their faces grim.

With a nod of agreement between them, the two women clasped hands and stood as one. Holding hands as they rose to their feet, their appearance rapidly morphed in a green and blue burst of color. Before the others stood the same two women, both still young, strong and capable—but robed as true sisters of the Thirteen—two mighty warriors as they held hands. In their other hands they held their staffs, the first glowing bright white, the second; flaming molten ash. As one they raised their staffs and struck them on the soft carpeting of the conference room floor. A blast of almost subsonic impulse erupted, rattling the panes of the windows—and setting off the fire sprinkler system.

Together they spoke, "We Fight"

From the far end of the table a glowing blue orb raced through the air down the long table. Stopping in front of the two women, Patch smiled and bowed her head to the two women and closed her eyes. Slowly at first she began to spin in midair, then faster and faster still, until she was only a blur of motion growing brighter by the second, until finally it was hard to look directly at her. Then, she stopped instantly in a final brilliant flash of blinding light.

As their eyes readjusted back from the blinding flash, Patch stood before the two women, her face painted in streaks of black and red, a leather buckler across her chest and a small two-handed sword brandished before her.

"We fight!"

"Well then." Ethan blinked and rubbed the water out of his eyes as the water pouring from the overhead sprinklers began to slow. "Firstly, we must leave this place if we are to accomplish even the smallest of things.

And for that I have prepared in advance." Ethan leaned his hands out onto the table and looked down the table, "I have a plan."

As the water from the overhead sprinklers began to abate all eyes turned back toward Ethan. Those that had stood found their seats again. All eyes except Annie's, whose remained fixed on the tiny figure in front of her.

"Can you do that any time you want?" She whispered.

The fairy gave a small smile and winked. *"Magic is powerful in the hands of the forces of light. Now revealed, the Keeper of the Long Promise can draw forth all of the potential of each and every magical creature. As long as I serve the true one, my light shall burn ever more brightly."*

Keeper of the Long Promise

"Several years ago, I felt that Mills House was too small a facility to host the kind of meetings necessary to accomplish the business of a growing state and its economy. As such I commissioned the building of this conference center. But, during the excavation in preparation for the building, we accidently happened upon a unique discovery. A large cavern was opened below the building and all construction was necessarily halted. Believe me the newspapers and media had a field day with the delays, and most especially, the expense for the governor's folly—my folly.

"Once I had cleared the workers and 'lookers' from the site, I contacted the dwarven nation and they delved the recess. What they discovered was a previously unknown expanse of avenues in the underground. But they also felt a force, a presence that guarded it and were reluctant to awaken it and so did not delve too deeply.

"As a precaution against the possibility of Fomorians, Thomas entered and traveled extensively in the underground passages. The way seemed clear for our safety, but in his travel in the darkness he met someone;

or something that predated even his ancient years. The being confronted him, questioning his presence by command, demanding an answer. For the question that it asked, Thomas had no answer. Because he could not answer the question, he was denied permission to explore further.

"For *Fear-giùlain a' Bhàis* to be turned aside, that being must possess the very power of the foundations. Yet, turned aside he was. We now believe that the escape that we must attempt from this beautiful brick prison lies on the path that even *Fear-giùlain a' Bhàis* feared to take. We believe that because of the question asked of him. Because we now know that we have the answer to the question.

"We have plans that we must make, but we must have the ability to move freely. Once we have decided how to best use our resources, we must escape to elsewhere, and quickly."

"Ancient one? What was the question? How can even the 'Bringer of Death' fear this?"

Ethan the Wise surveyed the room, meeting the eyes of each but stopped finally looking directly at Annie. Allegra reached and grasped Annie's hand as she also met the gaze of the druid and they rose again to their feet. Both knowing that the question was theirs to answer as soon as his gaze fell upon them.

"The being spoke this phrase, 'Go no further *Fear-giùlain a' Bhàis*' the way is shut before you. Go no further lest those you serve and those they love be struck from the earth and forgotten to all of the ages to come. The way is shut lest you answer my question. Answer and pass, or only death will remain behind you."

The eyes of the ancient druid never left the two women.

"They are coming. But the way is shut. The undead and the unclean rise from beneath us. Those that poisoned this earth. They are coming once again. Their numbers cannot be counted; they rise from the depths and seek to destroy the warriors of justice. Bring forth the lightning and the fire or begone and vanish beyond existence. Do you serve the lightning or bring forth the blue and the black?"

The druid furrowed his brows and finished, "For only they may pass."

All eyes were riveted upon the two robed women. Allegra straightened to full stature, and Annie gulped a deep breath but straightened as well.

"I am the Lightening!" Allegra flamed like a beacon in the night.

"And I…", Annie drew a trembling breath, "And I am the Blue…" another deep breath, "… and I am the Black… because **I am the Fire**." Her staff burst into dark flame and the sapphire of her deep blue robes rippled in glowing fabric of flame and ash."

"Well then, it is decided. The words of the being are ones that we have heard before. They are those of the Druid Stone recently excavated not far from here. They are words of warning but also words that speak to how immediate our response needs to be. So my friends," he looked around the room at the serious faces, "let us combine our strategies."

Tone of the Stone

The strategy sessions had continued for three days. All those in attendance chafed at the delay, not the least of which was Annie who was astounded by the number of details and the forces that might be required to accomplish even the smallest of them. But everyone also understood that mistakes at the beginning could mean devastating loss at the far end. In the end, all had been satisfied and anxious to begin in a forward direction.

Now it was time to begin. Annie dressed in her comfortable jeans and trusty poncho stood with the others before an ornate bookcase in the library of Mills House. Next to her stood Allegra, dressed similarly both shouldering backpacks. The three elves fidgeted, anxious to be on their way, and the four dwarves, now dressed entirely in battle armor stood silently. Colm McQuinn and Ethan Greyhame both no longer youthful in appearance paused and turned to the last of the group.

"We will see you my friends on the other side of this, whether here or elsewhere." Spoke Ethan.

"We will keep them entertained for a while. I can promise you that my friend." Michael stepped forward and clasped hands with him. "We will rendezvous on the other side. Trust the witches."

"Indeed, we must. And we will."

Turning back he took a breath and touched the spine of one of books of the shelf. "Wisdom In Time of Trouble, I really should read it sometime. Oh wait! I wrote it." He smiled and winked at Annie, and pulled back on the spine. Immediately, there was an almost silent swish and the entire bookcase panel swung slowly open. Turning to the dark shadow in the far corner, he addressed it.

"Thomas? Shall we away?"

Almost faster than sight, a shadow flashed through their vision and into the cavern beyond the bookcase opening.

"Ladies? As long as you know that Thomas is ahead of you, you are safe. Listen only to Thomas. If he tells you to retreat, then retreat you must. Many brave hearts are here to accompany you on this journey, but who may withstand and who may fall we do not know. But should it come to the hard spot, the rock and the hard place, do not allow yourselves to be separated from him. There is more than one reason for him to be known as 'Bringer of Death'."

Annie gulped and nodded. She looked across the other heads to Michael. At the last moment he pushed himself across the room and wrapped his arms around her.

"Dad... all of this... you know. I think I can stand it any of it, except the thought that I might never see you again."

Michael pulled back and met her eyes. He nodded.

"I understand my precious little one. Trust *Fear-giùlain a' Bhàis* he will bring you to the other side and we will see each other again."

Annie's eyes got bigger as she gazed into his and saw the tear that broke free and ran down his cheek. Then she looked down and reflected. Finally, she nodded to herself and met his eyes again.

"I'll make you proud Dad."

"I'm already am proud Annie."

She turned and stepped through the opening. Immediately, the temperature dropped ten degrees. Ahead of her a passage of cut stone extended into the distance and disappeared beyond the meager lighting of the doorway. From somewhere behind her a small whir signaled the arrival of Patch as she blazed into blue light, her sword drawn she faced into the subterranean night ahead of her.

"Follow me my queen. I will light the way."

"I'm right behind you Annie," Allegra's confident voice spoke quietly behind her. "We do not fear the darkness."

A gruff voice from behind them rasped. "Do not touch the walls please. I must ask the stone to waken."

"What?"

"Do not touch the rock."

Gunther, leader of the dwarves, stepped past the two women and into the dark tunnel. In a quiet voice he spoke over his shoulder, "Brothers?"

The other three dwarves also squeezed past Annie and Allegra and faced into the dark passageway forming a semi-circle. Gunther took a deep breath and with a strong voice sounded a single deep sonorous note, impressive with its volume from deep in his throat that echoed down the hollow hallway. One by one the other three joined, all singing the same deep note, a deep vocal chant, a chord that vibrated even within the chests of all the adventurers.

At first, it was only the deep sonorous sound of their combined voices, but as the moments passed another vibration joined it, this one a high-pitched crystalline tone. Then another and then still another, layer upon layer, until the narrow chamber sang like played music and the stone around them began to sparkle and glow. As the dwarven voices and the vibrations rose together in a crescendo of sound, the glow became brighter and brighter until the passageway ahead of them was bright with phosphorescent sunshine. One by one the dwarven voices tapered off, but the singing of the stone continued, a symphony of crystalline beauty. Sound upon beautiful sound, and the rock pulsed with light.

"Wow!"

Allegra stepped forward next to Annie, "Wow indeed," was the only thing Allegra could add.

"You may now proceed and need not fear darkness. Beware the warning of the Bringer of Death, but know that we are ready to defend and protect." Gunther turned and bowed to the two witches, then he stepped aside and swept a hand down the tunnel. "The song of the rock will follow us as we proceed, but do not retreat lest you do so in darkness."

The group began with the women at the forefront. Patch always just ahead of them alert for danger. Behind them the silent elves and swarthy dwarves shadowed them. The two druids, last in the procession, lagged behind as they studied the stone, rock, and all of their surroundings. And as the walk lengthened from morning time into afternoon the singing stone followed.

After several hours they came to a fork in the hallway and there they met Thomas—waiting. The passage to the right glimmered with faint light but the passage to the left was dark as a tomb. Thomas, no longer wearing the dark sunglasses, his red eyes ablaze in the dim light, spoke; "The way to the right is the way to death, the way to the left is the way to the creature. You must choose."

"Why is the way to the right the way to death Thomas." Colm McQuinn spoke up from the back of the group.

"The way continues downward; the unclean await below in ambush. But they cannot pass the creature. She will not allow it."

"She? She will not allow them to pass?"

"That which awaits is woman, not man."

Gunther spoke perplexed, "The passageway to the left does not sing as the other stone does, we must proceed in darkness. I do not know why this is."

"How much further is it until we encounter the creature, Thomas?"

"It is only a short distance. No more than one of your hours. It sent me here to wait for you; it knows that you approach."

"It knows that we are approaching? Is it normal for that to scare me a little?" Annie asked no one in particular.

"At this point Annie, I would almost expect it. I'm not exactly comfortable either." Allegra's voice also wavered a little. "What an adventure we are on, wouldn't you say?"

"Going to Disney World is an adventure; this is pretty different."

"*It is waiting for us in the darkness.*" Patch peered into the darkness, listening. "*I feel the life that rests there. See the life in all things, see the magic, truly it is a magical being. Magic is only good, we need not fear it.*" She started down the darkened passageway her blue glow once again shining the way.

"But we should also exercise caution. Remember the warning." Ethan Greyhame spoke up and Patch halted immediately.

"Perhaps it is wise that the women should advance first," she admitted.

"Here ladies, let me help a little." Colm stepped up past the others. "Ethan watch this."

He produced a glowing blue orb and handed it to Allegra. It immediately brightened in her hands. Then handed another to Annie. The blue immediately vanished and instead flamed bright red in her hands.

"Remarkable!"

"I'll tell you what. The first time I saw her do that I didn't understand, but now I know why. She goes her own way that's for sure, even when she isn't trying to. All that power is bubbling there but just beneath the surface."

"Guys. You do know that I'm right here and can hear you, right?" Annie eyes never left the dark passage as she spoke over her shoulder.

"Every time?" Ethan asked. "She can do that every time?"

"So far yes. I first saw it on the Paths of the Dead when she fought and defeated Lilith."

"Say not the name of the Dealer of Death!" Gunther exclaimed.

All four dwarves took a few steps backward.

"She is defeated?"

"Yes, defeated by Annie on the Paths of the Dead."

"Did I not hear this from you and see her before me, I would not believe. Can this be true?"

"She is defeated even beyond the reach of Thomas. Her amulet has been shattered and her power destroyed by a thirteen-year-old witch, the Keeper of the Long Promise."

"Aged beyond thirteen of your years it would seem."

"And she has already given the world one of the most priceless gifts we could have hoped for. Yet, unless we gain victory in this endeavor, it will mean nothing. Annie? Shall we go or turn back? The choice is yours to make."

"If I understand all of this—there isn't any going back." Annie raised the blazing red light in her hands and took a step. "But I'm not as confident as you guys seem to be."

She stepped into the darkened tunnel with Allegra next her and Patch just above her left shoulder. Thomas followed closely behind them. One of the elves and one of the dwarves moved to the rear of the group, weapons drawn, walking backward and facing any possible danger that might pursue from behind.

"What do you think the creature wants with us?"

"I can't even guess Annie." Allegra's voice was in a low whisper, "but from her words it seems to know of us. We must be careful. Guard your words."

"What if it's just all talk and she has no real power?"

"We are about to find out."

The floor beneath them remained smooth and straight before them. They walked silently, with the two small globes barely lighting their way for what seemed like a long time to Annie.

"How long has it been?" Annie asked

There was no response.

"Colm? How long have we been walking?"

Only the quiet of nothingness responded.

"Colm? Ethan?"

Both women turned around and raised the lights in

their hands. Thomas stood directly behind them, his body tensed in a crouch, his hands spread from wall to wall. There was no one else behind them. The elves, dwarves, druids and even the fairy had vanished.

"What!? Where did they go?"

A hauntingly deep feminine voice echoed as if spoken from deep within the stone itself answered.

"Nowhere."

Nowhere

Both women turned, incredulous. Immediately, the globes they held in their hands flickered and went out.

Allegra was first to recover, "Where did they go? Where are they?"

"Questions are mine to ask, not yours."

"Yes, my apologies."

"I know who you are, I know what you can become. Both of you. Always—I know."

There was nothing to see either ahead or behind them. Only the three of them stood alone in the stone hallway. The voice continued; "Those that would follow are here but not here. They await."

"Await what?" Annie blurted.

"Old but still young are you not? Patience must be learned or failure will follow." The voice was almost soothing as it continued. "They await the test that you must perform successfully. They await their ultimate fate, and yours."

Silence followed. It continued for a seemingly long time to Annie, but this time she did not question it but held her tongue.

"No questions. That is good, you have passed the

first hurdle. Now you may ask me one and only one. Then I will ask you the final question."

Allegra squeezed Annie's hand in the darkness, "Go ahead Annie."

"Who are you?"

The answer began with a light-hearted laugh, "A simple question; a harder answer."

There was a pause, then, "I am the doorway and I am the gatekeeper. As ancient as the pillars of the earth, as young as the seedlings of newest plants. I am both judge and jury, guardian of the secret way. Killer and lover of men, scourge of evil. Neither friend nor foe, but ally when need there is."

Light flared all around them. After the darkness of the tunnel, the light was blinding. So strong was it that Thomas was stricken to his knees, his hands covering his eyes. They found themselves standing in the doorway of a huge stone chamber. The room vast in its expanse, the ceiling vaulted high above their heads. In the center of it crouched a monstrous apparition, huge green eyes focused directly upon them. It had the face and upper body of a beautiful woman, but crouched on the four clawed feet of a lion.

"**I am Sphynx**!" Two huge wings spread from her sides, reaching almost to the cavern's walls.

"Prepare yourselves to answer me or death will befall all those behind you, and despair will follow you to your final breath."

Allegra reached and took Annie's other hand as they faced the gigantic monster.

"Lightning and Fire stand before me, yet power and reason are not the same. A riddle I propose to answer will open the way should it be correct. If it is not, no power you possess will stop the wheel that is now turning.

"Old as the universe, both chance and choice. To fight or to flee, to strive or retreat. Both true and false, both yes and no. When a question is complex and escapes reason, the answer is contained in the numbers of the two. A first chance or a last, give me the number that is key to all questions and the way will be opened."

"What? That makes no sense, both yes and no? Both true and false? It makes no sense." Annie looked toward Allegra, "It makes no sense."

"It's not supposed to make sense— unless we know the answer."

"What could be both yes and no? And if it could, how can that be a number?"

"Like I said Annie, it only will make sense once we figure out the answer. Remember it's a riddle, not a question. The nonsense of a riddle hides a deep truth usually. It's a brain teaser. The really good ones are the hardest to figure out. This is probably a good one."

"Great!"

"Right, so what are the numbers that we know of that mean anything? Let's start there."

"Um, there's perfect squares, like forty-nine and a dozen dozen, a hundred and forty-four."

"Yes. Seven is an important number, the number of completion. And forty-nine is seven times seven, the perfect circle is significant for change and inner strength in numerology."

"How about thirteen, the full coven of witches. The number of Jesus and the apostles."

"An important number to be sure, but probably not the answer to all questions."

Annie turned to the Sphynx whose gaze had never wavered, "How long do we have to answer your riddle?

Is there a time limit?"

"Until the last light in the universe blinks out."

"So can we go somewhere and think about it? You know and when we get it solved come back?"

"Here you will rest until the answer is given, as did the others."

"Others?"

"These others," she raised a great paw and pointed. Resting against the walls, unnoticed before now, lay clusters, countless numbers of the desiccated bodies of lost souls, some obviously once human, some elven, and some dwarves. All had rested there long ago, unable to answer the question and open the door beyond. "These who failed, guided by intellect untrusting of their hearts."

Allegra clutched Annie's arm, "Did you hear that? She gave us a clue."

"She's not supposed to do that is she?" Both women were speaking frantically. Annie wringing her hands with anxiety.

"How would I know, but a clue, any clue is big. Let's reconsider."

"So we should trust our heart, not our head?"

"Okay, but we still need a number. So let's put two and two together."

"What? Could that be it?"

"No I don't think so, doesn't feel right. Besides two and two can't be yes and no."

"True. Are there numbers for love or something. You know? Love's not supposed to make sense but everyone still does it. Didn't the Beatles or the Rolling Stones say that love is the answer?"

"Okay, thirteen is supposed to help with love, but so is forty-nine and a couple of others."

"There's not much chance that we're just gonna stumble on it is there?"

"Not unless I can tap into some other intelligence than my own Annie."

Annie was about to respond when she was caught up short.

"Well, that's something I forgot. Hold on a moment."

Annie closed her eyes and tried to relax her thoughts.

"Mathair? A bheil thu ann mathair?"

(Mother? Are you there mother?)

"Yes Anne, I am here. Always."

"Then you know my trial and the riddle of the Sphynx that I'm facing. Can you help me?"

"No child, the answer is for you to decide, and only you. I do not know it, because it is your answer and not mine own. You must trust your heart and take the chance."

"But there is only one answer Mother."

"Yes, and chance and fate collide at the moment of trust. Trust your heart, take your chance, the ultimate gamble that will answer your question and all others. Take the chance my love".

Annie opened her eyes and found Allegra staring back at her.

"Well, that is a wonder to be sure. How long have you been able to speak to your mother whenever you want to?"

"I just found out not too long ago. She's really great!"

"I know, remember, I knew Roison once. Was she helpful?"

"No. She just kept saying 'take the chance'."

"Take the chance? That's it? Anything else?"

"Nothing, take the chance, the ultimate gamble that will answer your question and all others."

"The ultimate gamble… the ultimate gamble… take the chance. Hmm…"

"The ultimate gamble? What… like heads and tails… the coin flip at the beginning of a football game. Head and tails, win and lose, yes and no. That could be it, right?"

"So what number is that, two?"

"Yes, two I think. What do you think?"

"I think it's the best answer so far."

"Should we try it?"

"If we are wrong, she will kill us."

Allegra took Annie's hand and nodded. Together they turned to face the inscrutable Sphynx. Giving the hand a squeeze she whispered, "A last roll of the dice Annie, perhaps, but yes let's try it. Let's take the chance."

"What!" Annie's breath wheezed out in a harsh whisper and she pulled her hand back and paced in a circle. Then bent over with both hands on her temples. "Wait. Just a minute. It's not two, it's… it's…"

Bending at the waist she took several deep breaths and then straightened up. Squaring her shoulders she stood tall.

"Forty-two. The number is forty-two."

The Sphynx slowly rose to her feet and circled the room, stalking ever closer, her eyes fixed upon her captives, seeming to grow ever larger the closer she got until she towered above them. Bending down she looked into Annie's eyes.

"Welcome little Seeker, the way is opened and you may pass and allies you now have at your back."

And the Dead will Answer

The great body of the lion then lay down in front of them, her paws crossed in front of her and she smiled.

"Your companions will arrive shortly. They took a small detour. A labyrinth actually, frustrating for certain, but necessary at the time." She shrugged, "I imagine the two druids rather enjoyed it actually."

"So... that's it?" Allegra was still slightly in shock. "Forty-two? The answer to every question? In the universe?"

Annie was still slightly shaken as well but first looked to Sphynx, who gestured her paw toward Allegra and nodded.

"Forty-two. Yes, and I wouldn't have gotten it if you hadn't said what you said. About the roll of the dice, one last time. It was the roll of the dice,"she looked to Sphynx for assurance. "Every chance, every decision we make with the best information that we have but every decision is a chance. 'Take the chance' is what my mom said. The ultimate gamble, take the chance—roll the dice. Mom knew the answer, she just couldn't tell me. I had to figure it out on my own. I had to trust my heart."

"Sooo...? I'm still in the dark, why forty-two?"

"Forty-two is the sum of all of the spots on a pair of dice. Every roll is chance, a 'crapshoot' is what my dad would call it. We hope it will turn out, but every choice is a chance."

"That is simply the most brilliant deduction I think I have ever heard of. I am blown away Annie, truly brilliant! Wow! Just wow!"

Allegra stepped forward and was about to embrace her but the sound of approaching voices and running feet interrupted them. From the passageway the three elves burst into the room, running at full speed, weapons drawn accompanied by the fairy. But they slid to a halt as they looked at the scene before them. They were soon followed by the lumbering dwarves, their hammers and axes held high until they too stopped short.

At the last the two druids walked into the chamber, their heads on a swivel looking at everything, taking it all in. As they looked forward, they too stopped.

"As I live and breathe, can this be true? After all these thousands of years?" Colm McQuinn stopped in his tracks and leaned forward, "Yes, it is! The meanest woman in this world or the next still lives. It **is** you!"

"Very funny *'wizard'*." The Sphynx sneered, "Yes, my old adversary. I still guard the way, vigilant when many were not. You have not aged well it would seem," the sarcasm in her voice was not subtle.

"Annie solved the riddle! She did in only minutes, she solved the riddle! The way ahead is cleared and safe for us because of her. Truly amazing!"

Colm McQuinn stepped forward, "Is that true Annie?"

"She answered and is granted passage. Unlike you Merlin."

"That is true," he smiled at Annie and shrugged.

"But the riddle you posed had no answer. It could not be answered because no solution met all the requirements of the question."

"Not true of course wizard, but you turned back, didn't you?"

"Yes. I could not answer so I found a different way."

"But not a better way?"

"No, not a better way." He sighed and stroked the scar on the back of his hand, "Definitely not a better way," he added almost to himself.

Then he brightened and smiled, "I gotta say though, you've made some major improvements to the labyrinth. It's really quite difficult. Ethan had never experienced it before."

"You do seem to travel with some of the most interesting characters Merlin. Greetings Grey One, your feet have walked many paths to here. I see the two before me, what of the rest?"

"Of the seven, five have been forgotten, their whereabouts are unknown to me."

"They have left behind answers to help with the ultimate quest. Those five stood against the evil and paid the ultimate price". She turned her head toward Annie, "but their legacy is written upon the stone."

"Stone?" Annie had been watching the exchange with awe. That the two speakers knew each other and knew each other well was obvious. "Are there five other druids?"

"Yes Annie, for a very long time the order was led by seven, but over the ages five of those have faded into memory. Where to or when that happened no one seems to know." Ethan Greyhame patiently explained.

"Seek the stones and feel their life. She just said their legacy is written upon the stone. Are those the stones that I've been finding?"

"What is this then?" Sphynx regarded the two druids.

Colm stepped up and crossed his arms, making direct eye contact with her, "Annie has discovered four stones that previously I had no knowledge of, all bearing the mark of the order. Each one proved to be true and each one led us on the path that we're on right now. You yourself, when you spoke with Fear-giùlain a' Bhàis quoted from the most recently found one."

"Ah… the Stone of the Mounds. Yes, she was a truly brave woman. She I knew. The unclean pursued her and her people. Smart but unwise, she wished to pass and would not suffer the riddle that I offered. They chose death over servitude."

"She brought them here?"

"Yes, a multitude."

"And they all chose to die?" Annie was incredulous

"Yes."

"That is horrific!"

"Yes. They rest, awaiting the command."

"The command?" Allegra too was confused.

"The command of the One, to rise and vanquish. The battle force of the druids—the Army of the Dead."

"What? You mean me? Me?"

"If you are the One little seeker, then they wait for you. You have only to ask to find out."

"Ask?"

"Ask. Stand before the Sentinel and ask."

"In the forest of the ancients? That sentinel?"

"Beyond the door that is now open, sound the tones and ask them to awaken." She leaned down close to Annie and held her gaze, "And the dead will answer."

The Tone of the Sentinel

"Your journey has been long to this point in time, Seeker but the crossroads approach. I wish you good fortune. It is time for your own 'roll of the dice'."

"My own 'roll of the dice'?"

"Yes, your fate has brought to this point, and now who knows what shall befall. But the choice will be yours to make. Yes or no, true or false. The roll of the dice."

"My mother said that chance and fate collide at the moment of trust."

"Wise words and true."

"So what now?"

"Now? Now we go to meet the Sentinel." Colm turned to Thomas. "Friend, the way is clear for us, but will you still accompany us?"

"I will bring the One to the other side. From this time on, I stand at her side."

"Good, that is good." Turning to the inscrutable Sphynx he addressed her, "Thank you. Thank you for all your services and guardianship. And thank you for the lesson that you taught me so long ago."

"The time passes wizard. The day has passed above us, and the way is still long. Rest here as I watch, and begin the next step fresher in body and mind."

"Thank you, once again. That sounds like a good idea. But we should at least attempt to reach the Sentinel before we stop."

"As you wish, but once you leave my chambers, the way will be closed behind you and you may not return by this road."

With a nod to the great woman, the group set out through the opening at the opposite end of the great vaulted room. As they went, once again the stones sang and the way was lit ahead as they proceeded. This time the elves proceeded ahead of the adventurers. Thomas was forced to stoop to avoid the ceiling and followed closely behind, his sunglasses back in place. Two dwarves marched behind him and ahead of Annie and Allegra.

The two druids now walked with purpose, no longer sightseeing, speaking in whispers. At the rear the remaining dwarves followed, their eyes on the passage behind them. All of them aware that the way was no longer guarded by the Sphynx and there could be enemies at each turn. The passageway curved ahead first to the left and then to the right, never straight. Their visibility limited to only a short distance and they could not know what was ahead or behind them for any distance. The elves were forced to range farther and farther ahead in order to ensure safety.

"How far do you think it will be before we reach the Sentinel?" asked Annie.

"There are many ways to approach the Sentinel. She is known to us and we have often consulted her on the events of the world above us. The Sentinel watches." Gunther spoke over his shoulder.

"Then this is not the only way to her?"

"Until now, we were not aware of this way. No, many

roads converge at the Forest of the Ancients. It is a gathering place, a solemn place where great matters and many treaties have been decided. I do not know the distance to it on this road; I have never delved here before. Perhaps we should ask the stone."

"Ask the stone?"

Instead of answering, the dwarf stopped and unshouldered his huge backpack. Opening it, he recovered a small silver hammer. Then he regarded the walls of the tunnel, searching.

"Ah, here's the one." He struck the stone he had selected with the tiniest of taps. The stone rang like a bell. The vibrating tone did not fade but instead it was joined by another and then still another.

"The tones. The dwarves speak of reading the tones. I have never seen it done before." Ethan's awed voice was a whisper.

All four of the dwarves each stretched one hand out and touched the walls. Closing their eyes they did not move for several minutes as the stone continued to ring.

"There is strife ahead. The unclean have breached the doorways. My brothers battle." Hecklif was first to speak.

"The Sentinel is attacked, the defenders are gathered at her feet." Gunther continued. "The elven warriors have joined the fight. We are close; we must go quickly else they are defeated. Come my brothers."

"Wait! Should we stay here? What should we do?" It was Ethan that spoke.

"Do as you must. If the Sentinel falls they will be here soon enough."

"We have to protect Annie and Allegra. You can't leave us here without your protection."

"Whether it is here or there, the fight is upon us."

With that he turned and ran down the hallway.

"He's right," Allegra whispered. "Here or there. We have to follow him."

"I know, but talking about it and actually doing it… my scalp is actually sweating." Annie's voice trembled

"I say go back." Ethan spoke again, "I'm no fighter."

"No, Allegra's right. If we run, they'll catch up to us. We've got to try and make sure that our friends win. That means we have to go forward." Colm said. "I think."

"We don't have to hurry though. Do we?"

"'Fraid so."

They hadn't run far before the sound of a fight echoed down the hallway. With each turn, the sounds became louder until they burst into a huge chamber. Vast beyond imagination, no walls beyond the one behind them could be seen in any direction. Instead, everywhere huge stalactites reached from the high ceiling and joined equally large stalagmites forming a forest of stone. The formations so thick that visibility in any direction was limited. But within the standing forest, they could see glimpses of figures weaving in and out and above all the shouts of battle and the clash of steel on steel.

The group moved forward, stealthily dodging from one thick 'tree of stone' to the next. Unnoticed, they arrived near the center of the great hall that opened into a vaulted amphitheater. There standing at the center, magnificent in its beauty and size, was the largest of the great trees. Fully ten feet thick and rising so high it disappeared into the darkness above, the great sentinel of stone had stood for all the ages of the earth.

The reason they had been undetected became readily apparent. At the foot of the Sentinel, the defenders of right stood, their backs to her facing outward. Their weapons held ready, they growled and shouted their resolve. Among them stood the three elves. Gunther and his three companions were among a dozen or so other dwarves. Completely outnumbered by the hundreds, they were resolved not to admit defeat. But defeated they were, and they knew it.

Surrounding them on all sides a great hoard of hideous creatures advanced. They jeered and shouted insults. Knowing that they would soon have the satisfaction of the kill they were in no hurry. They knew they had won and were enjoying a last celebration.

"I can't watch." Annie whispered, "they're about to be killed, aren't they?"

"Yes Annie. They're so many; we are powerless to help. Even with the powers we might use, we're just too few."

"But they'll die."

"But we can't help Annie," Colm spoke from over her shoulder, "We have to keep in mind the goal. We must protect you and get to the Red Queen. This is an important fight, but not the last. There are going to be casualties along the way, but we have to keep you safe. Let's see if we can find a way around them. Maybe they'll find a way to get away too."

"There are so many of them."

"Yes, way too many. What's worse is that this is probably just a small portion."

"How can there be so many? How can I, how can we, hope to win against so many enemies?"

"The last roll of the dice Annie." Allegra met her eyes.

Annie's eyes flew wide, then she considered her words. Looking up and meeting Allegra's eyes she slowly nodded. She stood and stepped out from behind the pillar.

"Annie! Get back here; we have to make a run for it!" Colm's harsh whisper was urgent.

"I sure hope she wasn't kidding," she whispered to herself. Taking a deep breath she shouted,

"Hey!"

At first a few faces turned toward the shout, then more. Those that saw who had shouted screamed for the attention of the other attackers. They could not believe the good luck; their prize had walked into the room seemingly defenseless. Half of them surged toward the little group hiding among the stalactites, shouting their hatred.

"Allegra? Could you stand with me? I'm a little scared."

"Well, I'm a lot scared." Nonetheless she stood and took Annie's hand, "What now?"

"Now, we ask the dead to join us. I don't have anything else."

"Okay, need any help?"

"I don't know. Whoever gets a practice run at this stuff?"

"Probably the wizard," Allegra quipped. "Here they come. You ready?"

"Oh sure, can't you tell?"

Annie stood up straight and in as clear a voice as she could muster she spoke, **"Sister! It is time, and the fight is upon us. Wake up!"** Then she added, "Please."

Nothing happened. The first arrows of the attackers began to strike both the floor and the great stalactites and stalagmites around them.

"Annie?"

"Hold on I'm trying. **Sentinel, I am here. It is time**

that the allies rise and defend. I'm asking them to arise."

Again, nothing happened. The wave of attackers stalking forward would soon be upon them.

In the very few moments left to her, Annie tried to calm herself. She had been frightened up until now, but now, she was terrified. She closed her eyes, but nothing came to her. There was no calming voice of her mother, no wisdom from the past. Opening her eyes she looked over the heads of the hoard at the great Sentinel and felt it waiting. Waiting for her, for her final act. At the moment of its own final demise, the Sentinel was waiting for her, Annie, to act.

"Ask him who he is." The voice of Colm McQuinn sounded in her memory. Ask him who he is. The wizard had advised her to ask the ancient willow tree for wisdom.

"I am the one; I am the many," had been his answer.

In that split second she found her answer. Taking a deep breath while another volley struck around them, Annie stretched her hands out and placed them upon the closest of the great pillars, "Sentinel! Sound the tone!. Awaken the dead! I am Keeper of the Long Promise. Sound—the—tone!"

BONNNGGGG

A great deep bell tone rang out, tolling as if from a high tower. So loud that the floor vibrated and shook beneath them. Another and another, the toll of the bell rang out;

BONNGGG—BONNGGG— BONNGGG—BONNGGG—

So loud that the great pillars began to vibrate and ring as well. The sound swelled until it was a deafening cacophony of sound, echoing and reverberating throughout the chamber and the tunnels beyond. The floor continued to shake as the attackers were stopped in their tracks. Looking around in shock, losing their balance as the floor moved and shifted beneath their feet. Covering their ears and squeezing their eyes shut, some fell to their knees.

As the great sounding of the tone continued, those defenders until now pinned against the feet of the Sentinel, surged outward, fighting furiously, destroying the evil creatures who were helpless to defend themselves against such ferocity, they advanced. Together they fought their way back to their queen.

The great tone stopped abruptly. In the echoing silence Annie's ears continued to ring, another vibration replaced the great deafening tone. At first it was hard to distinguish between whether it was sound or vibration. Felt more than heard—it was the sound of feet. Countless numbers of feet—building in volume—coming closer.

Pouring into the great chamber from every direction —

the army of the dead arrived.

With only the sound of their thousands of feet on stone, the Army of the Dead poured forward at a swift run, weapons held high. Uttering no sound, their faces grim, they fell upon the creatures of Cian, merciless, a storm of malevolence, cutting a swath through them like wind through a wheat field. Those that were the attackers only moments before were paralyzed with surprise and fear and where the dead went, only death was left behind. Annie and the others watched in awe. The violence, hard to imagine, much harder to watch. Even creatures that tried to escape were pursued and vanquished. The Dead, at last exacting their revenge upon those that had cursed them so long ago.

The fighters, elves and dwarves, arrived to where Annie and Allegra stood still holding each other's hands. The two had stood facing the host completely defenseless. The warriors formed a circle around the four and Thomas joined them, facing out, ready to defend once again. Two of the original dwarf defenders, Hecklif and Torbert, both still stood with the others, arrows protruding from where they had been unlucky during the fight at the Sentinel, but prepared to fight on.

The sounds of violence at last faded as the fight slowly ran its course, and the sound of destruction and carnage faded until the great chamber was once again silent and watchful. The defenders remained tense, ready, unsure of the vast army that now turned to face them, and approached.

From the center of their ranks, a figure emerged and approached. A woman, and as she drew nearer, she raised her hand in greeting and a gesture of peace. Her visage wavering in the light of the chamber; her substance thin, almost transparent. She smiled and spoke in a voice that sounded as if from a distance.

"Greetings. Thank you." She touched her fingers to her forehead and gave a slight bow. "We thank you, for the call to awaken. We have waited long in sleep, waiting for the One at last. I am grateful for this opportunity." She turned to face Allegra, "Greetings my Queen. At last the One is again among us."

"I am Allegra, Keeper of the Light, and soon to be Circe' sorceress and healer. The Seeker and Keeper of the Long Promise is this one. Not I."

The spirit's eyes opened large, then she turned to

Annie.

"I did not expect one so young. The lore did not speak of a child, so young, truly you must be one of great power. Forgive me; I meant no disrespect." She touched her forehead in a formal greeting gesture.

"Greetings. We stand ready to march with the One, we who can never again be killed." As one the lethal host of the dead dropped to one knee in a soundless gesture of respect.

Somewhat taken aback, Annie took a step backward; "My name is Annie. And who are you please?"

"I was Itzel. Once one of the seven. I am the forgotten sister."

"The forgotten sister! You left the stone for me. The one at the Mound of the Ancients."

"Yes. The mound of my people. My last act before we fled to the Sentinel. It was helpful?"

"We would not have found you and this place without it. It was very helpful."

Colm McQuinn stepped forward. "Itzel it's me, Merlin of old, Emrys before that. I was wondering what became of you after you had left for the New World. Also with us is Ethan Greyhame, Haldor Blackmane of old."

"Greetings wise one. I see only you. Where is the Greyhame?"

"He's right here," Colm turned to gesture but was stunned to see Ethan lying on the floor, the shaft of a single arrow sprouting from his chest.

"Not for long," Ethan Greyhame whispered to the ceiling. Then he turned and smiled, "not for long my old friend."

"Oh!" Colm dropped to his knees. Quickly he examined the arrow wound, then looking up he met

Ethan's eyes who nodded.

"Yes. I know Emrys." He raised an arm and shielded his eyes, "Ah me. Of all the epic battles that I've witnessed over the ages… I think I would have liked to see this one to the finish."

Looking up at Annie and Allegra he smiled at them and whispered, "Wow! Just wow.

And then—Ethan Greyhame was no more.

The End of Magic

"No!" Annie dropped to her knees next to Colm. "No! Do something! Bring him back!"

"I can't Annie. Believe me. I would do it if I could." Colm knelt over his old friend, tears coursing down his cheeks. "I would even trade places with him if I could Annie. I truly loved this man."

"C'mon Colm, you can do it!"

"No Annie, I can't. He accepted his fate. He didn't ask me—or you, to intervene. He could have, but he accepted his fate and stepped through the veil on his own. I can't retrieve him, nor can anyone else Annie."

"What about Thomas?" Annie leaned forward as her tears fell on the floor between her knees. She continued, the desperation obvious in her voice, "He can take him —you know, take him beyond. Right?"

Annie twisted on her knees and looked up to Thomas. "Thomas? Can you take him beyond. Please? Like you did with me once."

"It is not for me to do this. His time has passed; I cannot."

What? What do you mean, 'his time has passed'? I know, he's dead, but you can save him. Take him." She sobbed, "take him to the other side. Please?"

"I cannot."

"He's right Annie. His time has passed." Without leaving his knees Colm turned and placed a hand on hers. "His time; my time. Our time has passed. There won't be any next time. This age has passed, and the next one has not shaped itself." Colm took a deep breath and placed his other hand on the chest of his old friend. "Whatever we accomplish in the next days or weeks will decide if we, you, all of this, this magic that is the fabric of life will decide whether we will continue or disappear —forever more."

"Wait. So he's not coming back? Like he did in the past?"

"No Annie, he is not. From the time we started down this path, it has been the last time. For all of us."

Annie looked down at the still form of Ethan the Wise. His face still held the sardonic smile of the last words he had uttered. She took a shuddering breath and rose to her feet.

"Then we better make sure that we don't lose."

"We'll do our best Annie," Allegra stepped up and hugged her, then holding her shoulders at arm's length she made eye contact and said very slowly, "*we* will do our best."

Forgotten until now, the shadow that was Itzel appeared at the side of Colm McQuinn.

"The Greyhame's mortal form has ceased to be. We will take him among us and keep his wisdom in hope of the next age."

"Can you do that Itzel? Would you do that for us?"

"It is no burden. The Greyhame will instruct and rest for the next age. His fate and ours are one and the same. We gladly accept this great gift."

Itzel rested her almost transparent hands on the form of Ethan the Wise. She placed one on his heart and the other on his forehead and intoned, "My brother. My brother your form no longer lives but the wisdom that was once you lives yet. My brother, come join us so that we might yet dance the dance that is the joy of life yet again. Join us my brother."

Colm McQuinn placed one hand over Itzel's on his forehead. Annie reached out and placed one of hers on Itzel's hand over his heart. Instantly she felt energy flowing to and from the silent form.

"Please old friend? Join them." Colm spoke fervently.

Annie looked from one to the next. Then closing her eyes, spoke in a voice that was hers, but not hers, "Old One, we will need you soon. We will need your advice and wisdom when we usher in the next age of men and magic. This I believe. Join my Army of the Dead for now, until we come for you and the way is again safe."

As in the beginning, whenever she spoke from within the voices of her past she was staggered by the strength of her words and Allegra, with her hands on her shoulders, was quick to support her.

From under her hand she felt a painful twinge. The twinge became a surge of energy that burned its way up her arm only to burst in a bright flash in her mind.

To her amazement, there in front of her stood the robed and hooded form of a young man, his dark beard wild and long hair in disarray. He looked down at her and smiled. It was the smile of Ethan Greyhame, now Haldor Blackmane once again, and the smile extended into his eyes. The eyes of Ethan the Wise. With a nod of his head to Annie, he silently mouthed, 'Wow, just wow'. Then turning to Itzel, together they stepped away and vanished among the hoard that waited.

The Funeral of the Druid

Annie and Colm stood and watched in amazement as the multitude of dead warriors gathered together around them, each hoping to touch the robed figure of Haldor Blackmane. Soon Itzel alone appeared and approached. She did not approach Annie or the others, instead she stepped directly to Thomas and looked up at him, "Wañuy apamuq", (Death Bringer).

Thomas bowed at the waist and looked down at the small woman. Then speaking in the same language as her, he answered, "Ari', pitaq chinkasqa? (Yes, one who was once lost?)

"Wañuy apamuq, centinelaman pusamuy" (Bring him to the Sentinel.)

Thomas bowed and turning stepped through the small group. Once he arrived at the form of Ethan Greyhame, he stooped and lifted him into his arms. The body of the druid almost childlike in the arms of the huge Thomas. Turning, he nodded once more to the woman and swiftly moved toward the great pillar of stone with his long strides. The others followed more slowly, aware of the reverence in the situation they were about to witness and already grieving the loss of their friend.

Thomas stood in front of the great silvery pillar and spread his legs. Extending his arms he held the form of Ethan Greyhame out, presenting it to the Sentinel as the followers watched in awe. Slowly at first, Thomas seemed to brighten. As they watched the brightening turned into small sparks of light that began to dance over his great dark form. As the dancing lights increased in frequency and intensity, Thomas stepped closer to the great stone and raised his arms even higher. As he did so the form in his arms began to sparkle as well.

Soon millions of diamond lights danced and vibrated within the form in his arms that quickly turned into a glowing mass of star shine that pulsed with lights of every color and energy, losing its shape and form. The swirling in his hands became almost too bright to look directly into as it spun in a faster and faster whirlwind of light and color. With a blur of motion, it burst from Thomas' arms and directly into the great Sentinel herself. The lights of the chamber flared brighter and the room vibrated with the sound of the deep toll of a bell.

As one, the elves and dwarves dropped to one knee, their heads bowed.

"Is that what happens to druids? Like when you die? Is that normal?" Annie voice was hushed with wonder.

"Nothing about that was normal." Colm McQuinn was awestricken. He dropped his backpack and sat on it.

"I have never seen the ceremony of Fear-giùlain a' Bhàis. We actually may be the only ones that have ever seen it. I didn't even think it was a real thing. At least I didn't think it was a real thing." Colm rubbed his eyes, "It was said that long ago, there was a being that presented the worthy to a power beyond the limits of our worlds, perhaps even beyond our earth, so that they could become among the powers of the suns and the moons. Legends spoke of him presenting the great ones to those who predated even this planet to be judged worthy."

Thomas turned away from the glowing Sentinel and in his impossibly deep voice spoke, "She asks for the One."

"She?"

"She. She asks for the One."

Colm placed a hand on Annie's shoulder. Allegra reached out and took Annie's hand.

"It's okay Annie, we've already won. She is our ally, and she helped. It's going to be okay. Go ahead; I'm right with you."

Colm placed a hand on her shoulder, "Annie, the Sentinel may be the oldest thing yet on earth. She should not be trifled with but I would give anything to be asked to speak with her. Go ahead."

Annie looked into his eyes and he nodded. Letting go of Allegra's hand she stepped forward and held Thomas' gaze. He did not move from his place, but reaching up he removed his dark glasses and looked down at her as she passed.

"You are Keeper of the Long Promise. I stand with you." As Annie walked past, he turned and followed her. Finally placing an immense hand on her shoulder when they reached the foot of the Sentinel.

The sheer immensity of the crystalline pillar was daunting to be sure. It's surface grained and variegated, with great cervices and burls that glimmered and shimmered, giving it the appearance of a great tree cast in the finest marble. Annie arrived at the base of the Sentinel and looked back at her friends one last time, then reached out and placed her hand on its surface. Immediately, a velvety female voice sounded in her head,

"Greetings Anne L'Abbee."

"That's not my name. That was the name of a relative, a woman, from long ago. How do you know that name?"

"Not so long ago to me, young one. Anna L'Abbee was the last seeker, strong and powerful, the image of one who stands before me now once again."

"I'm Anne Abbott, not L'Abbee these days. But my name is such a small thing. There are so many big things going on all around me. Why do you bother knowing something as small as that?"

"I know many things, both large and small."

"But, my name? That seems a very small thing."

"Small things make up the most important things. Events turn on knowing the small things. A house of understanding is built one small brick at a time."

"Are you going to take me, like 'absorb' me? Like you did with Ethan Greyhame?"

"The form of the wise teacher was no more. I will hold and keep it safe for now, in hopes that he may again need it."

"So? You asked for me for a different reason then."

"You have sounded the tone and wakened the army of those that are dead. Only Morganna of old had that power to do so, yet you have done so. The roots of the standing forest speak of the One, Morganna of old, young in years and anxious to learn. They bid me make you welcome and offer what wisdom I might impart."

"The roots of the trees? The trees above? Do the roots speak of the Willow, my friend, the old One? Or do they know anything about the Red and White?"

"The old one has suffered greatly at the hands of the unclean. He was witness to the taking of the Red and White, betrayed from within their own circle."

"What? You mean that the traitor was or is one of the circle of thirteen? Another witch?"

"Witch? Yes, that is your word for those of power and knowledge. Yes, the traitor was among the thirteen. She flees."

"She better!"

"The Three are in pursuit, there is much conflict above."

"The Three are after the traitor? They know who she is?"

"Yes." Then after a pause, "As do you."

Annie pulled back her hand in surprise. She looked back at the others and their wide eyed stares. Taking a deep breath she turned back and this time, she placed both hands flat on the surface of the Sentinel, "What!? I don't know who it is. How could I know something like that?"

"Consult your feelings. See them in your memory. See them when you stood before the council." The Sentinel paused. Thomas increased his grip on her shoulder, "Feel. Feel who feared you most Seeker."

"Magda!" The name burst in her brain immediately. "Magda! She wanted me gone, she wanted me killed, but I thought she had changed after the battle of winter solstice."

"She has long worshiped the power of the underworld. She coveted the might of fear and pain over others. Now she flees. Once their goals had been met those whom she befriended have abandoned her to the mercy of The Three. She continues to create sorrow and suffering wherever she treads. Nothing can save her now. But still—even now—she hunts for you."

Will they catch her? What will they do?"

"I do not see into the future, only what is and what was. I have watched through the ages and I will watch for ages more. I am Sentinel."

The Sentinel Speaks

"The tones speak of conflict in many directions. The filth of the underworld continue to gain ground, desecrating everything that they touch, leaving destruction in their wake. Above, the minions of Cian, have assumed many positions of authority. They promote unrest and anarchy. The sow fear among the mortals in order to control them. The time of conflict has arrived."

"Sentinel? May these others approach? We are travelers together and would welcome your wisdom. May they approach?"

"Let one of each enter the circle of council."

Annie turned to the group, "Allegra, Colm, Micah and Gunther, she says you can step forward."

"What about me?" Patch's voice was tight, anxious.

"You too Patch."

Colm stepped forward quickly and immediately, raising his hands he looked at Annie, the look of delight evident on his face, impatient for the others. The other three were more cautious. When they were arranged surrounding the base of the great edifice, Annie reached forward and again placed her hands on the stone. The others followed.

For a long time, there was no sound, no voice in her head. Instead, she felt a deep silence, almost a tone but deeper beyond her range of hearing. A silence so profound that she could hear the high-pitched sound of her own nervous system singing in her ears. One by one, she felt the presence of the others. She realized that she looked into each one's thoughts and felt they could see hers.

She saw with the eyes of the elf, his thoughts almost lyrical, all the colors of life bright beyond description and the movements of life a dance. The dwarf, grounded in stone, his thoughts were muted in greys and shadow, his focus intense, anxious to accomplish. Allegra's beautiful mind glowed with light and joy; Annie felt her heart's deep connection to the world around her. Despite the circumstance, Annie felt herself smile in response. She felt the incredible strength and determination of the tiny fairy Patch and the wisdom she hid so well from the world. Colm's consciousness joined hers in a rush of depth and awareness. So powerful that her knees weakened and her balance failed her.

Behind her Thomas was quick to steady her. The incredible awareness of Colm McQuinn's thoughts of what was occurring and the depth of understanding was overwhelming. She suddenly saw and felt what each piece in this last final conflict meant, its importance and the dire results if their efforts failed. She felt the entirety of all of the threads coming together. She felt the wonder that he felt as this great and possibly last epic unfolded, and the confusion of not being able to see the end of it—or its eventual outcome.

"All have once sprung from the same grain of sand, yet all have taken a different path." The silence in their minds was broken by the deep voice of the Sentinel. "Each a brother or sister by birth and goal. Together they must see with the same vision but with a different eye. Only together will their strength perhaps be enough."

"Sentinel? What of the Red Queen?" Micah's voice, almost hushed, "Garnet of the Mountain of Smokes?"

"A great host approaches from the south. I feel the thunder of their feet above."

"Will she arrive in time?" Annie asked.

"The future is yours to make. Victory or failure hang in the balance of the small things."

"We must rendezvous with Garnet before she encounters the hosts of Cian, but where?" Colm asked.

"I see what is hidden within you druid, I see the Hammer of Stone that no longer sleeps. It is not yours to plan alone druid, the pieces on the chessboard approach with ever growing speed. Agreement within can only be accomplished by sharing among each and all. Each must know the other."

"I cannot see into that part of me Sentinel," Colm's voice sounded skeptical, "how is it possible that you see what I cannot?"

Rather than answer the druid's question, Sentinel turned her attention to Annie, "Seeker, look. Look with my eyes. See the malice that crouches within your friend. You must know and understand the Hammer of Stone."

The vision in Annie's mind clouded as another image slowly formed before her. Surrounded in heat and flame that she could actually feel, a terrible visage emerged, a wild-eyed demonic creature, the sheer ferocity of the face, terrifying. A great hammer held in its right hand; it stood crouched to attack. As she looked on the face turned to her and fixed her with a malevolent gaze with eyes that flamed bright red.

"He's a Femorian? The Hammer is a Femorian?"

"The druid is not. Not at this time, but when he descended into despair he discovered his roots in the ranks of the unclean. He demanded to take the transition and the druid masters allowed it. In fire and sorrow the evil ones undertook his transition; they created again the Hammer of Stone. They once hoped to unleash it upon the world. But the druid brotherhood controlled it, and he has also successfully leashed it until now, but if the ferocity is ever released, the result is unknown. The Hammer wishes only to destroy. The hand of the hammer must hold it in check. The Hammer is evil but not evil by itself."

"So the druid is not a Femorian?"

"I am not a Femorian." The voice of Colm McQuinn spoke in her mind. "But they tried to recruit me at one time. I withstood their pressure and was accepted instead as one of the seven. I have proven myself. But I agree, because of you, the Hammer has been awakened."

"Indeed." Again the Sentinel spoke, "the Queen of the Elves rides with a host at her back. A formidable force the like of which I have never observed before. She wields the Hammer of Iron. The daughter of Tam Lin is a formidable warrior and a clever general. The Three pursue the traitor and must succeed before they join in any other conflict of arms. The conflict above will involve those of the mortal world and because they doubt The Three, they have limited power among them.

The struggle against evil has never been decided in the mortal world. Therefore, the strength in battle and those that tip the scale will also be mortal born. The ones of power and knowledge must lead; the battle must hinge upon the power of the witch.

Because of his pledge, Fear-giùlain a' Bhàis will accompany the Seeker wherever her path leads. Therefore, once as in ancient times, he will wield the Black Prince in defense of the One."

"I thought that only The Three could wield the Black Prince?"

"The Black Prince was forged in the fires at the very birth of this earth, as was I. As such we have known of each other for all the ages of man and before. The Three did not appear until the need for them was great. Fear-giùlain a' Bhàis stood against evil until they arrived in a timeless battle that has spanned those ages—and he has stood alone.

"Fear-giùlain a' Bhàis stands to fight his last battle at the hand of the One. He fights with the Black Prince once again as he did at the very beginning. He fights for you Seeker that you may succeed. You have sought treasure, instead you have gained in knowledge and character. That is your treasure, allies in battle, friends uncounted and wisdom earned. The greatest treasure ever to be realized."

"How can we balance the scale against such numbers?" Gunther asked.

"You stand with a great host at your back. The Army of the Dead, stands ready, commanded only by Keeper of the Long Promise. They can protect, but the gateway to the world above is closed to them as a result of their long ago promise. They will only fight in the darkness, where they dwell forever. The forces that you have among you are the forces that you will succeed or fail with, but I see no others that will come to your aid."

"Do you know of Bracken? The leader of the true brothers, is there word of him in the roots?"

"Of the great dire wolf warrior of legend, I have no

word. The true brothers have passed from the earth that I know."

"Can we hope to succeed against these odds?" Colm's voice was subdued.

"You have the Seeker among you. The Keeper of the Long Promise is not to be discounted; her powers are growing and a formidable opponent even at this young age. At her back stands the Bringer of the Dead, whose skill in battle cannot be questioned. He is that will wield the Black Prince in the final conflict and he will stand at the foot of the first great queen of the next age when at last there is no longer hope. For better or worse, those are the tools of your conflict."

"The dwarves will march into battle, an army of thousands upon thousands," Gunther spoke.

"Indeed you must, for the very existence of this world, the ground you tread upon, hangs in the balance."

"What is your council then?" Annie asked

"The Army of the Dead may not leave this land of caverns. They know every step that may be taken within it. To close the ways behind you and to refuse the unclean from advancing from below would reduce the number you face at the final conflict."

"That seems like good advice," Annie said thoughtfully.

"The Black Prince must be joined with Fear-giùlain a' Bhàis that he may realize his worth. Seek the memory of Circe' to recover the weapon of the sorceress."

"The memory of Circe' is here among us." Allegra's gentle voice added itself to the conversation.

"Indeed, I sense her within you, but she sleeps."

"Sentinel? Can you help me remember, help me awaken her?"

"As she awakens, the Keeper of the Light must fade. Do you wish this?"

Allegra pulled her hands away from the Sentinel. She turned and stared out into the expanse of the cavern. There was a long pause as she stood in thought. Annie could feel the struggle taking place within Allegra. After a long moment she turned and placed her hands again on the Sentinel.

"I have accepted this fate. Allegra must fade and allow the wisdom of Circe' once again to appear."

"That is not so young one." The Sentinel's voice sounded soothing, "the two are forever one. Neither to be one or the other. They will walk together as one always."

"Is that true? Can Allegra still be Allegra?" Annie said in wonder.

"The legacy of Circe' must never be allowed to founder, and the skills of the Keeper of Light must be used in this final conflict. Together an ally and a friend. You are strengthened by each and both Seeker."

"Okay, then can you help me awaken her?" Allegra said hopefully.

"Even in sleep she is aware. She watches. You need only ask."

"I... I don't know how to ask."

"The Seeker knows."

"Annie? Yes, Annie speaks to her mother whenever she wishes."

"Not every time." Annie corrected, "but when I ask for her, she usually answers. All I know is that I have to really want to speak with her. I mean, I only ask for her when I'm in a real pickle."

"Well we're in a pickle, so let's give it a try okay?" Colm urged.

"What is a pickle?" The dwarf asked.

"They are delicious things to eat." Patch's voice was filled with smiles of satisfaction. *"There is no such thing as a bad pickle."*

"No, a pickle is a dilemma, a conflict... oh never mind. This talking while everyone is listening in my head is hard to get used to."

"So I can ask?"

"Unless you ask, the answer will always be no." The Sentinel intoned.

Circe' Awakens

"Can you take me to the place within, where she is Sentinel?"

"You are in that place already, and she awaits."

"Circe'?"

The familiar voice of the Eldest replied, "It's about time! Goodness but it took forever."

"Circe'? Really? I've missed you so much!" Annie couldn't contain her excitement.

"I offer you what wisdom I might add, but you Allegra, you must become who you are meant to become. You will not become me, nor I you, but my knowledge will become your knowledge. Do not hurry. Life is a joyful journey, do not hurry."

"We are approaching our final conflict eldest. Annie has awakened the Army of the Dead. We are about to emerge into the mortal world above, where the Femorians are waiting for us. The Red Queen is approaching. The battle will be joined." Allegra's voice was matter-of-fact. "Soon."

"Much to be decided. Who will win, who will lose? There are many chess pieces in motion. But in the end, the conflict, the last battle of the fey and the magic that is life, this last battle will be only some few. Those that stand before the Sentinel right now, the allies of the Red Queen, and an ally unlooked for. It is the threshold of the last battle for the race of men."

"What about The Three?"

"In the end, they assist, but the battle for man and this earth is for you to fight, not them. As it has always been. Their battle is fought as we speak. They fight for the souls of those who believe in the magic of life. That is their mission; that is their pledge. They are the Guardians."

"Fear-giùlain a' Bhàis will carry the Black Prince in the final conflict. Can you tell me how to find it?"

"The Black Prince will find the One. The Black Prince is the talisman of the Queen of the Druids. It wants to fight, but will only fight at the bidding of the One. Do not seek it, but trust that it will find you."

"How does it even know where we are?" Annie asked.

"Young one, I keep forgetting how young you are. The Black Prince senses conflict. It knows the battle approaches. Edward of Woodstock was the closest that has ever approached the skill and ferocity of Fear-giùlain a' Bhàis to wield the mighty weapon of old. The Black Prince will be there when the time comes. As it always has been."

"So we should go—and soon. Or so it would seem." Colm's voice was resigned.

"Yes," The Sentinel spoke, "but I sense your fatigue. Here you must rest for a time, for the way to above is close, and you must prepare."

"We must rendezvous with the Red Queen. They are coming from the south and will follow the coastline. If the choice is ours to make, is there a battle ground where we might have a chance to use what strength we have?"

"At the foot of the Inyo Mountains, in the land near the great Valley of Death. Defend the high ground. Let the elements be your ally. There the Red Queen will await you."

"The Valley of Death? Death Valley. Boy that's all the way on the other side of Nevada. It's a really long way from here."

"There are many paths in the caverns of the earth. Some are long and filled with wonder, others are short for those in haste. The dead can show you the way of your need. But first, rest here and take your ease. Here you are safe, then follow the dead and listen for the tones. The dwarf must alert those ahead of your approach. I thank you for who you are, such an assembly of strength in magic and life has not been in all my memory. Rest and take solace and then leave me to watch once again."

Walk to Tomorrow

The Army of the Dead moved without voice, only the shuffle of their many feet on the stone floor beneath them. The whisper of their feet was the only sound as Annie and the others followed behind. They had slept on that stone floor. Not so long ago, she would never have believed that you could sleep on cold stone, but sleep she had. She had dreams that when they awakened her she could not seem to remember. The sound of thunder and the smell of dust, and pounding, endless pounding of hooves on the earth, the only thing she could recall. But she had been able to go back to sleep each time and sleep soundly for the first time in a long time, secure in the knowledge that the Sentinel watched and the army; her army stood ready to protect.

In the caverns there was no day; there was no night. When you were tired you rested; when you weren't tired you walked. Today, another day, whatever day that it may have been, they had begun walking and as the hours had passed, the tones within the stone had slowly changed. The dwarves had stopped often to read them, reporting back with news from their distant friends.

"The dead have fought ahead of us. The enemies

have been swept from our path."

"Emissaries have been sent to alert the Red Queen so that she may know our point of rendezvous."

"There has been a gathering of strength. All warriors of our nation rush to the gateway above."

"There is no pursuit. The dead have sealed the way behind us."

The walk was long. They stopped to rest more than once and slept when they could, but eventually, the dwarves told them that the exit was close.

"The doorway approaches. The might of the dwarves has assembled and stands before it. They are ready for what lies beyond. They await the arrival of the generals."

"What does that mean Gunther?"

"We who stand at the hand of Keeper of the Long Promise. We who speak for all of our people. The final council of the Keeper and the Avengers of Ethan the Wise. We who stand at the forefront and fight before all others. For one last time Seeker. We are the generals that they look to."

The pitch and tone of the music of the stone changed abruptly, as one the dwarves stopped. Each hurried to the walls of the tunnel and placed both of their hands on the stones. The change in their posture and the immediacy of their movements alarmed the rest of the troop. Even the dead stopped shuffling forward, waiting. In place of the tones of the stone that had lit their way, a high-pitched hum was the only sound as the dwarves listened to the message in the tone of the stone. The hum intensified until Annie could feel the pressure building in her ears, making her eardrums pop.

After long minutes, Gunther dropped his hands to his side and lowered his head. He took several deep breaths while he digested what he had learned. With a final sigh, he turned to the others.

"The gateway is before us, only minutes away. The dwarven army has engaged the enemy at the gate." He took a deep breath, "Our losses are heavy, there are many more enemies than we but we still hold the gate and the space beyond. The enemy holds the high ground on the mountainside. There can be no surprise."

"I had hoped we would be clear of the entrance and free to pick our place to make a stand," Colm whispered urgently. "We are unprepared; this is too soon."

"There is more news. Also not good." Gunther lowered his head and stared at the floor for a moment before he heaved his shoulders and sighed, "Bad in fact."

Gunther stepped in front of Annie and then reached and took Allegra's hand in his. He looked into her eyes.

"The traitor has laid a devious trap," he drew her hands closer, "It is Magda that leads the army against us. The strength of The Three is broken." He looked away from her questioning eyes, "The Mariner has fallen."

There was a collective gasp. "But still they are marshaling the forces that hold the gate." He held Allegra's eyes, "I am sorry."

"No!" Allegra's knees sagged and she sank to the floor, tears springing into her eyes. "No."

"Broken? How can that be? They're invincible, aren't they? My father… is invincible. They can't have lost. How is that possible?" Annie dropped to her knees, speaking to Colm McQuinn but wrapping her arms around Allegra. "It can't be true."

Looking up at Gunther, "Can it be true?"

"The tones are sent and read only by my people. These are the tones that we have. The others here," he pointed to all of the other dwarven fighters that were with them, "have all read the same tone. We must believe that they speak truth."

Allegra continued to sag against Annie. Both witches sobbing together, one who had lost a father and the other who didn't know the fate of her own.

Thomas stepped forward and placed a huge hand on the shoulders of each woman. Gently but with his strength alone, he raised both to their feet. Then turning them to face him, he spoke. His deep voice echoed down the empty hallway.

"The three fathers of old would have you avenge them. Their fight is now your fight, and it is ever my fight. Perhaps it was their last fight, and perhaps my last fight as well. But you must win this last fight; we must win this last fight. I am Fear-giùlain a' Bhàis' and I am grief. I am Fear-giùlain a' Bhàis' and I am anguish and I am loss. No victory, no defeat can be without me for I am both. But I would have this one last glorious victory —then he looked away from them and added, "Before the dark takes me at last and I am Fear-giùlain a' Bhàis' no more."

Allegra raised her chin and looked into the red eyes of Thomas. "Can you help me Thomas? Can you help us?"

"I am anguish. I am grief."

"Can you… will you accept mine?" Allegra pleaded.

"All anguish and grief has purpose. To give it away, is to deny the lesson."

Annie looked at first Allegra and then up at Thomas, she was confused.

"Thomas can you help? Really?"

"I can unburden your hearts, but I cannot remove the pain in the lesson. I am Fear-giùlain a' Bhàis; I am darkness. Give me your grief but you must keep your pain."

"Please."

Thomas had been holding each by their shoulders as they conversed. Releasing his grip, he took each of their hands in his. His touch was gentle, but his hands were ice cold.

"You wish this? Truly?"

"Yes," they both replied in unison.

"Then it is done." Thomas released their hands and stepped away.

The two women looked down at their hands, then each other. They did not feel any different, but they certainly looked different. Standing up they turned and looked at Colm and the group of fighters who stood wide-eyed at what they had just witnessed. Finally, they turned back to Thomas who regarded them, his red eyes drawn down under dark eyebrows.

"No gift is without cost. No longer will the grief of this moment haunt your dreams. To give away such treasure, there must be a price to pay."

"I'll accept it when the times comes Thomas. I'll accept the consequence. But right now, I think we need to go and meet our friend Magda." Allegra's voice sounded strong, resolute and angry.

In the moments of the experience her appearance had morphed. The woman standing before Thomas was now an armor-clad warrior. Her now white hair hung to her shoulders and drifted over her face in the air drafts of the tunnel. Her face was drawn and matured with darkened circles beneath her eyes. At her hip was a great two-handed sword and in her left hand was the staff of Circe' the Elder.

"I agree."

In place of Annie, there stood Morganna of Old. Her

face once again, tattooed with runes of power, her face painted from left eyebrow to right chin in black. The sharpened toes of her spiked boots sparkled in the light of the cave. At her hip hung the great sword of Brian Boru, and in her spiked gloved hand she held the lance that had ended his life, the spear of Kehlen of the Twisted Teeth, her grandmother.

Colm took two steps backward, then when that wasn't enough, he took another. "How?"

"It is the cost. It is the cost of loss of sorrow. The consequence." Thomas answered.

Allegra turned to the dwarves, "Let's go!"

At first bewildered and then surprised, Gunther nodded, then with an embarrassed slight bow, he turned and raised his hammer, "To death and tomorrow!" and raced into the tunnel ahead followed by the other warriors and the elves.

"The loss of grief and sorrow is also the loss of empathy. The scale must balance, each must accompany the other. You will now be warriors forever more, but will also be cruel and vicious. The loss of sorrow is the loss of yourselves as you disappear into the world of vengeance." Thomas took a step closer, "And you become the givers of death."

"Okay with me," Allegra stomped the butt of her staff on the floor.

"Stop!" Colm stepped into her line of vision. "Stop."

Allegra tried to push past him but he pushed back. She looked at him, her eyes angry.

"Stop." He put his hand on hers. "My love, stop. To lose yourself in vengeance and revenge is to deny what your father wanted for you. It is not where your strength and talent lie. The way of a warrior is not what he wanted, nor was it your mother's way. Their gifts are your strength, not the way of the sword."

She tried to pull away from him but he gripped her hand and stared her down.

"Stop—and remember."

"No! Allegra shook her hands free. "Step aside wizard."

"Yes!" Annie stepped up. She looked at both of them, but then held the druid's gaze. "Learn learn you said. Learn the meaning of the lesson, not just the pain of it. Learn learn to see the wisdom that hides inside of the event."

"Yes! Yes, Morganna, er, Annie. Exactly! We must not be subject to the circumstance, we have to find a way to get beyond it. To gain the perspective and see something that wants to be seen, but hides within the tall grass of emotion."

"Talk to me when this is over! Now I'm going to see my father and the death that awaits me beyond that."

"Yes!" Allegra touched Annie's hand and together they ran to catch up to the others. As they ran, the staccato of Annie's steel-toed boots rang out from the stone floor. The rhythm was taken up by the walls and the tone of the mountain changed. It became hard, the beat of racing hearts and pounding feet. The sound built until it shouted. It rang in their ears, and the beat matched the pace of their feet. The stones rang with the call to war!

"To death and tomorrow!" They shouted in unison with the stone.

"To Death and Tomorrow!" they shouted when at last they sprinted into a vaulted antechamber at the end of the cave. The tunnel opening was elevated above a great hall of stone. At the end of their passageway, the three elves formed an arc of protection at the top of a stone stair, their weapons drawn. Before them a great cavern opened, reaching out toward the distant wide opening at the cave entrance. From where they now stood to that opening, the cavern was filled with hopeful faces all suddenly turned in their direction. From the elevated position of the tunnel entrance the witches looked down at a sea of dwarven warriors. Ranks upon ranks of soldiers, thousands upon thousands in ordered rows, ready to defend their world. All of them now with their eyes directed at her in the flickering torchlight of the cave.

The Strength of The Three

Annie's eyes were drawn to the center of the horde where two sets of eyes met hers. Almost twice as tall as any of the other fighters, two figures were pushing through the throng, rushing toward them. Michael Abbott and Rafer Tate were moving quickly in their direction, opening the way for those that followed. Behind them, a group of several dwarves followed them carrying something at shoulder height. It was the still form of Gabriel McDonald.

Both women turned and, led by the elves, ran down the set of stairs carved into the rock and rushed to meet them. As they moved into the army of defenders the ranks parted opening the way. All bowed their heads as they passed.

Finally, they came face to face with Mike and Rafer. Both were covered in dust and grime, their clothes were torn and several dark spots spoke of injuries underneath. Tears streamed down Rafer's face and his lower lip trembled as he stood facing Allegra. Mike's broad face was streaked where tears had tracked. He stepped up to Allegra and looked down at his shoes.

"I am sorry Allegra, we tried but... could not save

him. I am so, so sorry." Another tear broke free and ran down his face and into his beard.

The dwarves carried Gabe forward and then with great care gently lowered his immense form to the floor. Allegra stood back and regarded the still form from a distance. Next to her Annie looked on. Thanks to Thomas, she felt nothing. There was no stirring of emotion, no grief, no anguish—only a feeling of great emptiness.

Colm McQuinn, only now arriving on the scene, dropped to his knees next to the still form. "This is tragedy upon tragedy." He placed his hand upon the massive chest and then the other on his forehead. Immediately he was thrown backward with a howl, landing several feet away.

"Oof!" As he struggled into a sitting position shaking his head. His eyes were opened as wide as they could get. He crawled back to Gabe on his hands and knees and again placed his hands on the body. This time, he groaned and collapsed face down across the corpse of Gabe McDonald.

Both Allegra and Annie hurried to pull him back and then turned him over. When they did he laid on his back, his eyes wide open, staring at nothing. It was long moments before he stirred, taking in a deep breath and letting it out in a rush. He struggled into a sitting positon and looked over at the still form next to him.

"He's buzzing with energy! So much energy; it's like an electrical storm. I think he might even be still alive. At least something in him is, but I don't have the strength to help him. I can't even seem to touch him."

"He's my father; I can touch him." Allegra knelt next to him and put her hands over his great heart. "You see? Nothing."

"Let me see," Annie joined her on her knees. She put her hands on his forehead, "he was my friend." She closed her eyes for a moment then looked at the druid, "Nope, nothing."

"That can't be right. Let me see." Colm struggled to rise but after the last two shocks his balance failed and he put his hands on the two women's shoulders to steady himself. Instantly, a blast of electrical energy surged through all three of them. With the two women dividing the force, they were able to maintain their contact as their consciousness was flooded with intense awareness of great expanses of time and space, images bathed in multi-colored light and a sense of deep wisdom washed through them in wave upon wave. Between them Colm leaned forward, concentrating. In their minds his voice spoke,

"Greetings ancient one."

The current of swirling energy changed in their thoughts, becoming less random. It began to flow through them, filling their vision.

"Ancient one, can you hear my voice?"

Again the swirl of energy shifted.

"Ancient one, can you remember? Remember your purpose? Hear my voice?'

From out of the swirling vortex they began to feel another shift approaching, rushing toward them from the infinity of memory. A shapeless consciousness, sentient, aware regarded them from within.

"Greetings Ancient One."

"Greetings. Must I awaken? Once again?"

"Ancient one we ask this. Our need is great."

"Then I shall awaken I must repair the form that I inhabit."

Again, the energy swirled and shifted in whirling

eddies of light. The dazzling effect washed through their minds, filled with revelations of events and shifting awareness. This continued for long minutes and then abruptly coalesced into a flash of brilliance.

The still form beneath their hands rose and fell with a deep breath. Beneath Allegra's hands the great heart beat once, then again, until it began to beat in a regular rhythm.

"Leave me now." Was the voice they all heard.

The two women lifted their hands, fascinated. Colm wiped the sweat that had beaded on his forehead.

"That may be the most incredible experience I've ever had in my long life. What supreme consciousness and wisdom. Absolutely incredible!"

"So? He's going to be okay?" Annie asked.

"Seems so, it's really up to him now."

"Why couldn't I see his face, or hear Gabe's voice?"

"He is one of The Three Annie. He's not who you see lying here. He never was; it is only the vehicle he used. He is so much more than just an earthly form, as are we all really, but he more so than anything else that walks the earth."

Annie looked down at her hands. The spiked gloves she'd had on were gone. Instead she looked at her usual slightly freckled hands. Then she looked at her feet once again clad in her sneakers. She looked down at the form of Gabe McDonald, his chest rising and falling with regular breaths, and a tear formed in her eye. In the brief encounter, somehow Gabe had restored her heart. She felt the great burden of grief wash from her, and the sense of relief burst forth in a flood of tears.

She turned to Allegra. "I was angry. I still am. But I also have the memory of having fought and died when the numbers against me were too great. Learn learn, we need ruthlessness but not without squandering any resources we might have. We are going to have to fight with our heads—and our hearts. I didn't understand the lesson but now I think I do."

Allegra raised her eyes to meet Annie's. Tears glistened in them as she nodded, "Yes, anything else would have destroyed us and meant certain disaster for those we love. You're right Annie, we are better when we feel."

She looked down at the form of her father as his chest rose and fell with a breath, "Thank you Dad."

A great hand landed on Annie's shoulder and she turned to see her father, a smile on his face and tears streaming down his face.

"Dad!" She reached for him and he pulled her into his chest. "Dad! Dad...dad—daddy."

She pressed her head into his chest and inhaled the scent of him. The dust on his shirt, and the sweat of him, but most of all the scent of her father. "Dad," she sighed.

Her father pressed his lips into the top of her head, "Annie," he whispered.

They held the embrace while the events of their most recent experience played through each's mind. Finally, Annie was the first to break the embrace. She swiped her sleeve across her face to wipe the tears and sniffled.

"I guess we're a pretty long way from the beginning of the semester, huh Dad?" she sniffed again and wiped her eyes.

Tears, again, sprang from Mike's eyes. "Yes Annie, a long way. So much water under the bridge." Stepping forward he reached and took a long strand of Annie's hair in his hand and held it up. The once flaming red of her hair now shockingly white in his hand. "A lot of water under the bridge my dearest one."

Annie looked at the long white lock amidst the red of the others and smiled into his eyes. "Yeah Dad,—a lot of water."

"A long way from the history department at Lincoln College." He shrugged his shoulders and then looked away, "Do you wish it had never changed?"

She placed a hand on his chest and then reached her other and caressed the back of his neck.

"Not anymore Dad. I miss sleeping on a bed with a warm blanket, and I miss hot chocolate, and all that stuff. But no, not anymore." She shrugged up at him, " Things change." Then she took a long breath and leaned into his chest, "All that time… all that time, while you waited… waited for me" she looked away and sniffed back another tear, "Thank you Dad. I never would have known. Thank you, Dad, for giving me my childhood."

"Are you ready? Are you ready for all of this?" He swept his arm out over the massed fighters. "Annie? Are you ready?"

"More than you might have guessed Dad. Are you at my side Dad? I think I might be ready."

Allegra stepped up and touched Mike's shoulder, "Mike! Mike, she solved the riddle of the sphynx in less than ten minutes."

"What!? Seriously?" Mike stepped back incredulously.

"Better, she sounded the tone of the Sentinel and awakened the Army of the Dead, the lost souls of the mounds of old."

"She tolled the bell of the dead!?"

"And commanded them."

Mike put his hands on Annie's shoulders and held her at arm's length.

"Morganna of old no longer! The legends forever

more will speak of the Keeper of the Long Promise, Queen of the Fey, Annie Abbot, last of the Forgotten Sisters of the Druid brethren. **At last!"**

He pulled her into a deep hug and after a long breath let it out. "I did not think that after your mother, I could ever love anything so much again. Much less love something or someone more than I loved Roison, but you've proved that wrong over and over Annie. It breaks my heart with how much I love you."

Gunther approached and interrupted this last hug, which Allegra had enthusiastically joined.

"Keeper, we hold the gate. Outside the sun shines and the heat of the desert is strong. The unclean are weakest in the light of the sun, but we are disorganized and unready to mount an offensive. What is your wisdom?"

Annie looked at Allegra, who smiled back at her. Then she looked at Colm and he slowly nodded—once. Last she looked at Michael and Rafer who stood at his shoulder and she smiled.

"We will rest and wait for darkness. Then we'll kick their butts."

She turned away and along with Patch, found a place along the wall and lying down, curled into a ball and was instantly asleep. Patch, her sword drawn and ready settled down in front of her and dared anyone to approach.

The Black Prince

In what seemed no time at all, Annie was awakened by a gentle shake of her earlobe. She immediately sat up and was alert. Directly in front of her stood Patch, again dressed in a leather buckler, her face painted in the colors of battle.

"It is time. The sun has set for one hour. The starlight is all that will guide us."

"Is everyone ready? No wait, am I ready?"

"You are Anne of Present. You are my liege lord. It is time."

"So you say."

Around her there was the sound of movement. The jangle of equipment being lifted onto shoulders. The ring of axes of steel ringing against silver bucklers. And the collective strength of a mass of life rising to wakefulness.

As she pushed herself into a sitting position, a great figure stepped into her vision.

"Good evening! It's a good day to die."

"Hi... Dad."

He was dressed in leather from head to toe. He carried no weapons. He appeared to be unarmed in any way. Behind him Rafer Tate appeared.

"Good morning little one. Did you get some rest?"

"Yes." She rubbed her hair, "Yes. I slept better than I've slept in a long time Rafe."

"Are you ready daughter mine?"

"Daughter?"

"We are the fathers. You are the daughter of The Three, the Guardians. As you are Michael's daughter, you are mine as well. The Three are one."

"As you are the daughter of Gabriel, as well," Mike added. "We who have watched over you from the beginning. We are here at the end..." He looked away, "Or at the next beginning."

Annie pushed herself up and then stood up. She was surprised that she was the same height as Rafer; somehow she had missed that change. She was even just slightly shorter than her father now. She looked out at the activity on the floor of the cavern as they prepared for the offensive. She didn't need to be told that she was in over her head, she already knew it. She felt the burden of her youth, and she felt the shortcomings in her short life and she felt the pain that there might be no more life beyond today. She met the eyes of Allegra as she approached, and she felt her resolve. It matched her own. It was time.

Somehow, even when she had been sitting in English class back in junior high school, somehow even back then she had known that dangling participles was not her destiny. Even back in Junior High School, somehow she had already known that there was something that she had only to close her eyes to realize, and here it was. That one moment when she had fantasized herself as a Marvel superhero. Somehow now, without even trying, she was some kind of superhero to everyone she could see, and her superpowers were better super powers than any of the Marvel ones. She just didn't know how to use them or where they even were.

She closed her eyes and wished the biggest wish she had ever wished. When she opened her eyes the scene unfolding around her had not changed. There was no fluffy bed, warm from sleeping, no frilly curtains hanging from the windows. She was not waking up from a weird dream. The cold damp air was still cloying; the dim torchlight of the cavern had not brightened. The tension in the air was electric, and wherever she looked furtive glances were cast in her direction. A Marvel heroine with a target on her back, the world to save and the lives of countless priceless individuals depending on her strength. She would be a freshman in High School this year if it wasn't for this,'minor' speed bump.

With a long sigh, she shrugged into her parka and looked at Allegra.

"Is there anything to eat? I'm starving."

Patch swooped into her sight. *"Short rations before a battle. Too much food in your belly makes your reflexes slow. Warriors eat light and fight smart. Only short rations today— for all."*

"This isn't starting out very well is it?"

"It's really okay Annie. Out there it's really still very hot." Allegra pointed out toward the opening. "Once we leave the cool air of the cave the heat of the desert will try to suck all the energy out of you. The only thing important is water. Water will be the most important component of the fight today." She looked into Annie's eyes and added, "Unless we tip the scales early."

"Tip the scales?"

"Yes," she looked deeply into her eyes. "The Black Prince has been summoned but has not appeared. We must tip the scale Annie, we must call for the Black Prince and that's you. You must call for the Black Prince Annie, it's the only way to tip the scale in our favor and only you can call for it to awaken."

"Are you sure? Can't Rafer or Dad get it?"

"Only the true Seeker may command the Black Prince, only Morganna is master of the Black Prince. That's you Annie."

"But where? Where is it? I can't just conjure it up out of thin air can I?"

Mike Abbott stepped up. "With the passing of Circe', who was the bearer, the Black Prince was returned to the deep. It sleeps awaiting your call. But it senses conflict; it is drawn to it. It is close, but far away. It is not among us, but elsewhere."

"Elsewhere? What the heck does that mean? Elsewhere?"

Colm McQuinn spoke quietly, "It is where few are willing to go. It lives in the darkness of the dead."

Annie looked at him in horror, "The darkness of the dead!? Not the Paths! Seriously?"

"The Black Prince knows only the pain of conflict. It is the darkness of beyond the veil. There it dwells—and waits for the call to war. It is the only call it knows."

"Seriously? You've got to be kidding. This is like some dime-store paperback book. I'm supposed to go to the Paths of the Dead and somehow find the Black Prince and bring it back somehow. Just so we can have one more chance to die differently than we were going to die in the first place."

"Yes." Colm met her gaze and nodded. "But you cannot wield the Black Prince in battle. You can't even carry it, touch it even. It is not your weapon."

She looked at Colm and thought, who could bring

the Black Prince back from the Paths of the Dead without losing their sanity. The druid could, but he could not use it. He was not a warrior unless he was the very undependable Berserker. She looked around her, Allegra carried the staff of Circe' and her sword. She could not accept the Black Prince. Michael could not, the strength of The Three was broken and the fight of the mortal world was not his. Rafer couldn't for the same reason. The elves, although terrifying warriors were not up to wielding such a formidable weapon preferring their agile mobility in a deadly fight. The dwarves were mighty but wielded hammers and axes. She expanded her gaze and over the heads of the others she met the gaze of Thomas, and he nodded.

"I see." She crossed her arms and gathered her thoughts. "I see."

Thomas stepped through the small group and stood in front of her.

"I can show you the way, but you must wish it."

"Don't take such a journey lightly Annie, it can change your sense of reality." Colm almost read her thoughts.

Annie looked up into his flaming red eyes and considered the fate of her decisions,

"Okay Thomas, I guess. What do I have to do?"

"We go." Thomas reached and swept her into his arms. Cradling her in his great arms he leapt off at a great pace. Annie closed her eyes and leaned against the great chest as his stride lengthened and she felt the incredible legendary speed of Fear-giùlain a' Bhàis' and she experienced the terror that was felt by those who witnessed his passing. Together she raced with him, the Bringer of the Dead and the Fairy Queen—to the Paths of the Dead.

There was no wind in her ears, no changing lights flashing beyond her eyelids. There was only the sense of speed and purpose until there was nothing anymore, no sound, no light nothing, only nothing and the endless race to the dead as Annie clung to him feeling his strength— and his endless remorse.

In the bottomless silence that was beyond death, Thomas stopped and lowered Annie to her feet. She opened her eyes. Around her there appeared to be nothing, no substance, no floor beneath her, no sky above, only endless emptiness.

"Well, hmm, I guess I shouldn't have expected things to change much since the last time I was here. I gotta say Thomas, this isn't really as bad as the space between the minutes when I fought Lilith, but it's not much better. This isn't much fun either."

"It is the darkness of no hope."

Annie stopped and opened her hands, her palms facing each other. "Let's see. The druid can do this without even thinking about it. Let me think for a minute." She focused on her hands and instead of hoping for it, she tried expecting the result she wanted. But instead of conjuring a ball of light, nothing happened.

"Well poop. Let me try again."

"I do not require the light."

"I know Thomas, but for me it is a comfort." She thought for a minute. In her pocket she suddenly felt a small vibration. "Wait, hold on."

She dug her hands into her jeans pocket and drew out the five stones she carried wherever she went. Immediately they began to glow, within seconds they brightened. A bright white light, much brighter than anything the druid had conjured.

She turned to Thomas, "Where to?"

"I do not know, you are the Seeker, the dealer of death wishes for you to find it."

"Sheesh. This is all pretty new to me. Let me think on this for a minute."

"What you seek is before you."

The voice spoke from the darkness.

"What? Who said that?"

"We."

"We?"

"We, those vanquished by the darkness. Those defeated by the hosts of evil."

"Can you show us the way?"

"The dark one feels us, he feels the way. He who denied us the Elysian Field but brought you to it, he is the last hope of our kind. It is he who must avenge us. He alone we will guide to the Black Prince."

"Thomas? Do you hear this?"

"I hear."

"Are they right? Who are they?"

"They are the lost kinsmen. Those left behind when you last fell on the field of Brian Boru. They are your brethren. They are part of my eternal remorse."

"Follow them Thomas. You said you wanted this one last victory. Find the Black Prince then and avenge them." She stopped and drew herself up to her full height and turned to the darkness. "Show him the way! I command it! For your service, I will release you to the Elysian Field, I vow this."

"As you command, so may it be."

Far ahead of them a tiny bright light appeared. In seconds it grew brighter, and nearer. It rushed toward them at impossible speed, incredibly bright in this place of total darkness. In a flash of brilliance, it exploded before them and vanished. With the last flash of brilliance both Annie and Thomas were blinded, and bright white spots danced in Annie's eyes. She shook her head and tried to look around the blind spot. There was something directly in front of her, but she couldn't make it out.

As her night vision slowly restored itself the object began to come into focus in the light of the five stones. It was a small child standing patiently in front of her, a girl. Across her outstretched hands lay the great Black Prince.

Annie looked at the child. Her eyes widened and she looked again, "Wait. I know you, at least I've met you before. Isn't that right?"

"I was a child of Lilith until you freed us. You freed me. You granted me my peace. I am honored to offer this token."

"Oh." Annie dropped to her knees in front of the small child as a tear escaped and tracked down her cheek. "Oh, I'm so sorry." She reached out her arms but the child drew back.

"The great dealer of death may be wielded only by the great three, or as in the beginning by the Bringer of the Dead."

"Thomas, take it."

Thomas stepped forward and lifted the great sword from the child's hands. He leaned down and with incredible gentleness spoke, "Thank you, Enid; I remember you and will remember you always.'

"You know her name?"

"I know all of the dead; they are my kin."

Annie looked at the child, "Thank you Enid. We must go now." Turning to Thomas, "We must go Thomas, take me back."

Thomas slung the great sword and scabbard over his

shoulder and back. He reached for Annie and the darkness closed around her once again.

Trust the Witches

When the darkness cleared in her vision, Annie was standing in the same spot that she'd occupied before leaving. The group was still gathered around her. It only took a moment for her to realize that she had not just returned to the spot—she had never left it.

"It's a mistake to change your reality back and forth; you can lose yourself in it." Colm finished the thought that he had started only moments ago.

Annie looked directly at Colm, Thomas stood behind her, the hilt of the Black Prince extending above his great shoulder. Not one second had passed since before they had gone to retrieve it.

"You can't imagine my reality Colm."

"What?!" Colm again took a step back.

Allegra gasped, "You've gone? You've walked the Paths again? But… but… you've walked the Paths and are unaffected? Annie, that's not possible."

"Thomas took me. We have the Black Prince." She stepped forward and put her hand on Allegra's shoulder, "It is time sister."

Allegra looked down and took a deep breath. "I know."

Colm turned to Gunther, "We're ready my friend."

Gunther turned and strode to the top of the staircase. He raised his war hammer and shouted,

"To death and tomorrow!"

From below the sound of countless voices chorused back with a great shout, their hammers and axes raised in unison. They roared back, **"To death and tomorrow!"**

Then again, and again in an echoing chant,

"To death and tomorrow!"

"To death and tomorrow!"

Immediately, all turned and faced the great opening of the cavern. Their feet stomping in unison, their weapons ready. Then they stopped in unison and silence as they prepared for the advance of the generals.

Annie looked at the others. This was not what she'd envisioned when she daydreamed about high school. Certainly not for her first high school prom, not even her first boy/girl date. 'Things change', she had told her father. Indeed they had changed—a lot. She was about to walk toward her own possible death with her friends and family, and she was starting to be okay with that. Well at least she understood the reason she might have to. It was a lot to absorb for anyone, much less for a thirteen-year-old girl. Lately though, she'd gotten a lot more practice at it than she should.

She tried to conjure the warrior Morganna of Old but she did not respond. Then she looked deeply into herself and looked for the merciless warrior, her grandmother, Kehlen of the Twisted Teeth, Ceithlion Chaisfhiaclach, but again there was a vacuum in her request. Finally, she asked for her mother, Roison McQuinn of the West March.

"Mother? Mom?"

"Child, I cannot help you. None may. You and you

alone are the answer. It is you that we await. It is you. It is time at last for the shield and the spear."

But then there was only silence in her mind.

She turned and walked all the way to the stone wall of the cavern and gasped for breath. She and she alone. This was real, this was serious and she was on her own. Her breath slowed, and she gazed at the stone of the wall in front of her. To steady herself, she reached up and placed her open palm upon the stone.

"You face a great multitude. The scale is unbalanced. Are you ready?"

The quiet soothing voice of the Sentinel spoke in her mind.

"I don't know."

"Is there another answer? Is there another way?"

"None that I can see." Annie gulped and continued, "But I'm afraid - I don't want to die. I don't want to see anyone else die. Is this the only way?"

"I see what is, the wisdom of war and the mysteries of the heart I do not know."

There was a long pause. As the tenseness of the silence-built Annie waited, unsure of whether the connection should be broken.

"You know the answer. Trust the witches; only through them may victory be achieved. Small things make up the most important things. Events turn on knowing the small things. Trust the witches."

"But I'm a witch… apparently."

"Yes. Trust the witches and allies unlooked for."

The connection through the palms of Annie's hands ended. She drew her hands back and stood silently for long moments. Then she drew a deep breath and turned to the others.

"I don't know much, but more than anything, I

know there's no going back. I don't know anything about war, or fighting. I don't understand the need to fight or kill because what I want is better than anyone else's, but I know what we're doing is righteous."

She took another breath and looked from one to the other, "I'll do my best."

Of all the people in the group, all of them nodded in agreement, but Thomas stepped into her vision.

"Never. Never before have I fought to restore right. Only to stem the tide of evil. At this very last I now fight for a future."

Annie looked up into his red eyes. Until then she hadn't seen the gentleness of his face. She smiled up at him, "Thank you Fear-giùlain a' Bhàis. I know we've done this before together, but I can't remember those. But I know that out of everyone here, I can trust you to fight and defend us completely. At least this time, I won't forget you." She reached out and gripped his ice cold hand, "Thank you. Maybe for the last time." Her eyes welled into tears, and they ran down both cheeks.

"For one last time." The deep voice repeated.

Annie wiped her eyes on her sleeve and turned to the rest, she sniffed and smiled. Then as cheerfully as she could, she said, "Well then, let's go."

"This will be the fight of the races Annie. We will help if we can, but it must be your fight and that of your friends. But we will be right here. If the need becomes dire, we will come." Mike hugged her perhaps one last time.

It was a long walk from the staircase to the entrance of the cavern. As they strode through the gathered ranks of the countless dwarven warriors, each dipped their heads. When they arrived at the great opening, Annie was stricken by the beauty of the desert's night sky. The star shine was so bright that it lit the landscape in sunset light, the greys not so dull, the colors not so dim, the great expanse of sand bright like moonlight on snow.

Before them, a great rabble of troops of the unclean stretched out into the distance. Their vigilance unfettered they screamed their defiance at the newcomers. The sound of their screams crescendoed as each of the generals stepped to the forefront.

As Annie stepped forward and Thomas stepped into their vision, the screams of defiance stopped. Instead they drew back, looking to their comrades from side to side, confused, and daunted for the first time. They had been prepared for warriors and weapons, this was unlooked for, and for the first time they were suddenly afraid.

Annie and Allegra stepped out into the sands of the desert, both appearing as they did in the mortal world. A beautiful woman, clad in a robe of green, black in the dark of the night, and a young girl in a robe of the deepest blue, also black in the darkest of night. And behind them something of swirling shadow towering over them. Together they faced the throng of evil gathered against them as the horizon to the east began to glow with the promise of morning.

"Show them what you've got sister," Annie spoke from the side of her mouth.

"Close your eyes!"

A tremendous beam of light burst forth from the Keeper of the Light. Blinding but with the power of a lightning bolt. The light swept through the crowded rabble leveling everything in its path as she moved her vision from side to side.

"You can open them now."

Annie had been slow to shut her eyelids and now had

another blind spot to deal with, but there could be no mistaking the sounds of agony and suffering that came from the field in front of them.

"You think you can impress us with your magic tricks? You will tire long before we are defeated, and then you will pay and we will enjoy watching you die witch!" A great giant stepped out of the ranks of the evil ones. "We don't fear the light or you, but you should fear us."

"He's right," Allegra whispered, "I can't do this forever. Eventually, I'm going to need to rest."

"I trust you Allegra, we'll be fine."

Close your eyes again Annie."

"No wait. What was that? I heard something."

"I don't hear anything."

"Me either," Colm McQuinn spoke from behind them.

"There." She held up her hands for quiet, "There I heard it again. Listen."

The mass of evil warriors began to edge forward. They snarled and growled, hurling insults and shouting filth.

Annie took a deep breath and shouted at the top of her lungs. **"SHUT UP!"**

The sudden shocked silence that followed was profound, magnified by the silence of the desert after midnight. Everyone leaned up on their toes, listening. And then they heard it and their eyes were drawn to the horizon to the east. Something moved in Annie's peripheral vision, a silhouette backlit by the growing morning as it rose at the crest of the mountain ridge. Then they heard the sound again, echoing off the face of the cave cliff, and filling the valley. It was the howl of a wolf. It was the sound of an 'ally unlooked for,'. It was

Bracken, lord of the True Brothers, and cresting the ridge more shadows appeared and their howls blended with Bracken's. The last of the True Brothers poured down the steep mountainside while they howled the song of their ancestors and came to war.

Allies Unlooked For

With incredible violence they crashed into the attackers. Even in the darkness of the moonless night, the shadows of the evil victims were thrown about, and their screams of pain and frustration sounded into the silence. They were helpless to defend such ferocity that they had not expected or prepared for.

The last of the True Brothers attacked with unrelenting ferocity, their effect devastating as they drove a wedge deep into the ranks of the gathered enemy. One shadow broke clear and raced toward the witches. Skirting the throng of evil doers with incredible speed only to stop within inches of Annie.

"Greetings my friend." He panted, "I have fulfilled my promise; I have found my brethren. We are yours to command."

"Bracken! Oh Bracken, I have missed you so much!" She rushed forward and buried her face in his shaggy neck.

"With every day that passed, I wished to be at your side. Finally, we will fight together again. If you would have me."

"Bracken! How can you say that? We are friends; you

are my friend always. I cannot think of a better friend for this fight."

Bracken took a step back and met her eyes, "Then you will have me?"

Annie smiled, then gathering the length of her robes in her hands, she grabbed a handful of fur and vaulted onto his back.

"If we're going to fight, then I'll do it with you my friend." She looked toward Thomas, "and with my new friend. Allegra, if you would, can you do that thing again, please?"

Bracken turned away from the cave entrance and facing outward, he howled to the sky above. The vibration from his chest radiated through Annie as she sat astride and she felt the call as well.

She drew a deep breath and shouted **"To me!"** at the top of her lungs. Then raising her right hand in a fist, **"To me!"**

From within the riot of the attackers from the underworld, the great dark forms of the dire wolves broke free and retreated through the space they had just won and those already vanquished and on the ground. Breaking free of the horde and skirting it, they raced to Annie. Turning as they arrived, they formed a great arc of protection in front of her facing outward. At the same time, behind her came the sound of thousands of feet as the ranks of the dwarves stepped out of the tunnel and spread across the valley behind her.

Bracken turned to Micah and dipped his head. "My brother, select your mount. At last we battle together once again."

Without a sound Micah vaulted astride the lead dire wolf. Mink and Link followed on each side of him. Micah turned from his seat and looked back at Annie, "Now you will learn the way of the warrior my Queen." Then he laid down along the great wolf's back, his face only inches from its great fangs that were drawn back in a snarl. "Greetings Shey!"

"Greetings Micah, it is a long time."

Patch appeared in Annie's vision. *"There is something else Anne of Present. Do you hear the song of the morning? Listen?"* She cocked her head to one side, *"The voice of the sunrise, can you hear this as well?"*

"What? The song of the morning?"

"Listen carefully Anne of Present."

"I hear it plainly," Bracken spoke over his shoulder. "Only once in my long life have I heard this." He turned back and snarled, "They are coming!"

"What? Who's coming? Is it the Red Queen?"

"I hear it too! Allegra stepped up next to Annie, astride a great red wolf. "The legends are true, it is the morning's song, unbelievable!" she gasped.

Then Annie heard it at last. It was a sound, soft and musical, finally distinct and growing in volume. It seemingly came from nowhere but everywhere, as if from the thin air. The evil ones, still recovering from the attack of the dire wolves raised their heads and cocked their ears listening as well. From within the music, separate voices emerged, singing harmoniously. In the distance, at the far end of the desert valley, a small light appeared moving toward them. As it drew closer, the light separated and became two. Then it became four and as the distance closed it became a vast number spreading across the barren landscape.

The song gained in volume as thousands of the distinct blue lights raced toward them. Countless blue orbs spread across the valley floor, dodging obstacles, shifting. Again Patch hovered in front of Annie demanding her attention. When Annie furrowed her eyebrows in a question, Patch winked and flashed. Instead of Patch a bright blue orb hung where she had been.

"It is the war song of the Fey, the morning song for the Fairy Queen. The Army of the Fairies, Anne of Present. Yours to command. But how they are here, at this time, I cannot guess."

"It is Thomasina. I have asked her to gather the woodland and the Wind River fairies and follow. It is Thomasina that has marshaled their strength. I hear her voice in the song."

"Bracken, thanks. That was a stroke of genius. Another ally unlooked for."

"Yes! I get it, thanks Patch. Allegra? Whenever you're ready. Patch, let's give them something, um… oh,", she paused, "well I thought I'd be able to think of something inspiring, but my mouth's too dry. Let's just do our best."

"You have only to command Annie." Colm stood at her side, his face solemn as he looked out on the countless enemies. "We're all going to try and do our best."

"Patch. Give them hell! Let's give them some hell!" then changing her tone, she commanded. "Now Patch!"

Patch flashed from a glowing blue ball of light into a blinding white star. She began to sing joining the other fairies in their song of war. From out on the desert floor, one by one the blue lights that raced forward exploded into blinding flashes of white as they crashed into the rear of the great horde. The Fairy Army sang as they slashed into the surprised enemy.

Allegra leaned down over the great wolf's neck, "Let's go Diodre', make me path," and she too exploded into a great bolt of lightning that swept through the front ranks. The great wolf leaped forward howling. Together the other great wolves answered and sprang forward in a wide rank that raced into the forefront of the confused enemy. Behind them the dwarves broke their ranks and with a great shout, their weapons and shields raised, they too raced forward.

Fight to the High Ground

"Annie, make for the high ground; we must win the high ground." Colm touched her knee, "There are too many for us to fight on level ground. The fairies can only distract them so long."

"Gunther!" Annie yelled, "Work to the high ground! Force them from the mountainside!"

Gunther raised a great battle horn and winded it, the haunting horn impossibly loud and deep. With a sweep of his great hammer, he pointed to the mountainside and blew the horn again. As one the great army of the dwarf nation shifted, forming a phalanx of attackers, and began angling to the flanks of the unclean, forcing them from the hillside, the sheer ferocity of their onslaught winning the ground in inches.

The sound of the tempest of war was deafening as weapons struck weapons and shouts of anger and pain filled the air. In the crush of attackers and defenders, it was difficult in the dim light to identify specific individuals. The bright lights of the fairies continued to dart in and out of sight, a swirling vortex of coordinated attack. It was clear wherever the mounted elves traveled, mayhem followed as together they charged through the massed evil attackers. The attack of the dwarves was relentless against the others who were now suddenly facing attacks from multiple directions and they slowly cleared a path to the higher ground inch by inch.

Below them the dire wolves roared as they fought shielded within the blinding light of Allegra. The countless flashing beacons of fighting fairies darted in and out of the enemy, disappearing instantly, only to reappear and attack again. The fight on three separate fronts for the enemy was confusing enough that they began to retreat in order to regroup.

"Bracken can you get me up there?"

"As you wish, but are you prepared? It will be a difficult fight."

"No, I'm certainly not prepared. But we need to be able to see what's going on, and that's probably a good spot."

"I will make you safe Anu. Follow me."

"What did you call me Thomas?"

"He called you Anu. Mother of the Earth, mother to us all. Anu – Annie, hmm, I never thought of it that way before, but that makes complete sense to me now." Colm said with wonder in his voice. "He'd be the one that would know that's for sure. Boy that explains an awful lot. Anu indeed."

"That's just nuts, but just for a second there…" she cocked her head to the side, trying to put her finger on the thought that had just escaped her, "oh, um, nothing I guess, but just for a second there was something." Turning to Thomas, "Let's go then."

Thomas, a tall shadow, darkness upon darkness burst away and toward the mountainside in his great strides. Bracken ran to keep pace with him. Reaching over his shoulder, Thomas drew the Black Prince from its scabbard on his back. As soon as it was in his hands it flamed into life and Thomas leaped forward, his progress so swift he became a blur of shadowed motion. Wherever the shadow traveled, the flaming light of the Black Prince rose and fell, sweeping from side to side, like an artist painting only with light.

"It is the Black Prince!"

"The Black Prince fights once again. Run for your lives!"

The voices of those lucky enough to see it before it overpowered them were raised in panic.

"Quickly now Bracken, the high ground."

Bracken trotted up the slope that Thomas had swept clear. Near the top, a bolt of energy struck him in the side, knocking him down and throwing Annie clear. As he struggled to rise, another hit him and he collapsed senseless onto his side, his dazed eyes open and his breath escaping through clenched teeth.

Annie struggled to her feet. Stunned, she looked around, spied Bracken's motionless form and hurried to him.

"Not so fast!"

Annie turned and thirty yards away, Magda stood with her staff pointed directly at Annie's chest.

"You've caused way too much trouble already you silly little girl. I'm going to enjoy this more than you can imagine."

Slowly, Magda advanced. Annie was frozen in place as the sounds of the battle around raged but were no longer her priority. She looked in both directions, where any allies she might have were engaged already, struggling against the renewed energy of the unclean. She looked down at Bracken's unconscious form and then faced Magda.

"Hello Magda." She struggled to keep the tremble out of her voice. "You've wanted to kill me from the beginning, haven't you?"

"Yes."

"You killed Ash."

Magda smirked and nodded, "Easy peezy."

"And you killed Circe' too. Didn't you?"

"Circe' was the more difficult. The battle of the Winter Solstice gave me the perfect opportunity. She never knew what hit her, but in the end, she avoided her final fate and escaped into Allegra. Allegra, that equally annoying daughter of the White Witch. But I'll remedy that before the day is out as well."

"So now," Annie drew herself up straight and looked her in the eye, "so now it's my turn."

"Oh yes," she closed her eyes and gave a small shudder, "oh how I've dreamt of this moment. Little silly Annie Abbott, you can't imagine how insignificant you are but Morganna of Old, now that is something indeed. Oh yes, this is what I've imagined over and over."

The head of her staff began to glow as she stepped closer.

"You cannot win Magda. The good will win in the end."

"A pity you won't be here to see it then." The staff's glow increased into a bright red flame.

"It's you who won't be here Magda."

A scarlet bolt of energy blasted from Magda's staff and struck Annie in the chest and she disappeared in flame.

Sunrise and Storm

Throughout the battlefield a shock wave reverberated. Patch, who had been rushing forward as soon as she saw Bracken fall, pulled up in shock, *"No!"*

The dwarves turned their eyes up at the flaming staff and its target, momentarily rendered paralyzed. The dire wolves stopped their attack and looked up, then with tremendous snarls they struck out through the crowd toward the two battling witches. The lights of the fairies began to flicker, turning from white to blue and some even winking out. Instantly the evil ones from the underworld sensed a momentary advantage and attacked.

Magda lowered her staff and smiled. As the burning flash from the tip of it died, she gasped in disbelief. Twenty yards in front of her stood a dark figure, drawing what little light there was into it. It slowly raised its head, smoke trailing from singed locks. Annie no more, before Magda a figure looked back at her with flashing eyes—one a blazing blue, the other burning red. At her side once again, the great sword of Brian Boru, and in her left hand the great spear of Kehlen of the Twisted Teeth.

"Congratulations Magda. You've managed to accomplish what I couldn't bring myself to do. You awakened the memories of my forebears and made them one. Welcome to your ending."

"No! How is that possible? How...?"

"How? How did I do that? I didn't do it, you did Magda." Annie brought her hands into her chest and then flung them wide and a bright red flash erupted from her chest. Now in her place stood Annie Abbott, her angry face painted with runes of war down the right side, two long black stripes from her left eyebrow to her right chin. "I didn't have to become what I already was. Now..." Annie lowered her spear and pointed it at Magda. As the end began to glow, "Now to business."

From over her shoulder an arrow flashed and struck Magda over her heart and she staggered backward. Shocked she gazed down at it as another struck inches from the first. She raised her eyes, questioning wonder on her face as a shadow stepped into view, a great wolf and rider.

Slowly the rider slid to the ground and stepped forward. Micah spoke; "You are the traitor and murderer of my long mate. Ash would have vowed to avenge my murderer, just as I have. Your life was mine to take and no other. Now I have avenged her death, and may your fate be beyond the Paths of the Dead to the unknown world beyond."

As Annie looked on in horror, Magda slid to the ground, her eyes still disbelieving. With horror she realized what she had been about to do herself, and she dropped the spear. As Micah turned away he looked at her and gave her a small shrug.

"Your strength is in your innocence my sister. To have done this would have changed who you are. It is done, but not on your hands."

"We must get to the high ground, the battle has turned against us." Bracken's voice was urgent as he struggled to his feet. As others turned away, Annie couldn't bring herself to. Thomas stepped forward and nodded to her. His sword was sheathed and he reached down and placed a hand on Magda's shoulder. Magda looked up and understood. Smiling, she nodded once, and she was no more in this world or the next.

In the short minutes of her battle with Magda, the battle in the valley below them had turned. The advantage now belonged to the underworld army that outnumbered the dwarves many times over. Now they surged outward in all directions, taking advantage of the defenders' momentary loss of strength. The dwarves were being forced back, pinning them against the cliff face. The fairies had lost their source of energy when Annie was attacked, and Bracken had been injured.

Annie turned and gazed down the long slope. "We're losing."

"Yes. It was probably inevitable in the end. There are just too many." Colm panted up the hill. Turning he looked down the hill as the elven riders and the dire wolves fought while slowly being forced backward. "It would take a miracle."

"Well then, I know where to find one. Gunther blow your horn, good and loud!"

Again Gunther blew his horn and across the mass of fighters two men stood in the entranceway to the great cavern and looked up at her. Annie signaled, swirling her arms, and then making a fist and slamming it into her other open palm. The two stepped forward as a sudden wind swept in from the desert.

In no time, a gale force began to blow. The desert

sand rose from the ground, blinding everything from sight and great cyclones of dust, static lightning flashing in its midst, smashed into the mass of warriors. The combatants covered first their eyes, then their mouths and throats as any thoughts of continued fighting were out of the question. The fight literally blown out of them as the lightning continued to strike among them.

As quickly as it had risen the wind ceased and the sand settled once again. Above a dark overcast began to form as clouds swept in from the west and the landscape darkened.

The dwarves, partially protected by the very cliff face that moments before had all but spelled their doom, were first to recover. Leaping to their feet, they gathered their weapons and formed ranks. But the unclean had lived in forbidding places for millennia, no recovery was necessary for them. They appeared unaffected as they turned away from the dwarves. They now had eyes for only one target. They began the climb the slope of the mountain toward the few gathered around Annie.

The great horn of Gunther sounded again and the dwarves attacked from the rear, but there were too many evil ones. They were soon being pushed back again.

Again Gunther's horn bugled out into the valley. Annie raised her fist in the air, "To Me! To Me!"

More than a dozen great dire wolves, the three elves still mounted, broke free from the melee and climbed to the Keeper of the Long Promise. The three elves slid to the ground before Annie and smiled. Each saluted, but then one by one they stepped forward and embraced her.

"We normally reserve the display of physical affection for long mates and newborns—but for you I will gladly welcome your embrace." Micah smiled

"I know you've said that once before."

"But one that we so love, we would gladly return your embrace each day." His green eyes flashed. "We count you one of our kind—always."

Micah swept out his long knife and tested the edge with his thumb. Then unslung his bow and tested the string and counted his arrows. His quiver of arrows was almost empty. Then with one last smile at Annie, he turned and clapped Mink on the shoulder. As he looked down at the advancing horde, he laughed, "A good day to die, don't you think?"

Mink unslung his bow and laughed back. Together they stepped forward and raised their bows gazing down the hill. Link barged in between them, "Private party?"

"No, we are not picky—anymore. We'll even take you."

"Good thing," He laughed. He counted his arrows before slinging his quiver over his shoulder. "How many have you got? I've got eleven."

"Fifteen," Link spoke over his shoulder

"Nine," Micah said quietly, "it will be close work after that."

"Well, I wish they would hurry up and get here; I would like get this over so we can get some breakfast soon."

The dire wolves moved forward as well. Forming a semi-circle in front of Annie and Bracken they stood shoulder to shoulder, their hackles raised and teeth bared as the first volley of arrows from the attackers began to land among them.

"Well this should be fun." Colm also stepped forward, his hand on the small silver hammer he wore around his neck. He looked up at Annie as she mounted Bracken once again, "Shield and Spear Annie. It is time for the Shield and the Spear. I had hoped we'd have more time together Annie." He touched her arm and smiled up at her, "But we always think we have more time than we really do."

He gripped the hammer and disappeared into the visage of the Hand of the Hammer. His eyes flamed red as he turned and swinging the great hammer, stomped down the slope, taking a position in front of the three elves. All three of whom, their eyes opened wide, stepped back several steps and out of the reach of the great hammer.

"Well, I guess that spoke volumes." Annie watched as the hideous creatures scaled the slope and came within the range of the three archers. Several of those in front fell as the elves opened fire. With a scream of hate the underworld broke into a run, closing the distance between them rapidly and the Hand of the Hammer strode forward to meet them.

She looked down at her father. Even from this distance she saw the distress in his face as he shook his head, no. She raised the great sword of the last king over her head in a final salute. "Let's go Bracken, let's get this over with."

Bracken crouched to spring forward but stopped his ears pricking up. From behind them, at the top of the slope a great horn sounded. He turned and faced uphill as the first rider appeared at the crest of the hill. The horn was joined by another, and then by dozens, then by hundreds. At the crest of the mountain ridge, riders appeared and stretched from one end to the other, an army of tens of thousands upon tens of thousands. Across the valley the rising sun flashed as it crested the ridge, shining beneath the dark cloud cover in a brilliant display of color.

All eyes looked up the crest of the mountain as the morning light struck the riders that crested the hill and stood in the blaze of light. From the crest into the distance, left and right of both horizons, the silhouettes filled their vision. Then in the stillness of the desert dawn, the war horns of the Elvin Army sounded again, together, the sound of tens of thousands of battle horns.

The great ride of the Red Queen was over.

The Red Queen

One great horse stepped forward from the rank, and the rider leaned forward. A woman on a great war horse. On her head she wore the headdress and helmet of the queen, and in her hand she carried a great hammer. She placed her hand on the saddle's pommel and leaned forward. It took only seconds for her to take in the situation below her. Finally she looked down upon what she had come to do to fulfill her vow. She raised her great hammer and with a great wave of it, she wheeled her great horse in a circle and brought it forward, pointing down the slope.

"To the Queen!" She raised her voice and she spurred her mighty horse forward.

Behind her the elven warriors sprang forward, they poured over the crest and raced down the slope in a great shout and the blowing of horns. Rank upon rank, as wide as the ridge was long. Their charging horses stampeding toward war, adorned in battle armor of their own.

The great war horse of the Red Queen rode at the front of the horde, her long blond hair streaming out from her helmet, and her battle gear flamed red in the morning light. In her hand she held the great Hammer of Iron high over her head as she laid down low across the neck of the great stallion. The great war horse threw back its head and whinnied into the air. It was answered by the other horses as they plunged down the steep slope and their speed increased.

Behind her rode her fearsome captains, the elven kings of old. Wraiths from another age and time, frightening shadows in the morning light, their horses silent with flaming eyes of fire. Their riders silent, their faces grim. There rode Tam Lin, husband of Titania, last great queen of the fairy realm and the last to fight in the elven wars. He who had fought and fell in the last battle against the underworld of ages past, at his side Finwe', King of the Noldor and Ingwe' of the Vanyar, named high king of all elves of old.

The attacking filth of the underworld immediately understood that the chessboard had tilted. Veterans of war and unrest, they tightened their ranks. Pikes and spears were planted in the ground and pointed up the slope to stop the charging cavalry. Their archers stepped forward, firing volleys into the oncoming crush of warriors.

Without breaking pace as she approached the cadre surrounding Annie, Garnet leaped to the ground near the small group and digging her heels in, slid to a stop. Her horse unperturbed continued its headlong charge, anxious to fight, whinnying again as it crashed into the front line of the filthy underworld attackers unaffected by the spear and pike points that glinted in the new morning sun. Behind them, the kings of old followed the charge as well. The sound of their collision one-sided, as they made no sound, but the others did. While the unfortunate attackers disappeared under the great hooves of their war horses, the Elven Kings made no sound.

The great kings wheeled their mounts around and taking three separate directions, they opened a path through the front ranks of the Fomorians. Again, Garnet's war horse whinnied and the charging front of the elves narrowed forming a great thundering spearpoint and dove directly through the opening where they attacked with vigor. Their skill and their coordination with their horses awe-inspiring, both a beautiful ballet and terrible dance of death.

"Greetings, at last!"

"Um… greetings Garnet. I'm Annie."

"That's not what I hear," she pulled her glove off of her hand and offered it as a greeting. "You're Annie, but from what I hear, you are a whole lot of other things too."

The great Red Queen of the Elves bowed at the waist and then stepped closer and took Annie's hand, "We have waited for you since before the time of my father." She turned and looked down the mountain where Tam Lin wove in and out of the great battle, his great saber glinting dully in the bright sunshine. "At last the time is come. For better or worse, I bring all the combined strength of my race. We are here to save our world and the world beyond or to fight and die on this battlefield today."

Annie was embarrassed and stepped back but squeezed the Queen's hand at the same time.

"I'm just Annie. Just Annie." Then she smiled and added, "Unless you make me mad," she shrugged and winked, "then I'm not promising anything."

Garnet squinted at her and cocked her head to one side, "So I've heard." Then she nodded, "Good to know… Annie."

Looking down the slope again, she gasped. "A Berserker? How is that possible? And… wait… is that?" She placed her hands on her knees and squinted into the dusty fray, "He wields the Hammer of Stone?" She turned back to Annie, surprise and disbelief on her face. "The Great war Hammer was lost ages ago. And," she returned her gaze at the wonder, "and the last Berserker died at the feet of the king. Can you draw those that may help from the Paths of the Dead to fight your battle? Is this possible?"

"This from someone whose three toughest fighters have been dead for like what… a thousand years?"

Garnet pulled back again and regarded Annie with respect. "Touche.'"

Then she looked down at the battle; her elves were being slowed. The spears and pikes were forcing them to narrow their charge and blunting their strength. The dwarves were stalemated, unable to advance nor retreat.

"What now… Annie?"

"I'm not a warrior Lady Garnet. At least not right now I'm not."

Garnet gave her a serious look and then shouted over her shoulder. "Dwarf sound your battle horn."

"I am named Gunther, king of my people."

"Gunther blow your horn—blow it until I say to stop —please. Annie, Allegra join me will you? We're going to need to fix that Annie."

The Red Queen raised her hammer over her head and stepped forward to where she could be seen from below. Annie, her red hair blowing in the wind, drew her sword as Bracken stepped up next to her. Allegra, with the staff of Circe' in her left hand and mounted on Diodre' did as well. Gunther stepped forward and blew a great blast on his horn. Taking a deep breath, he blew again, then again.

As the horn continued, eyes turned up to the sound. What they saw was a huge dwarf fighter, a mighty war horn in his two hands, and the three most powerful women to walk the planet at the same time standing together. Challenging them. Challenging their fighters to greater deeds.

Garnet put two fingers to her lips and whistled a piercing note. As one, the mounted elves turned and spurred their horses away from their fight and up the slope to their queen, outrunning the evil ones still struggling up the steep slope. Upon reaching the rocky outcropping where the three stood, they surrounded them. Turning their horses to face downhill they formed into ranks. Ranks upon ranks, weapons held ready, presenting a formidable sight.

The dwarves backed away and taking a position at the base of the cliff, drew themselves together, shields outward, an impenetrable wall of defense, their war hammers held high.

"Allegra? If you please." Annie understood, it was her time. She smiled a sad smile at her. "Call them to me."

The staff of Allegra blazed and a flash of the whitest light shot upward into the darkened sky where the sunshine was no longer a factor. From everywhere, the fairies flew, their forms dark in the overcast light of the morning. As they approached they once again began to glow. They flew to Annie and gathered around her and their glow began to blaze brightly again. Patch, blinding in her brilliance, took a position directly over Annie's right shoulder and Thomasina her left. If there had ever been any doubt who she was, there could be no doubt now. She was surrounded by countless swirling lights now so bright that it was difficult to look directly at her.

The Girl Warrior

"Are we ready my old friend?' Annie leaned down and spoke softly into Bracken's ear.

"You are the One. I am ready." Bracken's voice rumbled and the dire wolves shook their great heads and together, snarled down the mountainside. Bracken stepped through the wolves and then slowly down the hillside through rank after rank of elven fighters until he stepped out in front of the vanguard.

"I'm sorry Bracken." Annie laid herself down along his great back and stroked his face, "I'm sorry if any of this is my fault, please help me be brave."

"You have shown me more courage than many of the greatest warriors that I have fought beside. I will hope that you can help me to do the same. Perhaps, when we meet on the other side, perhaps then we will live in peace and joy."

"Is there another side for us Bracken?"

"The good may live forever; the bad must die when they die. I am ready, I am ready my queen—to live forever."

"Well then," Annie closed her eyes, and when she opened them they flamed once again. One blue and one red, "well then—**GO!**"

Bracken squatted on his haunches and raised his snout and howled a great howl. Then stepping forward he began a slow deliberate march downhill. His howl was answered by the True Brothers and they leaped forward to the front, howling in response. The horns of the elves brayed out and the front rank stepped forward in a slow walk, marching downhill in a vast line, menacingly deliberate, silent but for the horns sounding, their spears pointed out in front of them. They were followed by the second rank, followed by the third. Their pace maddeningly slow.

Pushing out to the front, Garnet, now mounted once again drew up on Annie's right side. Allegra and Diodre' quickly stepped to the left.

From the side of her mouth, Garnet said, "Did somebody make you mad, or did you do this yourself?"

Annie looked across to her, her brows furrowed and a frown on her face. "My birthday would have been next week. I would have been fourteen-years-old. All of you, all of this," she swept her arm out across the landscape, "did this to me."

Slowly, one step at a time the dwarves advanced, their shields up. Pushing against the attackers, slowly but surely forcing them away. Not attacking, only pushing forward. Pushing them into the advance of the elves.

Rafer Tate and Michael Abbott, shoulder to shoulder acknowledging Annie in the distance, paced forward, directly toward the hated ones, seemingly unarmed.

Garnet twisted in her saddle and looked back at her army. Turning to Annie, "We're ready... Annie."

"To ME!" Annie raised her voice and pointed her sword downhill, "To ME!" And Bracken leaped forward and sprinted. "One last sprint Bracken, to fight or flee.

Today we fight!"

Around her a great swarm of blinding lights lit the way. From the staff of Circe in Allegra's hand a great beacon of light blasted out and into the ranks of the attackers. Behind her the elven army broke into a headlong gallop, their horns silent, replaced by the thunder of the hooves of the countless charging horses. Below the dwarves, hammers high slammed into the rabble invaders. Rafer and Michael quickened their pace, raising their hands in unison as the thunder of the first flash of lightning sounded from above.

Almost as one, the many forces of elves, dwarves and men collided with the great mass of Underworld attackers in a seismic clash. The ferocity of the allies unparalleled in their attack as they compressed their enemy, squeezing them together, forcing them so close together that it made it more difficult to defend themselves.

The Red Queen, her face set in grim lines, swung her Hammer of Iron from horseback, the effect devastating wherever she passed. The fearsome Berserker strode downhill, the great Hammer of Stone violent beyond imagination, clearing a path of those doomed to face him. The great lines of the elves, smashed into the evil ones leaping over their outstretched spears and pikes, one rank after the other, like waves crashing on the beach. The dwarves began making progress, their shields pressing forward, their axes bright in the increasingly overcast light.

Bracken, his ferocity unparalleled, fought everything in his path. From his back, Annie swung her sword to no avail. Everything and anyone that even came close to her was immediately crushed by her three elven friends, once again mounted on the dire wolves. As they wove in and out and all around her, none survived coming close.

She didn't know whether to be relieved or frustrated. She wanted to be brave, she wanted to show she could be a warrior too. Everyone else was a strong warrior, capable and deadly. She wanted to do her part, but the sword didn't seem to fit. It felt awkward in her hand, big and clumsy. She looked all around her at the great valiance of the elves and dwarves, brave beyond belief, fighting for the right to even exist. She saw her father and her friend Rafer, seemingly unarmed, stepping directly into harm's way. Lastly, she looked across at those of the underworld creatures, their hideous faces, the smell of death and decay that permeated them.

She felt the incredible weight of their hate. Hate that had no place in a world where magic actually did exist. In a world where because of magic, she belonged. She closed her eyes and took a deep breath as she gathered a handful of Bracken's fur and squeezed it. She felt his great form beneath her and heard the battle unfolding around her. With a flash of clarity, she realized she was home, and this is where she was meant to be.

"That's right my love, you are at last, the One." The voice of Roison echoed in her head.

Another vision replaced her mother's, another woman, clad as a warrior, a great sword at her side, a dagger on her hip, her red hair in long braids, her face painted for battle. She looked deep into Annie's thought and cocked an eyebrow,

"Magic only exists for those that believe in it. Strength is the same. You are we, you are Anna L'Abbee, you are Roison McQuinn, her mother and her mother's mother, you are we. Find your strength. We are strong; you must believe."

The sounds of battle all around her became muffled

as Annie felt a great stillness settle over her. In response Bracken stopped moving and stood silently, knowing the time had come. Annie sat calmly astride Bracken and drew several deep breaths and then opened her eyes. Looking around, she knew, finally knew her role and purpose.

Annie sheathed her sword. She had been right, the sword did not fit, it was not her weapon. With sudden clarity, she understood the 'Shield and the Spear' at last.

She was the spear, everyone else, all of them that fought with her, protected her, were the shield.

She looked down at the horde and the battle between life and death. Death for all the races, and death of the next world, the mortal world. The mortal world, her world no more. She closed her eyes one more time, *'We... we are strong.'* She drew a deep breath and slowly let it out, *'We... are... strong.'*

Opening her eyes again, they once again both appeared sky blue and she smiled to herself. She reached into her jeans pocket and drew the weapon that she had had all along. In her hand were her five small stones, their amber tones beautiful in the morning light —the five small druid stones. "Small things make up the most important things. Events turn on knowing the small things," had been the words of the Sentinel. And so it was to be exactly that.

In her hand the stones began to glow and quickly the glow flashed into flame as bright as starshine in her hand. She took a deep breath and threw her arms open wide and threw her head back. With a great 'thrum' a shock wave swept away from her; vibrating; subsonic, both felt and heard. It spread out, sweeping over the dwarves, the elves and the fairies, harmless to them, the same as them, as magical as they were, but devastating for the evil ones. Sweeping through them like a sickle through ripe wheat. They fell where they stood and in only moments it was done and the field had been swept clean of their filth.

The Consequence of Bravery

In the shocked silence that followed, Annie slid slowly from Bracken's back with a long sigh. Her legs weak and nerveless, she staggered forward clutching at handfuls of his hair until finally reaching his face.

"Bracken..." but then she lost her grip and fell first to her knees, and then with another sigh, face forward to the ground.

"NO!" Bracken tried to turn her over. He gave a great mornful howl to the sky, "No!"

Others rushed up, Allegra dropped to her knees next to her, and the Red Queen turned her over. Michael knelt gently down and cradled her head.

"So brave, my little one."

Colm McQuinn, no longer the terrifying Berserker, rushed up and dropped to his knees. He touched her forehead and placed a hand over her heart. For long moments he didn't move as those gathered held their breath. At last he dropped his hands, "She's gone."

"She's gone?" Allegra's tone was tragic. She stared down, disbelieving, "Oh Annie."

Straightening up she turned her back as the first sob erupted from her chest. She looked around at the crowd of warriors that had gathered, all faces showing shock and dismay.

"She is gone, killed by the very power that she carried within her." The Red Queen rose as well. "The legends have never spoken of such valor before. This child warrior."

Garnet shook her head, almost in disbelief. She looked around at the wreckage of war that surrounded them. Then at the great crush of allies gathered around them, "She must be carried in honor from this field of destruction." Then she looked down at the small form at her feet. "This victory is bitter indeed, and our loss cannot be measured."

"No one may touch her save us." Micah stepped out of the ranks. "She is our kin, neither witch nor elf, nor fey, mortal no more. We and we alone may raise her to the bier, for she was our sister."

A stretcher of spear shafts was lashed together. Three elves and Patch, along with dozens of other fairies, lifted the inert form of Anne Louise Abbott and carried her to the entrance of the cave. Michael and Rafer, with his hand on Michael's shoulder, followed both unable to contain their grief. Without warning, for the first time in years, rain began to fall in the valley, pouring down its sadness on all.

They carried her into the great cavern in a silent procession and laid her on a high stone table in the center of the room. Allegra lovingly finger combed the tangles in her red hair, and arranged her comfortably. Garnet removed her buckler and laid the great sword at her feet. Stepping back the two women drew a great sad breath and their shoulders sagged. Annie's face was composed and at peace. Everyone that witnessed her beauty wept openly and many stepped forward to see her up close one last time or to touch her.

Outside the rain wept down upon the fallen dead of the unclean and they began to dissolve. The clean rainwater melting them, dissolving their remains into the cleansing sands of the desert. Erasing their memories and the hatred they had stood for. Rafer Tate stood in the opening, shaking with grief. Michael approached and together they looked out into the rain.

Behind them a great hand gripped each shoulder. Turning around, the great form of Gabe McDonald, leaning on a long crutch for support, sniffed back a tear and then embraced Michael. They held the embrace a long time as the rain began to taper off and then stop as the overcast clouds began to break up and drift away.

"She's gone, Gabe," Mike whispered.

The Toll of the Bell

A deep bell tolled and echoed through the cavern. The sound vibrated, slowly fading until it was more memory than actually heard. As the echo of the bell slowly faded, it tolled again. Slowly it tolled out thirteen times and then stopped.

"Thirteen. Thirteen tolls of the bell? The Sentinel is sending us a message. Thirteen?"

"Thirteen, of course!" Allegra turned back to the funeral bier. "Thirteen, the number of the circle, the circle of the sisters. A full coven."

"We don't have thirteen witches around here." Garnet frowned, "what do we need them for."

"We need thirteen. Thirteen for a full circle!"

"To do what?"

"Please, Lady Garnet, take a position at the head of the table. Michael, Rafer and Gabe please? Could you stand at her side?"

Michael and Rafer assisted Gabe into position.

"Boys. Please take a spot along the side of the table."

Micah, Mink and Link stepped up and stood next to Rafer.

Looking around, she nodded, "Patch you too, and

Thomasina as well."

"Bracken please?"

The great wolf pushed through the crush of onlookers and placed a great paw on the table.

"And Gunther, please? Now counting me that's twelve. We need one more for a full circle." Frantically, her eyes swept all gathered.

"I am Thomas; I am thirteen."

The great form of Thomas stepped forward. The Black Prince slung across his back, he bore the evidence of many wounds from the battle. Those gathered drew back from his presence as he stepped to the foot of the stone table. He met Allegra's questioning gaze.

"I can no longer take her beyond. That age has passed. She has risen above me. I am the thirteen. It is my oath."

Allegra's face at first skeptical, softened. She nodded, "Very well. Everyone, find a place to touch her."

Each in the circle reached forward and found a place to touch her. Thomas was last as he grasped her sneakered foot. Allegra began to chant,

"Leanabh na cumhachd, a ghaisgich shoilleir, till thugainn a-nis, till don t-solas"

"Leanabh na cumhachd, a ghaisgich shoilleir, till thugainn a-nis, till don t-solas"

("Child of might, warrior bright, return to us now, return to the light.")

The chant was taken up by each of them, over and over, they repeated it. With each repetition their intensity increased until it was a shout. It was taken up by the many warriors until the room echoed with the sound. At last they stopped and gazed down at the still form. There was no change; her face did not register any sign of life.

Crestfallen they withdrew their hands and lowered their heads. Rafer again began to sob, and Gabe hugged him, his own eyes misty.

"No! That is not the way. It must not come to pass in this way." Thomas' voice was imperious. With one great leap he stood astride the stone table and straddled the girl. "As I spoke to her, perhaps this was our last fight, and perhaps my last fight as well. But you must win this last fight; we must win this fight. I am Fear-giùlain a' Bhàis' and I am grief. I am Fear-giùlain a' Bhàis' and I am anguish and I am loss. No victory, no defeat can be without me for I am both. But I would have this one last glorious victory and she must live to see that victory. As I have vowed to this One, I must fulfill my vow if I can."

Then he looked down at the small form below him and smiled in gentleness. "She must see the victory." His flaming red eyes blazed bright and then died out. In their place a pair of warm brown ones glowed instead, and a tear wept from one and dropped down to the girl. Straightening again, he swept the great sword from his back. Flames danced up and down the blade, then spread into his hands and raced up his arms. As the fire engulfed him, he shouted and raised the sword high over his head,

"Now the dark takes me at last and I will be Fear-giùlain a' Bhàis' no more."

Around him a great cloud of shadow gathered, swirling and growing, engulfing him. He disappeared into it as the fire extinguished. The darkness gathered and then rose to the ceiling in a swirling mass of smoke and ash. There it stopped moving and rained down upon the still form on the table.

No one moved. Stunned by what they had just witnessed, unsure if Thomas would reappear or what the meaning of his last words really was.

On the stone table, the silent form of Annie drew a long breath.

Thank you for reading *Annie Abbott and the Race to the Red Queen*. Continue the upcoming adventure in book three *Annie Abbott and the* and the Revenge of the Red and White by clicking the button or scanning the QR code above to stay updated on new releases.

Bonus Feature:

Download a free short story!

About the Authors

Isabelle Nelson is a currently at Saint Ambrose University double majoring in English and Secondary Education with a minor in ESL (English as a Second Language). Her plans are to become a high school English teacher and later teach English abroad. She hopes to pursue her master's degree following a few years of teaching. She has always loved to read and recently discovered her passion for writing. She credits her love of it to her parents and many educators who have supported her endeavors with the craft.

Michael Nelson is a retired physician who also writes under the pen name Michael Deeze. After thirty-eight years in a rural house-call practice, he retired to pursue hobbies, and be near his adult children and grandchildren. In his spare time, he decided to write down some of the deeply personal memories of his life before practice, and the wonderful experiences of a house-to-house practice with he and his team in the Amish communities of northern Wisconsin.

This is the fourth novel for him, and in his opinion the most fun because he shared the work with his young daughter. "Imagine the treasure of working with your treasure to produce treasure. What a gift."

www.ingramcontent.com/pod-product-compliance
Lightning Source LLC
Chambersburg PA
CBHW060251100726
47907CB00003B/840